BASTARD BROTHERS OF CARNAGE

CONVICT

BLAKE BLESSING

Blake Blessing

Convict

Copyright © Blake Blessing 2023
All rights reserved
First published in 2023

Blessing, Blake
Convict: Bastard Brothers of Carnage #2

Cover: Vicious Desires Design

Editing: Heather Long & Leavens Editing

Copy Line Editing: Lunar Rose Services, LLC

❀ Created with Vellum

FOREWORD

Hey! Welcome back! I'm glad to see you again.

If you're here, it must mean Addict wasn't too dark for you. I can tell you, while there are still dark themes throughout the book, there are not any direct SA scenes like you encountered in book one.

That's not to say the series won't go darker, but just a heads up so you know what you're getting in *this* book.

As always, in case you're new to forwards or it wasn't overtly obvious in Addict...

This story is a reverse harem romance, meaning that the female main character will not have to choose between love interests.

Have fun. ;)

RECAP

If you're struggling to remember where Addict left off...
you're in luck!

Grey's fight with Bruno was moved up and during the fight,
it became painfully clear something was wrong. Grey
started to go down, and the brothers left Amorette alone to
save him.

Cue Amorette getting taken. Again.

This time to Matías.

The brother she never knew they had.

*"Hello. My father tells me you're mine." A dark velvet voice tickled
my brain. "My name is Matías, and I also hear you used to belong
to my brothers."*

PROLOGUE
PARKER

S*ix years old*

I CROUCHED behind the pillar in the residential wing, waiting for Gregor to come around the corner. I'd show him. He'd never break anything of mine again.

It only took a few tries to steal the lard from the kitchen. Gregor loved it in his food. Nasty man. Mia said she saw him eating it straight out of the tub.

Footsteps echoed around the corner, and I shifted my weight from side to side. I was the cat waiting to pounce.

He'd never break any of my toys ever again. Not after I broke his face.

No one ever went against Vicente because he hurt people first. He wasn't a nice man, and I didn't like him. I didn't even think he liked me. But people left him alone.

This part of the mansion was always deserted during lunch. All the men were working. The women were in their rooms on the other side of the property. The staff was only ever allowed to clean during very specific times.

Except for Gregor. The guard. Why was he allowed to sleep on the residential floor, and I wasn't?

It was Vicente's place. But each of his favored women had a suite on this floor. Just Vicente, his women sometimes, and Gregor.

Who cared? What was important was that he was evil. And I'd taken his phone, so he'd have to come back here looking for it. He'd never know it was stashed with the dog food.

The footsteps got closer; the sound bouncing off the ceilings. Around the corner, the tip of the first black boot popped.

Then a separate set of angry footsteps pounded from the other end of the hall, coming from the courtyard.

Andre ran right toward the lard spread out over the white floor. His arms pumped and his face poured sweat as he locked eyes on Gregor.

"No!" I popped out from behind the column. But Andre sidestepped the lard like he knew it was there.

"Gregor." He stopped and braced his knees while panting. Then he extended one hand, holding Gregor's phone.

How did he know where that was?

"You dropped your phone outside."

Gregor glared down his nose at Andre. "Where outside?" he asked, because Gregor wasn't outside this morning.

Andre was about to get beaten, *estupido*.

"Not outside. At the entrance to the dining hall. Isn't this yours?" Andre straightened up and examined the phone. "Maybe this is someone else's?"

"It's mine." He snatched the phone from his hand and tucked it into his pocket. "Get out of here. Both of you.

Vicente would flay your hides if he knew you were in this part of the mansion. Consider that a favor, bastards."

Bastards. I sneered up at him, but Andre jerked on my arm and I turned my glare to him. They loved that word. Like it made us less. Or small. Or...what was that word we learned in lessons the other day...

Insignificant. They used that word like it made us insignificant.

I'd show him. I started forward, and Andre yanked me back again, my shoes squeaking across the floor as he wrestled me back.

"We'll leave. We were just looking for you." Andre dipped his head and started carting me away like we had less of a right to be here than Gregor.

"Let go of me!" I whispered, kicking my legs, trying to catch his knee or ankle. He was too tall. Much too big for me to actually hit him.

Andre shoved me into one of the servant stairwells and waited for the door to shut before pushing me against the wall.

"*What is your problem, Park?* Do you want to die? I can't always save you! You're lucky I saw you sneak into the kitchen. I would have been here sooner, but Pilar was trying to take me to the chapel." He grimaced. We all hated the chapel.

"I was about to kill him! He would have slipped and cracked his head! Do you know what he did? He broke my favorite car. Mia got that for me for my birthday." Andre might pretend to forget things, but I didn't. I huffed and rammed my shoulder into his stomach. He grunted but didn't move.

"Parker, listen to me. He wouldn't have died. Only you would have. You're my baby brother, and I can't lose you.

You and Grey and Lafe...you're all I have. Stop being stupid." He gripped my shoulders. "Now, let's go clean up the floor before Vicente falls and really takes our heads."

"It's not fair," I cried, balling up my fists as he turned me toward the door. "Why is he allowed here with them, and we aren't?"

That wasn't necessarily true, either. Andre was allowed in here sometimes. When Pilar was here. But I didn't have a mom to call for me like that.

"It's not so great here. I'd rather stay with you all in the servant's wing than ever come here," Andre whispered like he didn't want anyone to hear his secret.

When we made it back to where I'd smeared the lard, the marble floor was squeaky clean. No trace of grease.

We glanced around, but there was no one there. Had Grey or Lafe followed us up here? I snickered. Not Lafe. He was a coward. Maybe Grey.

"One of the maids must have seen you. Let's go before anyone else notices us." He squeezed my arm and pulled me back toward the stairs.

Whatever. I'd have to find another way to take care of Gregor.

1

GREY

Andre's fucking voice beat at my head like ice picks to the ears. What was he yammering on about?

Parker's voice joined in. But both were too muffled for me to make out what they were saying. Bastards. Couldn't even let me sleep off my hangover in peace.

I readjusted my head on the pillow. Holy fuck. That hurt.

Groaning, I stopped. Their voices stopped too.

"Grey." Andre's voice echoed around my head as he touched my shoulder. "You alive, you fucking asshole?"

He needed to get the fuck away before I taught him another lesson in the gym. It'd been too long since he'd sparred with me. Even with my body on fire, I could still kick his ass.

Why was I hurting like this?

I reached for the last thought before I went to sleep. The recesses of my mind were so thick and my thoughts so jumbled I couldn't pick out the last thing I did. Or saw.

The strain of searching increased the throbbing pain in my temples. What the hell had happened to me?

I peeled my eyes open and found Andre bent over me.

His lips were pressed together like when he was livid with one of us. Too fucking bad if it was me. He had a better chance of getting Lafe clean and sober.

"You with us now?"

Blinking again, I raised my hand. "Water," I croaked.

My mouth tasted like shit and I was dehydrated as hell.

Andre rolled his eyes and walked away. I closed mine and opened them again when I heard him coming back. The lid crackled as he broke the seal.

I slowly pushed myself up and sat back against the pillows. He handed me the water and I took long, healthy pulls from the bottle. Parker had his arms crossed and his chin tucked as he leaned against the wall. Lafe sat in the window seat with one leg up, staring out the window.

Glancing down, I caught sight of the red and purpling bruises over my chest, stomach, and sides. Damn, I didn't think anything was broken, but I should still see Doc, just in case.

If I wasn't mistaken, this was the hotel on the other side of Vicente's city.

After finishing off the bottle, I tossed it into the trash next to the bed. Andre had started pacing, muttering under his breath.

I snapped my head up. Where was Amorette?

"Where is she?" I growled, fisting my hands against the sheet. If they let her run...

The fights. And Bruno fucking drugging me.

"*Where the fuck is she?*" I yelled when none of my goddamn brothers answered me.

Andre sighed, running a hand through his hair as he turned to face me. "I guess I'll be the damn adult." He tossed Parker and Lafe a glare. "Vicente took her."

Lafe tensed like he had something to say, but he remained quiet.

"Then we fucking get her back." I tried to swing my legs over the side, but pain radiated down my leg. Bruno had caught me on my fucking hip with his meat tenderizer.

"Sure, Grey. Let's walk right into Vicente's hands after he tried to have you killed." Andre paused to take in a deep, calming breath. "We can't go off half-cocked to get her back when we don't even know where she is. Do you think he'd just leave her at his mansion?"

"We don't know if we don't check," I grunted, scooting to the edge of the bed. "Lafe, call your boys up. I need painkillers. Fucking strong ones." I could see Doc later. I needed to numb the pain enough that I could lay Vicente's men out if I needed to. It wouldn't take much. Outside of Bruno, they were brainless muscle with no strategy behind their fighting.

"Donnie was already here. He gave you a shot." Lafe continued to watch the air outside.

"Well, it fucking wore off."

"Use your goddamn brain, Grey!" Andre shouted. "You're not even asking the important question. Why would he take her in the first place?"

I shrugged. Like, I gave a damn. Amorette didn't belong with Vicente. Andre could ask those questions when we had her back. I pushed up from the bed, my knee and hip popping.

"Where's my phone?" I glanced around the room. It was pristine. Like they'd walked me in here ten minutes ago and tossed me on the bed. The sun was setting over the water, so Vicente had Amorette for almost a full twenty-four hours.

"We don't fucking know. It was a burner." Andre tossed up his hands.

I narrowed my eyes at Lafe, then at Parker.

Lafe was probably beating himself up, thinking Amorette left on her own. She wouldn't have. Not there. But Parker... He had a smart mouth and started shit for no reason. He should be eating this up like the giddy fucker that he was.

Instead, he worked his jaw and glared at the floor.

"What's your fucking problem?"

He glanced at me without raising his head. "We need to call Jorge. See if he's heard anything."

"Don't you think you've fucking done enough?" Andre whirled around. "If we call anyone, we'll call some of my contacts..."

"Why are you two being stupid about this?" I hobbled to the kitchenette and riffled through the cabinets. I doubted there was any medicine here, even the kiddie stuff, but it didn't hurt to look.

Shit. Nothing.

I returned to the little circle my brothers had created by the window.

"Our baby brother—"

"Andre!" Parker yelled, pushing away from the wall.

"What's wrong, Parker? You don't want Grey to know the truth?" He sneered.

Lafe kept his gaze trained on the outside. Who knew if he was even listening to anything they were saying.

"I can't help it if you're content to sit and rot under Vicente's thumb. That's not the life I want. It's not the life I've ever wanted." Parker balled his fists up at his sides.

"Your baby brother," Andre repeated, pointing at Parker, "is most likely the reason Amorette was taken."

Red descended over my vision.

Parker clenched his teeth and tensed his shoulders. I

didn't think twice. I didn't ask questions, and I certainly didn't wait for answers. His body language was enough to tell me Andre was right about something.

Cocking my arm back, I let it swing and caught Parker right in the cheek under his left eye. He didn't block his face, because the fucker expected it. That was the thing with Parker. He fought with words. He fought with shady behind the back action. On occasion, he'd fight with his fists if needed.

But only when he felt guilty did he let me wail on him.

He staggered back and cursed, clutching his face.

"*Mierda dios mío!*" he grumbled, righting himself against the wall.

My entire body raged from the swift movement, but the pain only incited my anger. I turned to Andre. "I'm getting her back. And if I find out this was your fucking plan to—"

He hit my shoulders with both hands and shoved me back. I grunted, struggling to keep my feet.

"Fuck you! If I wanted to get rid of her, I would have chosen a different way than to lose her to Vicente while I was saving your ass!"

I stepped forward, ready to shred my body to pummel his face which looked just like Vicente, when Lafe jumped between us.

I was so shocked, he didn't even have to use any pressure to push me back.

"Stop. You're all being fuckwads. This is getting us nowhere."

"And where do you stand, Lafe?" I let out a breath and relaxed my body.

"He wants her back." Parker stepped up next to Lafe. "We're going to get her back. That wasn't ever a question. Right?" He pinned both Lafe and Andre with a glare.

"We're *going* to get her back," Andre confirmed, exasperation coating his words. "Sit your ass back down. Lafe, get him some meds, Parker, just... get out of my fucking face."

Satisfied they were on my side, the only side, I shuffled back to the bed and gingerly sat down on the edge. Parker threw himself over the couch like a spoiled brat, and Lafe resumed his window seat.

Sighing, Andre propped one hand on his hip as he spun around, giving us his back. Then he scrubbed his hand over his head, leaving his hair sticking in different directions.

"We have to do this very carefully. Vicente taking her means that he doesn't give a fuck what we think or what we'll do to retaliate."

"The bastard is expecting us to hit back," Parker ground out. "He *wants* us to."

"We have networks. All of us have men and women we work with. We call them," I tossed out. It wasn't like Andre to be so dense or hesitant, like he was afraid of his shadow.

"No," Andre gritted through his teeth. "We have to be smart about this. If he's going against us this openly, people will notice. And if they think they can curry his favor by turning on us, they will."

No one said anything. Andre was right. The only people we trusted with our lives were in this room. And even then, we didn't like each other. This was a forced bond.

Everyone else? They'd slit their own throats stepping on each other to get Vicente's approval. He thrived on enticing that kind of chaos among the masses.

"Call Pilar." Lafe turned his head to stare at Andre. "Call your mother. She won't go against Vicente, but she will tell you if Amorette is there." There was a tightness to his voice that indicated he wasn't sure what he wanted that answer to be.

Fuck that.

Still, Pilar was a good option. Andre was the only one who still had that option available to him.

"Shit. Okay. I'll call Pilar." He pulled his phone out of his back pocket and dialed her number, pressing the button for the speaker.

The blaring ring grated against my sore ears. Like hell I'd ask him to turn it down though.

It rang five more times before clicking over to a generic voicemail. Andre hung up without leaving a message. Pilar might love Andre, but if Vicente took her phone, there wasn't a damn thing she would—could do about it.

His hand barely lowered before it rang.

He picked it up immediately. "Ello."

"Andre," Pilar whispered into the phone.

"Pilar. What's going on there?" His words were rushed. Urgent.

"Son, what did you do?" She was livid, her voice shaking.

"I'm not sure what you mean, besides Vicente taking something of ours." A blank mask settled over his face. He hated when she questioned him.

"Why? Why bring that girl here? What did you do for Vicente to do that?" A door shut on the other end of the line as she was moving farther away from someone.

Lafe and I both perked up. Parker remained in the same position, as if he were listening to a boring call from his men.

"Is she there?" Andre asked in a measured tone.

"No! Of course not. You think Vicente would leave her here? You think he's so kind?" She laughed, the bitterness leaking through the phone. "You *pendejo*. If you cared about this girl, you should have never brought her here."

I stiffened.

"You'll be lucky to ever see her again."

"Where did he take her?" I jumped up from the bed and Andre tried to wave me away. I didn't give a damn. "Pilar. Where did Vicente take her?" I growled.

Silence filled the line.

"She's not your girl at all, is she, Andre?"

Andre glared at me. "She belongs to us. Do you know where Vicente took her?"

She sighed. "No. He wouldn't tell me such things. I doubt he even knows where she is. He has men for that kind of thing. Don't call me again until you're back on his good side."

The phone beeped three times, and he dropped his hand and lifted his gaze to me. "Are you satisfied that she's not at the mansion?"

I curled my top lip. "It's not like Pilar is in Vicente's inner circle. She could be there, and Pilar would never have a clue...although it's a start." I turned to Lafe. His shoulders slumped and his eyes drooped. Too fucking bad. Now was not the time to check out. "I need those fucking drugs."

Each bruise was like fire under the skin, and the longer I was up, the more my body smarted. The places where he'd caught me with the hammer hurt even worse.

"Okay." Andre paced the small space between the couch and bed. "Okay. If we were Vicente, where would we take her? Is she bait or collateral damage?"

She better fucking not be collateral damage. This dodge-and-kill game I played with Vicente would stop, and I'd raze his operations and his legacy.

I smirked.

He wouldn't die until his legacy was a bad memory, and even then, I might have too much fun killing him.

2

AMORETTE

The food on the coffee table was steaming hot. Some kind of seasoned rice with juicy shredded pork. Different from the clean-eating Grey fed me. Or the barren cabinets in Lafe's place.

My stomach was a tangled web of knots, and even though the smell made my mouth water, the richness also made me nauseous.

Somehow, I'd passed back out after the "brother" tried to scare the shit out of me. When I woke up fifteen minutes ago, I was on the couch in a posh living room with only a mild grogginess. The double glass doors were open, and noises from the kitchen floated through the room.

A nasty, unwelcome case of déjà vu hit me square in the chest as my heart refused to listen to reason. No, that useless organ tried to kill me every time voices came close to where I was.

There was someone else here besides that man. The brother.

Maybe a man, but if it was, his voice was high. When the

voices moved farther away, I stuck my head out of the living room and glanced around. I needed to find a bathroom, or this brother would have another reason to hurt me. With how clean and new everything seemed, he wouldn't take kindly to a puddle on the new rug or leather couch.

The space was fairly open, like a receiving area of some sort. Much bigger than the apartments. A door was partially opened across the room; from what I could tell, it had a tile floor. Possibly a bathroom. I darted over and shut the door behind me.

Gently.

I was still in the red dress and my underwear was still intact, thank God.

Pulling my panties down, I started peeing before my ass ever hit the seat. Then I ran into a dilemma. Flush or not. If I did, this brother would know I was awake. If I didn't, he might be grossed out.

Hell, I went for it. I flushed and went back to the living room.

Which brought me to now. In the few minutes I used the bathroom, splashed water on my face, and had a good long look at myself in the mirror, someone had dropped food off for me.

"I see you're awake."

I snapped my gaze to the door. How the hell had he snuck up on me so quietly? The floors were hardwood, the place echoed like a museum, and he was nowhere to be seen when I'd rushed from the bathroom to the living room.

"No words? Cat got your tongue?" A hint of a smile curled his lips, but it did nothing to replace the cold calculation in his eyes.

He was everything I remembered from my drugged state

and so like Andre on the surface, maybe too much. Except, there was no warmth to him. Andre burned hot.

This man ran as cold as ice. I half expected my next exhale to fog over.

He had his hair buzzed, even shorter than Parker's, and his eyes were a brown somewhere in between the deep brown of Andre's eyes and the black of Parker's.

I committed as much of him to memory as I could. If the brothers had never mentioned him, there was a reason.

"Who are you?" My voice was rough, scratching up my throat.

A teasing huff escaped him before he pushed into the room. "I can tell from the recognition in your gaze that you remember. What do you think you'll get by playing dumb?"

"You said you're their brother, but I don't believe you. They never mentioned you." I backed up step for step as he moved forward. But his strides were longer, and by the time my back hit the wall, his chest was inches from my face.

I fucking hated tilting my head back to see him. It made me feel small and powerless. But I wasn't. I would never be powerless.

"Matías," he said, the accent thickening over his name.

"Ma-tee-as," I repeated.

He nodded, the hint of amusement wiping from his face. "I imagine you haven't heard of me. They don't claim me as their brother. Not even when we were brats running around the mansion."

I sucked in my stomach as he pushed forward even closer.

"Why am I here?"

"Because they've been playing a very dangerous game, and Vicente—you know who Vicente is, yes?"

"Yes," I said quietly.

"My father never loses. And he plays with his food before he kills it."

Was he referring to me? Or the brothers?

We stared each other down, my breathing the only audible sound in the room. When I didn't make any attempt to engage him in conversation, he stepped back. "Eat. The food will be cold soon." He walked toward the door but stopped just before he crossed the threshold. "You're not a prisoner here, but neither are you free. Don't leave the house, and let me know if you need anything."

Then he was gone, leaving me staring after him dumbfounded.

Shit. Matías could be a hitman, an estranged brother, or an undercover cop. I had nothing to go on. No information to match up against. Except that he was being kind.

At least in the only way these men knew how to be kind. If Vicente was into head games like Matías said, could dropping me here, offering limited freedom and basic comforts, be a ploy?

But what did I matter in the grand scheme of things? I didn't.

Except as leverage over Grey. The other brothers could probably give two fucks if I lived or died.

I walked back to the food and sat on the couch. I needed to eat. I'd been gone at least twelve hours. When was the last time I ate?

Sucking it up, I picked up the fork and dove in. Flavors burst on my tongue, and even though I knew it was delicious, it still tasted like ash. I made myself eat half before I felt like I'd toss it up.

So many competing thoughts fought for brain space.

Was Matías as bad as Vicente?

Would the brothers ever find me here?

Should I escape? Could I?

I shook my head. I'd promised I'd stop being stupid. This time, I wouldn't trust someone blindly, not after the last time. I shivered as the memory ghosted down my spine.

But I wouldn't lie to myself. The possibility of this man sending me home was tempting. Just the hope of seeing Grace again warmed my chest. If Parker could be believed, I would see her again. One day.

I didn't need this man to let me go.

What I needed was to get back to Grey and his brothers. I at least trusted them to a certain extent.

Voices picked up again, and I stood slowly. My shoes were gone, but I didn't need them. I crept to the living room door, listening to see where Matías was in the house.

I followed the voices down a hall, passing a sprawling double island kitchen, another guest bathroom, and a few bedrooms. Matías lived very well. From what Lafe had told me, this could be Vicente's mansion.

Maybe.

Would Matías live with his dad? He was at least in his late twenties.

Spanish fired back and forth between Matías and whoever his guest was. I could pick out his voice even if I couldn't decipher the words. The door at the end of the long hallway was open a crack, and I stopped just out of eyesight.

A gruff, slender man perched on the edge of a chair tossed his hands up, angry about something. Matías leaned on the desk in front of him with his arms crossed, watching the man with an unimpressed stare.

When the guy paused, he must have expected an answer. Matías gave none. He jumped up out of his seat, and Matías immediately clutched the man's neck. As Matías stood, the man was lifted to his toes. As his feet left the ground, he started choking and clawing at Matías' hands.

Matías brought his mouth to the man's ear and spoke softly.

I couldn't understand a damn thing! But I'd stopped breathing at the display of sudden violence. I should be used to it by now. I should be. But I wasn't.

Taking a step back, I froze when a board creaked. Matías glanced my way, then turned back to the man in his grip without even blinking. He didn't care at all that I witnessed this act of cruelty.

Leave or stay?

Just when I was starting to get comfortable in the apartments, I was thrust here, and now every decision was weighed as if I were playing an entirely new chess game.

"Don't be shy, Amorette. Come in." Matías' accent was thick. Thicker than even Andre's. Had it been that thick earlier? Or was this a sign of his emotions running high, even if he appeared calm on the outside?

The man tried to look my way, but Matías gave him a shake.

"You don't have to worry about her. She's not your concern. If I were you, I'd carefully consider how you're going to stay alive."

The man's face was purple, and spit spilled from his mouth, yet Matías only seemed to be squeezing harder.

Matias ordered me to enter, but I didn't. I couldn't. I was stuck in a state of shock a-fucking-gain. Just like when Grey beat that man to death. Matías continued to hold him up, and the man continued to struggle.

"Do you have anything you'd like to say? This is your last chance to save your hide." His droll tone reminded me slightly of Parker, but not quite.

The man was too busy fighting for air to answer. He didn't react to the words at all.

Then the man just stopped. In slow motion, his body relaxed. First, his hands, then his feet. Limb by limb, he seemed to just...give up.

Finally, Matías tossed him in the corner and grabbed a tissue off the desk, wiping spit, or maybe tears, from his sleeve. He sighed as he threw it in the trashcan next to his desk.

"Cleanup is never fun." He moved around the desk to take his seat, moving the mouse to wake up the computer.

I hadn't moved and when he looked at me, blood coursed through my frozen body.

"Surely my brothers haven't shielded you so much you haven't seen death?" he asked as if that thought hadn't actually crossed his mind until then.

I shook my head. That wasn't it at all. It must be the residual shock from being taken. Or maybe because I was processing what his actions said about him. I wasn't sure.

"I've seen death. I've killed too." The admission tumbled from my lips. I think a part of me wanted him to know I could be dangerous too. He wouldn't believe it. No one ever did. It was why I was so successful as a junior lawyer. Why I had been successful...

One side of his mouth kicked up. "Cute." Then it was like I didn't exist.

The rest of the day, I explored his house, which had to be upwards of ten thousand square feet. It lacked personality. Lacked any warmth. Yet it was as beautifully decorated as any home I'd ever seen.

The way my own footsteps echoed back at me was eerie. I constantly looked over my shoulder, but Matías never joined me. Not that day. And outside of bringing me food, he didn't talk to me the next day either.

For all the violence trapped under his skin, he didn't seem to want to direct any of it at me.

Yet, I couldn't bring myself to be grateful. Not when it felt like he could be set off at any moment.

3

ANDRE

"Sorry, Andre. I have nothing for you."

I hung up on the motherfucker. He'd been in my circle for years, ever since I took up my part of Vicente's business. He was the last fucking one I could see who had any idea where Vicente would have taken Amorette.

I spun in my chair, dropping my head back with a bang. Had I even slept over the last three days? Hell. *How does Lafe function without sleep over one day, much less several?*

Scrubbing my hand down my face, I let my mind wander through colleagues and adversaries. What favors was I owed? Which favors were a waste to call in?

Two favors had been blown already.

"Andre," Grey barked as he slammed his fist on my office door in greeting.

"If you put a hole through my wall, I will fucking kill you," I mumbled and closed my eyes again.

"Stop. Just fucking stop."

I opened my eyes to face a very irate Grey. I was furious too, but I was also at my wit's end. Exhausted. Depleted.

And what had Grey been doing over the last few days? Stalking around and punching anything or anyone that offended him. Very fucking productive. "What do you want me to do that I haven't already done, Grey?"

"Fucking find her!" He yelled so loud my ears rang.

The tips of my ears burned as I threw myself forward, pressing my chest against the desk and spearing the clean glass surface with a finger. Damn it. It was goddamned smudged.

"What do you think I've been doing? Sitting on my thumb and having a good whirl? I've called every single person I can think of to probe about Amorette. She's a fucking ghost as far as the Institution is concerned." I sucked in an irritated breath. "I've called in two favors to have Vicente's properties searched, and nothing. We wasted good fucking favors for absolutely nothing." I tossed myself back against the seat.

Grey curled his lips, and his eyes sparked. "This is your fault. Your fucking fault!" He leaned over the desk until our noses were centimeters apart. "You were supposed to watch her while I fought!"

I shoved up out of my seat, and he straightened up. "And let you die? Absolutely fucking not! I'm trying to get her back! I'm killing myself trying. But in no fucking universe would I let you die to save her."

"Hey. Hey," Parker waltzed in with his hands in his pockets. Not his typical self with the dark bags under his eyes. "What's going on?"

"What the fuck is wrong with you?" I threw my hand out to encompass how off he looked. Grey glanced at him and dismissed him in the span of two seconds.

"If you want to lay blame, look at your own self in the mirror. You wanted to take her to the fights. You made a

show of kissing her. She's on Vicente's radar because of *you*."
It was a low blow for anyone who cared. That obviously
wasn't Grey.

He shook his head. "She would be on Vicente's radar
because she lives with us. She's with him now because I
couldn't trust my fucking brothers. Call in your favors, pin
down your contacts, fuck his whores. I don't give a damn.
But we're getting her back. You have a week. If you don't
have her back by then, I'll take over the search. And you
won't like the way I do it."

Damn right, I wouldn't. He'd get himself spiked on a
pole outside the mansion before he found her.

Grey growled and spun around, punching a hole
through the plaster.

"Fuck you, Grey!" I yelled as he backtracked and
punched Parker for good measure.

"Argh!" Parker howled as blood poured between his
fingers. He didn't go after Grey, and that was very telling.
Usually, they'd be rolling around on the floor, choking and
hitting each other.

I grabbed the tissue case from the back corner of the
desk and tossed it to him. He caught it against his chest
with greater reflexes than I expected, with his face
covered.

"Why are you still here?" I asked as I sat and watched
Parker clean up his face. He didn't get all the blood smears
off, not that he cared.

"I still haven't heard from Mia," he sneered, his voice
nasally.

"Not my problem." It was his own damn fault that he got
Mia in hot water. And hers. She knew how reckless he was.

"What if he's holding them together? Or hell, killed
them both." He linked his hands behind his head as he

stared out the window. Anger zinged through every tense inch of him.

"I'm sure, knowing you, you have a never-ending stream of plots to get away from Vicente. Why are you even still here?" I rolled my mouse to wake up my computer. Over the last few days, I'd consumed myself with getting Amorette back.

Parker and his motivations didn't deserve the headspace, and I could give two fucks if he left. That was clearly what he wanted. To get away from us.

"Fine. Be a bitch." He twisted one of my chairs to be angled toward my computer screen. "I expected nothing less. When your feelings get hurt, you pout. But this is bigger than your fucking feelings. Yes, I am most likely the cause for Vicente taking Little Love. I'm most likely the reason for him doing whatever the fuck he's done with Mia. But I will not—*will not*—pretend to look the other way while you fumble on getting them back. You want to be angry. Fine. You want to get pissy and fight me? Fine, too. Although, brother, I will fight you back. The only reason I haven't fought back with Grey is that he's truly attached to her. You're just scrambling to bring her back, so Grey doesn't detonate and get himself killed."

Not true. I curled my fingers into tight fists next to the keyboard. He would think that. And maybe that would have been true a few weeks ago, but I did feel some level of responsibility for her, damn it.

Even if I wouldn't change a damn thing about jumping in to save Grey.

"Don't lie to yourself or me. You just don't like your things being taken away from you," I growled.

Ignoring the comment, he slammed his hand on my fucking desk. "Goddamn it, Andre! We need to call Jorge.

We need to call your man in the mansion. And maybe even Maikel. He owes Lafe for not putting his head on the chopping block."

I sighed and faced him. "No on Jorge. He has no connection to Vicente, so he'd be useless. We need to keep what happened as close to the vest as possible." He worked his jaw, but he didn't argue. "My man in the mansion is a loose rat. I can't trust him not to turn us over under the right circumstances. As for Maikel. Fuck you."

Parker's brows dropped over his eyes and he bared his teeth. "What do you think is going to happen, Andre? No, really. I want an answer. What do you think is going to happen? Your entire fucking life you've tiptoed around Vicente to keep us all alive, and for what? So we can literally get shit on any time he feels like it? So we can live in a cage of his making and call this the good life?" He scoffed in disgust. "By taking Amorette from the fights, by letting Bruno almost kill Grey—rigged or not, he declared war on us. This isn't a time to hem and fucking haw around each potential contact and determine the five fucking consequences that could happen as a result. I would wager every fucking body in the Institution knows we're on the outs. You have got to stop fucking pussy footing around and make some goddamn decision, *pendejo*.

"This is when you call in your favors, use blackmail, and make an example of the men who betray us. Otherwise, we might as well shoot ourselves now and never look back." Parker panted through his anger as he pinned me with his dark gaze. "I didn't tell Grey this, not that I needed to, but the likelihood of getting either Mia or Amorette back is slim. If we do get them back, Amorette especially, we stand an even lesser chance of her mind being intact. She's strong, but she's not that fucking strong.

"We can work together on this, or you can fly solo and get us all fucking killed." His laugh was like broken glass pricking my skin. "I might get us killed too, but you know what? At least I fucking tried. We talk about Lafe being the coward, but you're the coward too. You just don't show it the same."

He stormed out of my office, leaving me to sit there in shock. Two brothers in less than five minutes reaming my ass.

Parker's words sunk into my thick stupid skull. I was being an idiot. Approaching this from the same lens I'd approached everything in this cursed life. And where did that get us? Fucking nowhere.

I spun back to the computer and unlocked it. Opened my contacts and catalog of favors.

Blackmail. That wasn't such a bad idea. Who did we have shit on that would have some idea of what Vicente would have done with her?

Against my better fucking judgment, I started exactly where I knew I shouldn't. Dialing Maikel, he picked up on the second ring.

"Andre, to what do I owe this pleasure?" The smug note in his voice made me wish he was here in person so I could shove my foot up his ass.

"Maikel," I responded coolly. "I have some questions for you."

"Oh, that doesn't sound very good. I should first let you know that Vicente is my brother. If your questions are related to a certain *pequeña perra*, my loyalties first lie with my brother."

One side of my mouth twisted up. Maikel was loyal to no one. If he couldn't steal it, he broke it. He only used his relationship with Vicente as the cover to act as he fucking pleased.

"Is that right?" I hated this, but maybe Parker was right. I needed to push my limits to get the answers I needed.

"I like you, son. But not enough to stick my neck out for you."

"Let me tell you what I think, Maikel. I think you've been skimming the business for a long time. Longer than this most recent infraction. We have proof. We've been good little boys and sat on that information because it didn't serve any purpose for us to get you killed. Or tortured. The loyalty you say you have for Vicente—he has none for you. Not a surprise. Psychopaths can't feel true attachments like that. As soon as you stop being an asset to him, you're done. And we both know you're not an asset, right, Maikel?"

His labored breathing got worse with each word that fell from my lips. "Now, I would hate to turn that over to spite you. But I would. Because I have no loyalty to you either. Now, are you going to answer my questions?" The words were light, but my tone was cold.

"I don't have any answers for you. Save your threats. I haven't seen her."

As much as I hated to let out any kind of reaction, I blew out a relieved breath. Part of me had thought he would have sent her back to Randall. Given her to the man who would torture and brutalize her just because of our apparent attachment to her. But he wouldn't have seen that as an actual punishment, not when his favored women still worked the Gallery.

"You haven't even heard whispers about her?"

"No," he gritted out. "The only thing traveling through the circuit is how you fucked up, and he took your toy."

"What's that rumor?" I pushed. "Why are people assuming we fucked up?"

Maikel laughed. "You're his enforcers when he needs it. You four run different lucrative businesses for him. The only reason he'd so publicly go against you is because there's an expiration date on your lives." He paused. "I don't know what you did. But I'd watch your back. Consider that a good favor, nephew."

The three beeps of an ended line were harsh on my ears.

Was this good or bad news that Amorette wasn't at the Gallery? My one favor at least confirmed she wasn't at the mansion, so she wasn't in Vicente's Gallery either. Not that I expected her to be.

Pilar, as much as she hated the position I was in, would have told me if Amorette was anywhere near her.

My stomach sank as I scrolled through the list of leverage we had on members of the Institution. Most were useless in finding Amorette. But I scrolled anyway.

It would destroy Lafe and maybe even Grey, if we didn't find her.

Alive.

4

LAFE

The small canister weighed heavy in my pocket as I headed toward the movie room. On the one hand, watching movies while Amorette was being tortured or worse felt wrong. On the other, it was the one place in the compound where I felt like I could escape without the help of drugs.

My hands shook so bad I missed the handle two times. I caught it on the third try and shoved it open. The door banged against the wall and bounced back, slamming into my shoulder.

"*Helvete,*" I cursed and kicked the door shut.

Then kicked it again.

And again, as I let go of my rage.

When I splintered the wood and nearly ripped it from the hinges, I fell onto the couch. The movie room was in our private hall. No one but us was allowed in this hall. Our men knew they'd die if they pushed this boundary.

Some of the wildness under my skin settled with the outburst, but my heart still beat too fast. I still felt out of place inside my own body. A hit would make me feel better. Clear my mind.

But every time I reached for the powder, I curled my fingers instead. I never used at the compound. It was my clear line in the sand. One I broke because I'd needed to when Amorette was a fool. And possibly a traitor.

I laughed.

A traitor to what? She didn't have any loyalty to us.

The darkness in the room soothed me more than I would ever admit. I could have turned the TV on to something mindless, but I'd much rather sit here in complete silence with nothing except my thoughts.

That was probably a terrible idea, but it made me feel better. Not need the drugs so bad.

Had Amorette even been taken? I exhaled long and slow.

As soon as she was gone, I'd struggled to come to terms with Vicente taking her. But what if she took the opportunity to escape? The more time passed, the more I wasn't convinced.

Andre was a beast when he was on a mission. He would have found whispers about where she was if Vicente had taken her. It was more likely that she left when she had the chance. Found her way back home.

I hadn't shared my thoughts with any of them. They wouldn't believe me. Parker would say I was just paranoid. Andre wouldn't say anything at all. Grey...

Grey would knock me in the face like he did Parker whenever they were in the same room together.

So what if Vicente did take her? Or she left?

At the end of the day, she wasn't with us anymore. She couldn't cause problems. She couldn't fight us. Wasn't that what I wanted?

I fucked up in taking her in the first place. Right?

Scrubbing a hand over my eyes, I pressed my head back against the couch. Even without the TV on, there was still a soft hum in the room. It was louder with no windows, with no light.

Six days since the fights.

Six fucking days that we had no idea where she was. Maybe she was back home. Any minute, Feds could storm our doors. We'd see them coming long before we were actually in danger.

For the moment, my paranoia was at bay.

Except, I kept thinking about her. Every time I was alone, Killer was the only thing on my mind.

When I was with any of my brothers, she was forced to the front of my thoughts.

Killer consumed my entire being.

"Brother, are we protesting?" Parker asked through the hole in the door, causing me to jump.

"Bastard." I relaxed back against the couch, pretending I hadn't jumped two full inches off the seat.

Parker sighed as he twisted the handle and politely stepped in, and shut the door behind him. Sometimes, Parker was too much. Too cultured, too smooth, too classy. It was hilarious because he could be the dirtiest of us.

"What are you doing here?" I closed my eyes when he took a seat on the other end of the couch.

"I happened to be returning to my apartment to think when I noticed the door splintered to hell. Care to explain what the door did to you?"

"Like you fucking care." He didn't care about anything unless it impacted him or it provided amusement.

I could practically see his shrug. "Are you staying away from the powder?"

"Again, like you care."

He didn't answer, and I didn't expect him to. I enjoyed that about my brothers. For the most part, they left me and my bad fucking decisions alone.

We sat in silence for several minutes. It was odd that Parker was in here at all. Outside of Grey, I was the only one ever to use the movie room. Andre was too busy, and Parker was gone more than he was here.

"Do you honestly think Amorette was taken?"

"Lafe, how many times are you going to ask that?" Parker let out a manic laugh, completely at odds with how worn down he seemed when he entered.

I stiffened. I hated how they treated me like a fickle, confused kid.

"Until I know for sure that she was actually taken. There's no evidence. None. I want to believe she wouldn't have walked away from us—"

"Do you want to believe that? Are you sure, brother? Because I'm not convinced that's what you really want. I think you've been obsessed with Little Love since the day you stole her away from the Gallery."

I opened my eyes in time to see him lean toward me. If there were more light, his eyes would have twinkled with his brand of cruel mischief.

"How much does it kill you to know Grey fucked her before you?"

All-consuming rage seethed just below the surface as I growled and tackled Parker. He was faster than me, but I had been trained by Grey just like he had been.

I reared back and clocked his chin while gripping his collar to pin him against the couch. He laughed, the wet bubbly sound grating against my ears. I hated that fucking sound.

I pressed against his throat, using my forearm to cut off his air. That was the turning point when he'd had enough. With his own snarl, he slammed his hands against my chest and propelled me backward. I tumbled to the floor as he straddled my waist and punched once, twice, and just when I thought the third hit was going to land, he gripped my shirt and banged my head against the floor.

"Stop fucking around! Between you and Grey, we're all going to get concussions, and where will that leave us? Ripe fucking ducks for Vicente." He pushed off of me and stalked to the other side of the room, hitting the lights. The last time they'd been on, they were dimmed, giving just enough light to make out expressions and body language yet leaving the details fuzzy.

The scuffle lasted less than two minutes, but I couldn't make myself get up. I was drained, aching for sleep I knew wouldn't come, even if I downed a bottle of NyQuil.

My heart pounded in my throat as I laid there, waiting for whatever bullshit Parker was about to spout. Whatever it would be, it would be about Amorette.

Everything was about Amorette.

"Care to ask yourself why you lost your winning disposition to one innocent little question?" Parker reclaimed his seat on the couch.

No. No, I didn't want to ask myself anything.

"You're a bastard, Parker. You don't care about getting Amorette back. Not like Grey does. Why are you even in here?" I tossed an arm over my eyes.

"Vicente has to die. He's the root of all our miserable problems." Parker's voice lost its amusement and I pushed up to my hands. He braced his elbows on his knees as he narrowed his eyes.

Fear trilled up the back of my neck, and I shuddered.

Those kinds of thoughts were what signed death warrants in the Institution. I'd seen enough death, caused enough, that I didn't want any part of it.

"No. If you want to risk your life to leave us, go for it. I've seen what happens to those that try. Being his bastard son isn't going to save you. We'll get Amorette back, for Grey," even that felt like shit on my tongue, "but that's it. We find a way to get her off his radar and then go on as normal."

"Lafe, Lafe, Lafe," he said with a small smile, his cheek darkening into a coming bruise. My eye didn't feel much better, but the throb lessened some of the withdrawal.

"Stop patronizing me."

"Stop thinking with that worthless spine you have. Or lack thereof. Vicente has already made his intentions clear on where he stands with us. Whether we get Amorette back or not, we're blacklisted with the equivalent of a bounty on our heads. And make no mistake, Vicente will have *fun* watching different factions of his men kill each other to bring him our heads. The more pain and suffering they can cause before that happens is just a bonus."

I squeezed my eyes shut. We'd had this conversation. When we'd first taken Grey to that hotel room, when Parker confessed it was most likely his fault that Vicente put us on the chopping block. That was six days ago, however.

Six days of nothing. No attacks, no threats. Not even a whisper of where he'd taken Amorette, if he'd taken her at all.

The lack of action made this all seem like a fever dream. We could go on and live our pathetic limited existence.

Was Parker right? I almost laughed. Of course, he was. I was just sticking my head in the sand, leaving my ass exposed for a good fucking.

"What are you suggesting, Parker? What's your plan? If

you're here, you've already tried to convince Andre. I'm not sure what getting me on board would accomplish."

"Well, *hermano*, that's the burning question that's been plaguing my mind for years. The first step is getting Little Love back. For us to actually stand a chance at working together, we need her."

A dark smile twisted the corner of my mouth, and I pushed a little payback at him. "You're telling me the only reason you want to get Amorette back is so Grey will stop using you as his personal punching bag?" We all noticed his choice of...women since Killer walked into our lives.

But I wouldn't bring that up now. I'd sit on it until it would be like tossing gasoline on a weak flame.

He grinned, catching me off guard. "I like Little Love. I never said I didn't. It's you assholes who walk around with all that ignorant panache." he snorted as he waved a hand.

I gritted my teeth and pulled one knee to my chest. "How are you going to get her back? Andre has been trying to all week." Parker was trying too. He wouldn't sit on the sidelines; he just wouldn't advertise it. But if he had been successful at all, he would have crowed it from the rooftop.

"I'm working on it. I put the feelers out with my most trusted men. Or at least, men who have something to lose." He shrugged. "Who do you know, Lafe?"

"Who do *I* know?" Why was that even a question? I barely spoke to my men unless it was necessary. I certainly didn't make friends. Absolutely didn't trust them. Vicente probably had a third of my men on retainer to keep an eye on me.

"Vicente either took her somewhere alone or used only one soldier. There's too much silence surrounding that night. Who do you know in Vicente's inner circle that we don't? You have to know someone. You can't have grown up at the mansion with absolutely no connections. It's not possible." He shook his head.

"You have the wrong impression about me. That's exactly what I did after..." I gulped. I still had nightmares. "I made it my mission to stay away from everyone."

"Funny that you took Amorette despite that, isn't it?" He smirked and pushed to his feet.

He was halfway to the door when I furrowed my brow. There was someone I knew at the mansion. But I didn't trust him. I didn't even know him. And it had been years since I'd thought about him. For all I knew, he could be dead by now.

But if we were grasping for straws, he might know something.

"There was this one kid. Around our age..."

Parker turned around with a wide smile plastered to his face. "Tell me more. Who is this mysterious kid?"

"A servant's son. But the last time I saw him, he was in Vicente's second tier."

"And why would you think this man would be willing to give us any information? Assuming he's still part of Vicente's men." Parker took a seat on the couch that was closest to me, his excitement palpable.

"Because when we were twelve, I saved his life."

5

AMORETTE

"Eat," Matías said as he slid a plate of eggs and toast over the island. From the moment I walked into the kitchen, he hadn't looked at me. Not that he stared, but he hadn't gone out of his way to actively avoid me over the last week.

After the first show of violence, he'd been...pleasant.

Except today, he was looking everywhere but at me. Locks of dark hair covered his eyes as he moved around the kitchen. Instead of pushing them back, he seemed to be using them as a wall or maybe a shield. Not that I believed for a minute that he felt the need to shield himself from me.

"Can I call Grey?" I asked, like I hadn't asked to call him, Parker, Lafe, or Andre multiple times over the last week. I was starting to sound like a broken record.

He shook his head and dropped the skillet in the sink. His white shirt stretched across his broad shoulders as he turned the water on and rinsed it out. "Shouldn't you be asking to go home? Weren't you abducted to go to Maikel's? How did you even end up with my brothers?"

I paused.

This was different. Matías was different today.

Every other time I'd asked, he'd given me a curt no and continued doing whatever he was working on. I'd leave it alone until the next time I felt comfortable enough to ask. He never left the house, giving me ample opportunity to bring it up. Matías didn't appear to get angry at my questioning. His mood was always even, regardless of my questions.

A few men stopped by, but he never let them see me. Matías did try to take meals with me, peppering me with questions I didn't answer.

Although, they were never about the brothers. All of our interactions were cordial, mild, and emotionless. Matías had a bland curiosity about me, but that was as far as his interest in me seemed to go. If he was asking about them, he wasn't as uncaring as I thought he was. And if he was asking about after I was abducted, he'd been talking to someone.

Something was off.

Picking up the toast, I took a bite while keeping my gaze locked on the food.

"What do you mean?" I'd never told him I was at the Gallery.

"You were at Maikel's. No one would want to stay here or anywhere within the Institution if there was a way out." He cracked his neck to the right, then to the left, while pouring orange juice for us.

My stomach went cold. "How do you know that?" My tone was measured and lightly curious. I'd been careful not to give him any voluntary details about my time with the brothers. I'd not shared a goddamn thing, and he hadn't seemed to know any other information outside of the fact that I was theirs.

So how did he know this?

"Sources, little girl. I have sources throughout the entire Institution." He grinned, but it was pained. Then he leaned against the counter to face me, finally bringing his rich brown gaze to mine. Raising a hand, he trailed one finger down my cheek. "I've been kind to you, haven't I?"

Goosebumps raced down my arms.

Matías also never touched me.

He dropped his hand and stepped back. His body language was too tense. His entire being was poised, trapped, but ready to spring at a moment's notice. I cataloged every nuance of his body language, ready for him to try to catch me off guard, but he only tapped his fingers on the countertop.

"You've been very kind," I drawled out, placing the toast back on the counter, preparing myself to push back and run.

"I haven't forced myself on you. I haven't hurt you. Despite my father's wishes, I've been a perfect gentleman." He sighed as if he should get an award for acting human.

"Do you want to do those things?" I was almost afraid to ask, but I had to know what I was facing. Was this a man reining in his depraved desires on a tight leash, just waiting for the opportunity to snap?

I hadn't gotten that impression from him at all. He reminded me so much of Andre with his dark hair, long and sharp features, and skin as rich as his eyes and hair were dark. Except Matías was colder in his demeanor and personality. Still, the small similarities made it hard not to fall into the trust I'd given them. Even if it was only a surface-level trust.

I trusted them not to kill me. I trusted them not to hurt me.

With Matías? There was no such trust even though he

hadn't touched me, as he put it. However, he made it perfectly clear that he could if he wanted to.

"Of course not," he said with a bright smile—so much like Andre's.

"Except you won't tell me why they never mentioned you. And you won't let me speak with them." I clasped my hands in my lap. For all the kindness he'd shown, I hated it. It was a ruse to draw me in, and I refused to fall for it. My palm itched to slap him to get a different reaction than dull curiosity and empty answers.

I needed him to show me his real colors.

"Tell me why Lafe took you." A command, not a request.

How did he know this much? And if he knew these details, why didn't he know more?

"Why do you want to know?"

"Call me curious. You've asked about them every day. What did they do to make you like them so much, when they had you trade one cage for another?" he mused, more to himself than me.

"Let me talk to them, and I'll answer your questions."

"No. But the better question is, what is a woman like you doing trying to make her way back to them instead of going home?" He continued to tap his fingers on the counter again, and the constant noise made me grind my teeth. I'd never been affected by things like this. People's actions, no matter how annoying, didn't get under my skin.

But I'd been here too long.

"What if I said I would take you home? Would you prefer that to my brothers?" His voice dropped to a smooth timber as he watched me with eerie stillness.

I stopped breathing.

This was everything I had hoped for. All that I had

wanted since I was abducted. But was that really what I wanted? Could I trust him?

The short answer, I'd learned my lesson. I refused to get taken in again.

A nagging feeling in the pit of my stomach wormed its way up toward my throat. "How can I go home when you haven't told me if Grey survived the fight?"

He huffed out a laugh and dropped his chin. "I have to give it to you, you're nothing if not tenacious. Do you care if he lived or died?"

"Of course, I care! I'm not a monster."

"No, you're Grey's girl."

I shut my mouth. Was I?

Damn it, I was. And just thinking about him left a pang in my heart. I hated it as much as I enjoyed the reminder that I was still alive. At times I thought I'd end up waking from a dream, still stuck in the Gallery.

"What do you want from me, Matías?" I woke up barely thirty minutes ago, and already I was exhausted. This particular stint in my abduction was different from the others. Not emotionally and physically traumatizing, like at the warehouse. Not equal parts frustrating and thrilling, like the compound. I did indeed feel safe here, as safe as I could feel with anyone wrapped up in this Institution. But there was something deeper going on here. "Are you afraid of Vicente? Is that why I'm still here, and you haven't sent me somewhere else or killed me?"

So many questions, yet we never answered the important ones. Everything was superficial with Matías.

He studied me, a faint divot appearing between his brows. I must have been such a mystery to him. Better a mystery than a useless nuisance.

"Eat your breakfast. Let me know if you need anything."
Then he stalked out of the room.

"Fuck," I muttered, picking my toast back up. That
wasn't strange at all.

By the time mid-morning rolled around, Matías found
me in the living room watching TV. He fell into the chair, his
attention glued to the documentary.

He didn't mention our strange impasse, and I didn't
either.

Sometimes, I got the feeling like I was a novelty to him.
He wasn't drawn to me like Grey was. Or even Lafe. But he
didn't seem to genuinely understand me either. How could
he, growing up in a criminal underworld?

The times he joined me here were more of an exercise or
an experiment than a desire to lose a few hours in fluffy
entertainment.

"You don't strike me as the documentary type of girl." He
propped his head on his hand and glanced my way. "Every
time I've seen you watch TV, it was something like old
sitcoms. I'm not even sure where you find them."

I shrugged. "Depends on my mood, honestly. Right now,
I'm craving something mindless, and the monotone narra-
tion of documentaries is the best for that."

"Not a true crime junkie?" A small smile played at the
edges of his mouth.

"No." I shook my head. "That's a little too close to home,
don't you think?"

He laughed, slapping his leg. Whatever had been
bugging him this morning seemed to be gone now. "And tell
me, Amorette, what crime have you been a part of?"

"Murder..." I whispered, then slammed a hand over my
mouth. I hadn't meant to say that. It just slipped. "Enough.

I've seen enough that I don't want to watch it on TV." My voice shook, and my pulse jumped.

His laugh tapered off, and a dangerous air settled around his shoulders. "This is fun and games now, but you should watch your tongue. It only takes the wrong word to the wrong person, and your life is forfeit. Often in a way you won't like," he said in a low, weighty voice.

I gulped and closed my eyes. What was wrong with me? This wasn't Lafe. He wasn't Grey. I needed to keep my mouth shut. Maybe it was time to start looking at escaping. Why hadn't I memorized one of their numbers?

"You understand, Amorette?" he asked casually, losing the threatening tone.

"I understand."

And just like that, the tense moment dissipated. Matías spent the next few hours watching TV with me. We watched another documentary, this one on lost cities.

After lunch, he joined me in the living room again, but he paced the floor instead of sitting down. Periodically, he'd look out the window then he would resume his pacing.

"You're making me nervous." I was only half joking. The longer he walked around the couch, the more my palms started to sweat. Was this it? Any minute I expected Vicente's men to come racing through the door.

"You never answered my question earlier. Why do you want to go back to my brothers instead of going home?"

I stood from the couch. "If you want that answer, I need one in return. Why don't you want to let me call them?" His increased edginess was making me anxious.

Something was about to happen. I was tempted to take my chances and run. I'd looked out the windows. We weren't around any neighbors, but I didn't see the ocean either.

"Because we're not close. We have never been. Why are *they* special?" He stopped prowling the room and faced me head-on. His jaw set as he waited for my answer. Just like almost everyone, he towered over me. I didn't think he was doing it on purpose, but I walked a few steps away to ensure he wasn't about to attack me.

He held up his end of the bargain with a half-assed answer. So, I gave a half-assed one in return. "They're nice."

Matías scoffed. "You're not naïve. From our limited time together, I can tell you wouldn't be taken by pretty faces and sweet words. What's the real reason?"

I narrowed my eyes at him. "How are you related to the brothers?"

He pinched his lips together, glanced out the window, then back at me. A look of...jealousy or something close crossed his face. "Just how close did you get to my brothers while you were with them?"

"That's none of your fucking business," I spat. I'd been lulled into a false sense of safety. Ridiculous, considering I'd watched him kill a man. Yet here I was, rebounding back now that it felt like shit was about to hit the fan.

Raising one eyebrow, Matías didn't seem impressed with my outburst. "I'm not your enemy here. I'm asking how much you know about their relationship with Vicente."

Pulling in a deep breath, I said, "I know they're the bastard sons."

That pulled a self-deprecating smile from Matías. "Well, there's your answer. Why do you think we would have grown up together but not at all?"

This whole time, I thought he would have been another half-sibling. Maybe even that his mother lived outside the mansion. But...it sounded like they grew up together.

"You're a legitimate son." Still a half-sibling, just a different kind.

"The apple of Vicente's eye," he sneered. "You can imagine how that would put a wedge between them and me."

"Are you their enemy?" Breathing became difficult as I ran through all the questions he'd peppered me with today.

Why did I want to go back? What made them so special? Why did Lafe take me?

This new piece of information put an entirely different spin on every interaction between us.

"They'd like to think so, but no." He shook his head, his shoulders slumping.

"If you're not their enemy, let me call them."

"Answer one more question for me. Give me an honest answer. Why do you want to return to them when I can offer you a way back home?" He tilted his head, confused as to how my mind worked.

That was fine–since my abduction, the inner workings of my mind had confounded me too.

"I don't trust you. Kindness doesn't spawn trust. And Grey, Lafe, Andre, and Parker– they've earned my trust." That was as close to the truth as he would get. "Your phone?" I held out my hand.

"No need. They're here. Just remember this. I helped you get back to them." Matías pulled out his phone and tapped on the screen.

Within a minute, Andre and Lafe were walking through the door.

6

AMORETTE

I stumbled back, reaching out to grip the back of the couch.

My eyes had to be playing tricks on me, but there they were. Andre smoothed a hand down his suit and glared at Matías as if he was barely worth spitting on. They were so similar in looks they could have been twins.

One angry twin and one cold unbothered twin.

Lafe clenched and unclenched his hands as he slid in behind Andre. His gaze swept over me. He started to turn toward me, then hesitated, returning his attention to Matías.

"Come," Andre commanded and held out a hand.

My first reaction was to sneer. I wasn't a fucking dog. But my logic knew that wasn't what they or I needed right now.

"Why don't you stay for a drink," Matías asked while curling his upper lip. He didn't seem to want Andre and Lafe to stay. The question was more of a taunt.

"There's no reason for us to stay. You're lucky we came alone." Andre dropped his hand and strode the ten steps separating us with dark purpose. When his gaze touched mine, I lost some of my bluster.

He looked like hell. His ebony hair was brushed back and his suit was impeccable, but his face was haunted by shadows. Purple bruises edged the bottom of his eyes, and his cheeks were slightly sunken in.

Before he reached me, Matías' voice cracked through the room. And I didn't understand a word of it. Whatever he told Andre made both brothers tense. Andre slowed to a stop and turned only his head toward Matías.

Responding in harsh Spanish, he spat on the floor. The exchange went back and forth as Lafe shook his head and moved toward me. As he got closer, I backed up another step.

This is what I wanted. Right?

I wanted to go back to the brothers. I wanted to make sure Grey was okay. But...why did it feel like I'd been betrayed?

Matías didn't owe me anything. He'd been civil while I was with him. Then he goes and calls Andre behind my back when I'd been all but begging to speak with them.

I was chattel—something to be bartered for.

Whipping my gaze back and forth between Andre and Matías, I sucked in a grating breath. "How did you find me?" I directed my question at Andre.

Lafe, who had been seconds from touching my arm, paused.

Andre angled his body toward me without taking his glare off Matías. "We'll talk about this at the compound. We need to go."

"No. Before I leave, I want to know how you found me." My voice rose with each word.

Lafe caught my arm but with none of the kindness I expected. His fingers bit into the muscle as he tugged me toward his chest.

"Did *you* find me?" I narrowed my eyes on Andre. "Or did Matías call you?" I switched my glare to his brother.

Both men stared each other down, silently daring the other to speak. Neither did.

I let Lafe wrap his arm around me, and when he did, I sunk into his chest. The trembling started, and his chest rose against my side as he pulled in a deep breath. I wasn't sure how I felt. Shocked, maybe. Maybe I was still in a state of shock.

Let down too.

Matías almost reminded me of the brothers, but when an opportunity presented itself, he was just like everyone else.

"He called me," Andre bit out. He seemed to want to say more, though not in front of Matías. That was the only answer I needed. Whatever kind feelings I might have had for Matías evaporated. I should be thankful that he hadn't raped me. Or worse. But sometimes, the most frustrating and painful hurts were the ones that hit your chest dead center.

I was a fool, and I only had myself to blame. Even when I thought I'd learned something.

As Lafe steered us toward the door, Matías walked to cut us off. Lafe growled as he pulled me deeper into his body, and Andre punched Matías' shoulder.

They had another exchange in Spanish, then Matías straightened his shirt and looked down at me. Some of the coldness seeped away.

"Take care of yourself. I'm sure we'll see each other again." He cut his eyes at Andre and stepped back.

Lafe pushed on my back to get me moving again. The house was silent in a way I hadn't noticed until now. We walked down the hall, through the kitchen, and out the back door. There was a black SUV caddy corner to the door, parked in a way that said they were in a rush.

To get *me*.

Lafe reached around me to open the door, and I slid in. He followed and shut his door at the same time as Andre. There were no sweet words, no concern, nothing. Andre started the car and peeled out of the driveway.

He glanced in the rearview mirror as I scooted to the other side. If Lafe noticed me putting room between us, he didn't say anything. Andre scanned the street while Lafe messed with his phone. Both were completely engrossed.

Once we pulled onto a long stretch of dirt road, they relaxed just a hair. Even I relaxed on their cue. As the danger had passed, Lafe leaned back against the seat and glanced at me with sad eyes.

Andre felt none of it and used a nervous hand to muss up his hair.

"I think we're clear," Andre said as he glanced at us in the rearview. "We have about fifteen minutes to the chopper. Then we should be good."

So many questions sat on the tip of my tongue, but I didn't know where to start. No, I did. The question I'd been asking Matías for days.

"Is Grey...." I couldn't finish the question. I just pressed two fingers against my lips, willing one of them to tell me that my worry had been unfounded. Grey was bloodied and beaten the last time I'd seen him, two seconds from a death blow from Bruno's hammer.

"Grey's fine." Andre paused, spearing me with a contemplative gaze through the rearview mirror. "The better question is, how did you come to be with Matías?"

I blinked. He didn't actually believe that I left with him on my own, did he? I didn't know anyone outside the men

I'd come into contact with at the warehouse or anyone they'd introduced me to.

"Why the hell would you even ask that?" Blood rushed to my cheeks. "Your fucking father had me drugged. Then dropped me off to him like I was some piece of meat. He told Matías that I was his now." I bent forward, trying to ease the sudden ache in my stomach.

Lafe rolled his head to face me, his lips pursed. He wanted to say something, though he was working up the courage. "Why did you look like you'd been betrayed when we walked through the door?"

"Because I was fucking betrayed!" I yelled. "I'd been asking to call you all for days. Every day. Every day I was there, I asked to call Grey. Call you, Call Andre. Even Parker. I asked if Grey was okay. I asked when he would take me back. He avoided every single question like the plague. But you tell me, what did you give him to come get me?"

I wanted to know exactly why they weren't close, but I was more concerned with why they appeared now, after a whole week. What did Matías stand to gain from it?

And why did I feel like I couldn't trust myself or my instincts?

Loud, bitter laughter tumbled from my lips, and Andre and Lafe stared at me like I'd lost my mind. Maybe I had. I was so relieved to be going back to the place I felt most comfortable that I could taste it. Tangy but sweet on my tongue.

Lafe straightened, shocked either by my laughter or my words. Ever since they'd walked through the door, he'd been eyeing me with suspicion. Now, though, he had a deep furrow between his eyes.

Andre cursed in the front seat. "Matias called us two hours ago. He didn't ask for anything, but that doesn't mean he won't. Just said that something that belonged to us was at his house. And to not make any noise when we came to pick you up."

Rubbing my hands down my thighs, I struggled to comprehend what that meant. It would be easier to put Matías in a neat box if he'd ransomed something for me. Except he hadn't.

"Why did he wait a week to call you, then?"

Tightening his grip on the steering wheel until his knuckles were white, he growled. "To make us squirm. To see how far we'd go to get you back."

I almost asked what they did while I was with Matías. Did they look for me at all? But I didn't. I didn't want to know the answer if they were happy to wash their hands of me.

Tears–stupid, betraying tears filled my eyes, and I turned my head to stare out the window. My emotions were all over the place. I always seemed to be doing fine, ignoring the new traumas dumped on my lap, but every once in a while, something would happen or not happen, and I'd break down in tears.

This wasn't me. I wasn't like this.

I hated it.

Warm fingers touched my temple, then tucked the fall of hair behind my ear.

When I turned, Lafe dropped his hand. He didn't say anything, but he kept his gaze locked on mine.

Then Andre pulled up to the pad, recklessly throwing the car in park, causing us to jolt forward.

"We need to go. Vicente could know we're here." He met my gaze in the rearview mirror. "That was the other option. Matías could be working with Vicente and this could have been a trap."

We slid out of the SUV and speed-walked to the chopper. Andre opened it up and I climbed inside as they raced around doing their checks. In minutes, we're buckled in and taking off.

I adjusted my headset, weighing how much of this conversation I wanted to have in the helicopter.

Turned out, my need for answers was too great.

"Vicente's your father. You're all his enforcers. Why would he be setting a trap? Why would he even take me in the first place?" Grey and Lafe had alluded to the fact that there was no love lost between the sons and father, but to trap them? That didn't make sense.

Lafe twisted in his seat, his bright sapphire eyes pinning me in place. He studied me as he pursed his lips like he was trying to come to some kind of conclusion. He shook his head and turned around, typing out a message on his phone.

"When Vicente took you during the fight, that was his sign that we're no longer blessed with his approval." Andre's voice came through slightly scratchy over the headset.

"Why?" I scooted to the edge of the bench as much as the seat belt would allow. "What happened?"

None of the brothers seemed fond of him, but they hadn't mentioned any issues before I was taken. I sat back. Why would they? I was just a nuisance to them.

They exchanged a look but didn't say anything. I wanted to push for more, but I wasn't sure they would react well to that. Especially after they came to collect me.

Too many questions swirled around inside my head. What did that mean if Vicente removed his favor from them? Were they targets? How much did he know about me, and if Vicente knew about me, could he know about Grace?

The likelihood that Vicente knew or cared about who I

was beyond his sons' interest in me was slim. I had been drugged during the transfer and had only given Matías my first name. He hadn't probed me with questions the way Grey and Parker had.

I steadied my breathing and didn't let my fear and annoyance show on my face. If they thought that I was a threat during their fight with Vicente, they might take drastic measures. I wasn't sure if they would. I hoped they wouldn't, but if I was on the outside, I needed to make a decision.

Stay and work for them as they'd offered or redouble my efforts to get back home.

The irony soured my stomach, when I could have been looking for an escape from Matías' low-security home. Except, I was trying to learn. I was constantly learning, but if their situation was as dire as they were conveying with their grim expressions and rigid bodies, what choice did I have than to leave any way I could?

At the end of the day, my personal feelings aside, I couldn't let anything in this new life touch Grace.

I'd die first.

7

PARKER

For the millionth time, I dialed Mia's number. It rang seven long and irritating times. The generic voicemail picked up, and after the maddening beep, I did something I never did. I left a voicemail.

"Darling. You know I've missed you. It absolutely breaks my heart that you haven't reached out to me. When you get this message, be a dear and dial back." I injected false cheer into my voice just in case Mia's phone had been confiscated.

Andre had been riding my ass about Mia, and while I was certain Vicente was behind her going dark, Andre wasn't so sure. None of us were angels, not even Mia. There was a minuscule chance that she was taken by police or a rival company.

Although that was highly unlikely. If she had been taken by the police, Andre would have heard about it. If she were taken by a company, her father would have lost his head in a wild show of defiance to get her back.

Two of my men in his house confirmed with me not twenty minutes ago that he was alive and utterly unaware of his missing daughter.

My phone rang, and I jabbed the green icon on the screen. "Yes?"

Harsh breathing beat down the line, then a low groan. My stomach dropped. Sex could be on the other end, but more than likely, that had been a pained noise. "Who is this?"

"Parker. This is Jorge. We have a problem."

"Fuck," I muttered, pinching the bridge of my nose. "What's the issue?"

"We were on the heist for the *Naked Dancing Ladies* painting, and we were made. They shot Benny, and Geo is down too. I called in a team for assistance, but this shouldn't have happened." A crash came over the phone. "*Mierda.* Something feels weird. I'll get the men out as fast as I can, but this should have been a cakewalk. The painting is stored in a small collection of climate-controlled storage units in an old warehouse."

I was familiar. There was a skeleton staff during the day and limited surveillance. For my men, that should have been practically a field trip instead of a challenge. Vicente had to be behind this.

Over the last week, he'd been silent. Hadn't required our presence, hadn't sent his soldiers to seek us out. It was a good strategy. Lure us into a sense of confused safety until we left the compound.

But this? Picking off my men, just because he could? That was an insult that couldn't stand. Andre could be damned. Vicente was going down, whether I stayed or not.

"I can't join you." I resented the words. I wasn't the most hands-on, like Andre, but I helped my men where I could.

"I don't expect you to. I needed to update you in case something else happens—so you'd see the pattern."

I ground my teeth. Jorge knew about Amorette's abduction. It had spread through the different factions of the Institution that Vicente's golden bastards weren't so golden. Or untouchable. Now Jorge was afraid this would be the first of many strikes to throw us off balance.

He was right.

"Noted. Thanks, Jorge, and let me know if you need additional backup. I'll call in some of Andre's people if I need to." If they were having a shootout in a fucking warehouse, these men were sent there as a hit. Andre's people could work in that situation.

I left my apartment, needing to move. Restless energy pushed against my chest. Fuck this shit. I'd been sitting out, letting Andre do this his way, and look where that fucking got us.

The only reason he had this lead to Amorette was because Matías, of all fucking people, called him. I couldn't wait to hear that story.

Without realizing it, I approached the gym. I was already in sneakers and gym shorts from my run this morning. I might as well go in and work up another sweat.

I could always leave the compound. Vicente wouldn't know if I didn't hit up one of my usual spots.

The rhythmic pounding of the punching bag echoed down the gym hallway. I perked up. Grey was here. Likely pissed he wasn't allowed to go on the mission to retrieve Little Love.

Grey stopped when I came into view. He grabbed the towel hanging in the band of his shorts to wipe his sweat as he glared at me. *Lovely to see you too, brother.*

This wasn't what I had in mind, but now that we were here, it would be nice to blow off a little steam.

"Taking your aggression out on the punching bag?" I quirked a brow.

"I don't want to fucking hear it from you. You're the reason Amorette was taken." He went back to killing the punching bag. Was it just me, or were these hits a little harder than when I first walked in?

"That's almost like victim-blaming, and I'm sure you know enough about society to know that's not okay." He threw the tape by the mirror as I walked over to the chair. I was in the mood for a real fight. I'd need the tape and Vaseline for that.

Grey snorted, yet there was no humor in it. Not surprising. Grey wasn't a funny guy.

"How are you the victim here? Your shitty actions landed us on Vicente's radar. Vicente, *qué cabrón,* decided to play cat and mouse with us by taking Amorette. You're lucky she's been with Matías this whole time and not gang raped." He paused, his shoulders scrunching up to his ears. "Although, if he touched her, he's dead."

"Mmmm." I flipped the top of the small tub lying next to the chair. "And you don't think that will catch Vicente's attention? Taking out his only legitimate son?"

Grey shrugged and started working the bag in a pattern. "Not my problem. He should have kept *mamí* out of it. It's not like Matías wants to be his heir, anyway. Otherwise, he wouldn't have called Andre."

I moved closer after smearing the Vaseline on, propping my hip on one of the posts for the ring. "And you don't think that's suspicious?" I still ached for a good fight, but this conversation was just getting interesting. Everyone up until this point had been pussyfooting around the issue, choosing to avoid each other than to actually figure out a way to take Vicente down.

Andre was on board, until he wasn't.

"Everything anyone does outside of us four is suspicious." He switched up his combination.

"Fair," I agreed. "But Matías isn't likely to want to help us. There has to be something in this for him. Maybe he's angling to take over Vicente's seat now." He'd never publicly shown his ambition, but nothing was as it seemed in our world.

Grey stiffened as he thought that over. "If it's a trap, he's dead." Then he shook his head and reached for the water on the floor. He squirted a long stream in his mouth, then over his head. "Why the fuck would Andre take Lafe instead of me? Lafe hates those kinds of jobs, and he's not as strong as I am."

I chuckled. "Are you jealous?"

He snapped his head in my direction, and his brows dropped over his eyes. "Do you think I'm fucking jealous?"

"I don't know. Maybe you should be. You know Lafe was the one that saved Little Love in the first place." I push away from the post, then bend down to slide between the ropes. "I've seen the way he looks at her. If you hadn't snatched her up when you did, it would only have been a matter of time before he took her to his bed."

Grey sneered. "What, and overdosed? He was so uneasy around her he had to stay coked out of his brain to deal with her in his space."

A grin tickled my lips. "You know his history. There's no other way our dear, sensitive brother would be. But the longer she sticks around—"

"She's not going any fucking where," he growled and approached the ring.

"The longer she sticks around, the more he'll see she can be trusted and that she's not going to fucking die." I paused. "Vicente taking her was a setback, I'm sure. However, he's already beginning to trust that Andre's not going to get her killed. Not again. What are you going to do when Lafe takes what he thinks is rightfully his?"

I curled my fingers into fists as he growled and jumped over the ropes, slamming his shoulder into my stomach. I laughed and wailed on his back until he flipped me onto my back.

Then it was on.

We traded punches, kicks, knees to the ribs. At one point, we grappled on the mat, each trying to get the upper hand. I had so much pent-up rage and anger from the last week; I wasn't the easy target Grey usually found me to be.

He caught my arm in an arm bar, but I dug my thumb into his inner thigh just above the knee.

"Fuck!" He yelled and let go. "I hate when you fucking do that." I laughed again as he cursed and jumped to his feet. He was ticklish in his inner legs, and when pressure was applied, it caused a sort of tickling pain.

That was what I loved about our fights—they were never clean. We fought with every advantage we could find, which was how Grey landed a left uppercut to my chin. I was fucking slow on that side.

Stumbling back two steps, I quickly caught myself and launched at Grey, hooking my left arm around his neck and punching his head.

He swept my feet out from under me, and I landed hard on my back. I groaned and tried to catch my breath. Waving a hand, I stopped his next assault.

"That's enough. I need a breather. The way you've sucker punched me this last week has my head dizzy." I saw his smug grin before I closed my eyes to stop the room from spinning. It wasn't bad, and it would settle in a minute, even though this fight had done precisely what I needed it to.

It wore out the wildness threatening to break out of my skin. From the slump in his shoulders and lowered lids, he was exhausted too.

"You're a motherfucker. You know that?" He lightly kicked my already bruising thigh. "You baited me on purpose."

I grinned, the copper tang of blood coating my tongue. I was sure it was on my teeth too. The last time he caught my mouth, I cut my lip on my front teeth. Even now, I could feel the sting and swelling.

He didn't look any better, with a darkening eye and swelling on his jaw. At least his bruises from his fight with Bruno were mostly faded to the ugly yellow of old bruises.

"Who said I was baiting you? Lafe did save her. He doesn't do that shit. Ask yourself why he saved her."

He pursed his lips and looked out the windows to the sunny sky.

"How are the injuries from Bruno?" I pushed myself up to a seated position and pointed at his hip. Out of all the hits he took, that one had been the hardest.

"Sore. Aching. Doc said nothing was broken, and our doctor here confirmed it. You're lucky I've been out of commission, or I would have wiped the floor with your ass."

He would have, but that wasn't our reality, and we only ever focused on the now. What pussies would we be if we constantly thought about how things might have been.

"You hear from Mia?" He cut his gaze to me as he fell into the metal chair. It creaked under his weight, but that old fucking chair was sturdy.

I sighed. None of them had asked about her after that initial day. I doubted they cared if she lived or died. Maybe I wouldn't either if she hadn't been my childhood friend. Once something was mine, in any way it was mine, I never let it go. It grated that Grey had a fling with her, and I had to share her with him.

Not that I wanted to fuck her. I didn't and never had the desire to. Her fling with Grey notwithstanding, I wasn't convinced that she liked men at all.

But Mia had been my friend, and in a world where true friends were a commodity, why did he have to take mine? Bastard.

"No. The tracker is off. Her phone rings and then goes to voicemail. So she's either purposely hiding, or someone is being very kind to charge her burner."

Grabbing his phone and water, Grey returned and dropped next to me. This was different.

When was the last time I sat with any of my brothers for any length of time, if it wasn't to talk business or beat the shit out of each other?

"I'm sorry. I don't want Mia caught up in this shit with Vicente." He took a drink while keeping his gaze on me.

I shrugged. I didn't want her to be hurt. Although, as much as it made me an asshole, I wasn't losing sleep over it either.

The only thing keeping me constantly miserable was the knowledge that I had potentially put my brothers on the chopping block. And sweet Little Love. She wasn't like Mia. She didn't grow up in this world, and she didn't understand it.

A savage joy filled my chest when Matías called. Vicente hadn't killed her, and now she was almost back in our grasp. Which, thank fuck. Her absence had made my brothers like bears to live with.

Now we'd get her back, and we could focus on bringing Vicente down in style.

Our phones chimed, and I scooted over a few feet to

grab mine. It had fallen out of my pocket at some point. Probably when he hurtled me through the air.

Lafe: We caught the little bird.

That was it. Nothing else was needed to convey his message. "Those bastards got her."

Grey started to dial someone on his phone, but I slapped the phone out of his hand. "Chill the fuck out. They would be on their way back and in the air if Lafe texted us. You're not going to be able to talk to them."

He scowled at me and grabbed his phone. Stuffing it back in his pocket, he jumped up and started racing around the gym to close it down for the day. Grey was nothing if not meticulous in his gym cleaning rituals.

Excited energy was nearly bursting at the seams as he turned off the lights and left me sitting on the mat.

"Fucking asshole." I hopped up too. We were about to get Little Love back, and I couldn't wait to hear all about her stay with our estranged half-brother. That was probably too kind of a description. Matías had never been one of us, and he never would be.

Already, I was salivating over the information she could have gained and how I could use it to our advantage.

Yes, Little Love, I can't wait to see you.

8

AMORETTE

As we dipped toward the pad, Grey and Parker stood off to the side. Parker was busy with his phone, casting glances at us periodically. He looked like he'd rather be anywhere else.

Grey...He had his arms crossed as he watched us with focused intensity. I searched his face for any sign of the fight, and there were plenty. Dark bruising lined his jaw and under one eye, and then some swelling I could make out from here.

I'd wanted to come back to them. Then they found me, or rather Matías gave me up. Either way, I was right back with my hands tied behind my back, unable to leave, unable to have freedom over my own life. Was this what I genuinely wanted?

I wasn't sure...

The wind whipped through their hair, ruffling their shirts until strips of their toned stomachs flashed us. They didn't seem bothered by the force or sound of the landing. Grey, at least, seemed impatient for us to land.

My heart fluttered in my chest as I got a good look at

him. He seemed fine. Larger than life, really. The bruises were much darker up close, mottling one side of his face around his eye and mouth.

We'd barely landed when Grey was there, opening the door. He reached in, deftly releasing my seatbelt and plucking the headset off my head. The dying sound of the engine roared in my ears without the protection, and my nerves rioted in my stomach as I just watched him. He tossed the headset into Lafe's lap, grabbed my hips, and lifted me from the helicopter.

"What the hell, Grey!" I squealed as he tossed me over his shoulder, landing a hard swat to my ass. "Ouch, you asshole!"

Another swat as he started us toward the house. As soon as he turned, I faced Parker, who had his gaze glued to where my ass had been. Andre and Lafe were coming around to the back of the helicopter, both slowing to a stop. All three watched us with some level of fascination as Grey turned to the side.

Parker with an amused smirk and a slight shake of his head. Lafe with a furrowed brow, and Andre with an unreadable expression.

"Grey, put me down. I can walk."

"No," he grunted when the door bumped his hip. Men prowled through the commons, some stopping to stare. I almost expected them to catcall since most of my ass was hanging out under the cotton shorts, but they didn't. They lowered their gazes and looked away.

He headed straight toward their residential hall and double-timed his steps to reach his door. I didn't bother trying to reason with him anymore. Part of me was so extremely happy to feel him. To know he was okay and wasn't laid up somewhere recovering from shattered bones.

I let myself have a few minutes of dirty pleasure by smoothing my hands down his back. His strong muscles firm under my fingertips. I closed my eyes and reveled in the feel of him.

Then I was airborne and bounced on the bed. He said nothing as his gaze burned through me. We stared at each other, breathing hard.

"Grey," I whispered.

That was all it took. He stripped me down in record time, growling unintelligibly. Each yank lifted me from the bed and I landed back with a small grunt. He wasn't gentle. He wasn't soft or sensual.

There was a pure unbridled need in the way he touched me.

I didn't have any time to react as he fell to his knees and lifted my ass, bringing my pussy straight to his face.

"Mine," he groaned and licked a swath from my ass to my clit. I gasped and reached down to slide my fingers through his hair, gripping the strands when he repeated the motion.

I dropped back, pushing my hands through my own hair and pulling to offset the intense pleasure rocketing through me. He tongued my clit, then sucked on it, rising away from my pussy until just a bit of pain registered. Then he released it and dove back down.

It felt like he had eaten me for hours, but it had to only be minutes. Each dig of his fingers into my ass, each bite and nip along the inside of my thighs, drove me insane. He knew exactly when I was close and moved away. Not letting me come.

After another week of constantly being on guard, not knowing when I would be rescued, if I was rescued at all, I needed to come. I needed the release, to let go of everything that had happened since I was taken and live in the moment.

Grey slowly circled his tongue around my clit, the soothing rhythm sending burning sweetness through my core. I gasped as little soft noises escaped my throat. Just when I could feel it, that dark abyss rolling closer, Grey backed off and bit the apex of my thigh, hard.

"Ouch!" I tried to scoot back, but his grip was too much. "What the hell are you doing?" I screamed at him and pulled his hair.

"Teaching you a lesson." He watched me with dark, blazing green eyes. No, they weren't green right now. His pupils were so dilated from desire that they nearly looked as black as Parker's.

"I was taken!" I struggled against his hold, and he bit me again. This time, I thought he drew blood.

"You didn't fight. Where was my fierce, wicked little love?" He dropped my ass to the bed and pinned me down with a forearm across my stomach. Then he thrust two fingers inside me. "You were in enemy territory. No one but my brothers and me were safe. Yet you let yourself be fucking taken."

He twisted his fingers hard and curled them against my g-spot. The pleasure competing with the pain hurt so damn good. My eyes rolled back in my head.

I forced myself to focus. This was not my fault. There was nothing I could do. I bucked again and screamed, trying to dislodge his arm. He pulled his fingers out and smacked my clit. I groaned.

"They drugged me. I never saw them." I groaned as he pushed his fingers back inside, adding a third and fucking me within an inch of my life with his thick, calloused fingers. "I was worried about you, you fucking bastard! I thought he was going to kill you!" Tears burned my eyes just like the image of him falling to his knees before that man had been branded in my brain.

"Oh no. You don't get to play that card." He fucked me faster, and my core started to light up with white fire. I held my breath and curled my toes. Needing something to grip, I dug my nails into his forearm. "I was never going to die. Vicente wouldn't kill me, and my brothers wouldn't let that happen either. They should have fucking stayed with you." He bared his teeth in a feral snarl.

"It wasn't their fault," I groaned, squeezing my eyes shut. He was punishing me. That was what this was. A punishment.

One I didn't even know I craved.

"It fucking was. Just like it was your fucking fault. You should have stuck to them like glue. You don't leave their sight ever fucking again. If I'm not there, you stick to them. They jump, you follow. You're fucking lucky you weren't raped and killed!" he roared.

"You're fucking lucky they saved you! What the fuck is your problem!" I pushed against his chest, but he flipped me over to my stomach. I'd just started to push myself up when he curved his body over mine—his naked body.

His hard cock pressed against the top of my ass as he growled in my ear. "You know better! Not again, *mami*. Not fucking again. The next time you let someone take you, I'll fuck your ass for days with no relief. Hell, I might even invite Parker to watch. Would that make you uncomfortable?" He pressed down on my neck, keeping my face in the covers.

I groaned as vicious heat swept through my body. I didn't want that. I wasn't an exhibitionist. What I did with Grey against the glass was as kinky as I'd ever been.

"You like that, don't you? Your skin is flushed pink, and you're breathing hard. That can be his payback for you getting off to him." He raised up, smacking my ass.

The sound cracked through the room, and the sensitive skin smarted as he smoothed a hand over it.

"Fuck you, Grey! I'm not a fucking toy!" I braced my hands against the bed to push myself up, but he was too fucking strong.

He lined his cock up with my opening, notching his head just inside, then seated himself fully. I could feel how hot my face got. I whined, embarrassed by how needy it sounded. I didn't want this, yet I did. The only thing my body seemed capable of was to get him deeper. I pushed back against him.

"You're my toy, aren't you, my wicked love? You belong to me. No one is going to take you from us again. I fucking forbid it." He started to move, and my fingers curled in the blankets from the delicious drag of his cock inside me.

He was slow yet forceful, making sure I understood him completely. "You want to save lives, then fight. Because next time, I'll handle things my way, and you won't like all the blood I spill."

That was the end of our conversation as he pounded into me. The obscene sound of flesh smacking against flesh drove my pleasure higher. But I wanted to see him. I wanted to see the savage beauty of his face as he came. I ached for it.

"I want to see you," I whimpered, trying to turn my head.

He landed another hit on the side of my ass. "No. This time, this is for me," he echoed the words he'd said not that long ago.

He picked up speed, hitting that secret spot inside. Once, twice, then twice more. Waves and waves of acute pleasure started at my core and echoed outward. I quaked underneath him, and it wasn't long until his rhythm staggered and his guttural groans filled the room, eclipsing every other sound.

Grey dropped against my back, our sweat-dampened skin sliding together. He took us to our sides and wrapped his arms around me completely, tucking his knees into the back of mine.

Pressing a kiss against my nape, he nuzzled the spot below my ear. Now he was giving me the sweet attention I had wanted initially. Tears wet my eyes again as I sucked in a breath. He could have died. This could have been a dream if his brothers hadn't jumped down to save him.

"I won't regret them saving you." My voice wobbled, and he squeezed me tighter. "Just like I won't apologize."

"Just remember what I said." He smoothed his jaw along the side of my head. *Remember what he threatened.*

What did that even mean, next time he'd do things his way?

"Did you all look for me?" I asked. My heartbeat, which hadn't slowed, started to increase in tempo. It shouldn't matter, but at the same time, I needed the validation that I hadn't just been a problem they couldn't wait to get rid of.

It was ridiculous that I'd even care so much. This was classic Stockholm Syndrome. I knew that and still needed to hear him say how much they wanted me back.

"Andre spoke to everyone he dared to, trying to figure out where you were...Then Matías called." He sounded tired as he finally rested his head on the bed behind me.

What Andre confessed in the helicopter started to trickle back in as ice slipped down my neck.

"Andre said Vicente was after you all now." Not exactly his words, but that was the gist of it. "Is that true?"

He grunted, and my heart sank. "Vicente's playing his games. That's what he does."

I stared at the wall, bare except for a dresser and a darkly ethereal landscape portrait. That didn't ring true. It didn't even sound like Grey believed it. He was placating me, and for what? To keep me docile?

"But never with *all* of you. Not like this." It was a statement.

"Vicente's not happy with us right now." He avoided the meat of the problem. Not voicing what their reality really was. Because I was an outsider?

That burned in a different way, and I wanted to bang my head against the wall. I couldn't make sense of my own emotions because I was ecstatic to be back and hurt he wasn't telling me the truth. Although I understood why he didn't, it still fucking hurt.

It made me question everything.

"Why won't you say that he's trying to take you all down?" I whispered, anger winning out as my fingers bit into his arms.

"Because you don't need to worry about that. It's not going to touch you." He sounded so sure. His voice was strong, with a thread of darkness weaving its way through.

Wasn't it, though? If Vicente hurt them, I would go down with them. As collateral damage, if nothing else.

I squeezed my eyes shut, this time to attempt to block out the damning thoughts. For a week, I'd driven myself crazy thinking the worst had happened to Grey. He was here, alive, and plastered to my back. I needed to hold onto this reality–this pleasure.

But my brain couldn't be controlled.

Grey couldn't guarantee my safety. He couldn't promise

anything. Not when their world was full of backstabbers, killers, and manipulators.

Inky, horrible thoughts pelted me.

Would I be used against them again? I was self-aware enough to know when I was a liability. As much as it choked me to admit, Grey was right. I hadn't been as vigilant as I should have been because I let myself get caught up in worrying over him.

If Vicente got to me once, there was no reason to think he wouldn't target me again. And succeed.

Grace.

If not for them, I needed to think of my sister.

I sucked in a deep breath.

In the middle of a crime war, would my identity be safe? Would my sister?

A tear ripped through my heart. I'd gotten attached to this fucking asshole. I begrudgingly liked most of the brothers, even if I didn't understand them. The more time I spent around them, the more I saw them as men just trying to do the best they could.

But I had to think about what this fight with Vicente would do to the one I loved the most.

"Grey," I started, then paused. This was fucking hard after I'd worried about him so much. It felt so good to lie here with his steady heartbeat against my back.

"Hm," he answered sleepily.

"I want to stay with Andre." I held my breath as my words registered.

He stopped breathing, too. Shocked, I was sure, because there was absolutely no love lost between Andre and me.

"What did you say?" He couldn't believe his ears. I almost laughed. "Why would you want to stay with that *pendejo*?" Grey tightened his arms around my middle like he wouldn't let me go.

Because he was my best chance to get accurate information and maybe even an ally to leave their lives.

It felt like a lie to my own ears.

"I don't have to give you a reason. We're not dating. This isn't a fairytale."

He laughed, and it was filled with a nastiness I hadn't heard from Grey.

"You're being fucking serious. You want me to take you to my brother with my cum leaking out of you?" He flexed his hips, pushing his half-hard dick further inside me to make his point.

I winced. But I wouldn't be a liability to them. For all the doubt I had and the crimes I'd witnessed, they weren't the bad men I had initially wanted to paint them. For their sake and mine, I needed to get away from them. Otherwise...

Shit, I didn't want to think about worst-case scenarios.

He pulled out and shoved away from me. I almost mewed at the loss.

Raking his hands through his hair and pacing the room, our combined fluids drying on his cock, he laughed again. Then snarled, whipping his head back to me.

"No."

I jerked my head back in shock. "No?"

"Why do you want to go to Andre? The fucking truth, Amorette." He towered over me, a menace sliding through his gaze.

When I didn't answer, he scowled. "You think we haven't got your number? You have a hero complex. Maybe even a martyr complex. I don't fucking know. But as soon as I confirm Vicente's targeting us, you want to go to the brother who would kill you as easily as he would tie his fucking shoe?" He shook his head. "And don't think that's still the case, *mamí*. Andre was the one hunting for you. You won't get what you're looking for from him. So, no. You're not going anywhere. Especially drenched in me. Lay the fuck down and go to sleep. After you've had a nap, maybe we'll chat. If you're still spewing this bullshit, I'll fuck you again. And again and again, until you get it out of your *estupido* head that you can leave."

He stomped out of the bedroom and slammed the door.

I thought he would come back, but he didn't. The longer he stayed gone, the more my stomach twisted into vile, furious knots.

His stinging accusations rang in my ears with every breath.

Yes, I wanted to help people. I wanted to make the world a better place. A lot of people did. That didn't mean they had a hero complex. And making decisions based on the amount of trouble it would bring the people I cared about didn't make me a martyr.

I groaned into the pillow. By the actual definition, I could see how I fit both on paper. But this wasn't about saving other people. It was about saving *them*.

There was one last question on my tongue, but I never got to ask it. Grey would have laughed in my face, anyway. It was the only thing circling my mind as I fell asleep.

How was I going to fight when I didn't even know the rules?

9

ANDRE

The cool air from the fridge in the main kitchen washed over me, and I stood there, enjoying the shock of temperature.

Amorette was alive and unhurt. Matías had seemingly taken good care of her, but to what end? There had to be some hidden agenda I couldn't see. I had expected Vicente's men to ambush us as soon as we walked out. When they didn't, I thought they'd drive us off the road. When they didn't do that either, I was left fucking confused.

He was Vicente's golden child—the one who would inherit everything one day.

What was more surprising was the lack of staff at his house. He didn't have a mansion, not like Vicente's, though it was still a monstrous size. Usually, twenty to thirty men patrolled the area with the occasional maid or two.

There were two men. One at the edge of the property and one in the backyard on the roof of the detached garage. *One* of the detached garages.

I only knew that because I had a man on his team until

last year when Vicente stationed him with Maikel. Still useful, but it left a blind spot where Matías was concerned.

He'd told me about how slim Matías ran his ship, but I hadn't believed him.

"Are you going to share what happened? I'm dying for the details," Parker said dryly. I turned and shut the fridge, finding him leaning against the doorframe with his hands in his pockets.

He'd changed since they met us on the pad. Showered too.

"We got her back. It wasn't a trap." I went to walk past him, but he stopped me with a hand on my shoulder.

"Mm. No, *hermano*. We're all on the block—" I raised a brow, and Parker's nostrils flared, but he didn't acknowledge that he was the reason why we were all there—"and we should all be in the loop."

I pushed around him, heading to my office, nodding at a few of our men. Parker kept up with me step for step, with his hands clasped behind his back.

Once we were in my office, he shut my door and sprawled out in the chair in front of my desk. "Okay. Now that we're alone. No ears to hear, tell me what happened."

I sighed. "Then shouldn't you call Lafe and Grey in so we can have a group meeting?" The question dripped with sarcasm, but I was fucking tired of being the only one who cared about saving their sorry asses.

He waved a hand. "Lafe hates this stuff. And he was there, so he knows what happened. Grey's probably balls-deep inside Amorette right now. We can fill him in later." A smirk hooked one side of his mouth.

Using my forefinger, I rubbed the skin above my eyebrow. Fucking Parker.

"We got her back. It wasn't a trap. We need to keep our

ear to the ground to see what Vicente's next move will be. This could have been him just being his fucked-up self, playing with us." I leaned back against the chair, the wheels creaking from the shift in pressure.

"Uh-uh." He shook a finger at me like I was some kind of naughty fucking kid without a clue. "That's where you're going off course. Vicente's already making his next move." Fire flashed in his eyes. "Jorge called. His job was compromised, and some of my men were injured as a result. None dead, thankfully. He's cleaning it up, although there's no way this should have happened. Vicente's circling."

I stiffened. If Vicente was actually out for those men, at least a few would have died. This was a game of cat and mouse.

"What, you thought Vicente would just forget and forgive?" He scoffed in disgust.

That wasn't what I'd been thinking at all. I had been enjoying the reprieve while also trying to find the fucking bane of our lives. We needed time to regroup. Do research. Build alliances.

"Matías said he didn't harm her. He fed her and clothed her. Didn't touch her. And to remember that."

Parker jerked his head back. "No request for payment? No favor to call in at a later date?"

"No, unless you count that as a favor to be called in later," I said as I shook my head. I was just as confused. "When I asked if she'd been there the whole time, he said yes, straight from Vicente's hands. When I asked why he'd taken so long to call us, he said he had his reasons. That was the extent of our very stilted conversation."

"Hmm. That's a twist I didn't see coming." He rested his elbow on the arm of the chair and propped up his chin.

"You think he's trying to take over Vicente's place without waiting for the old man to die?"

I blinked. Parker and I... didn't have brainstorming sessions. I worked on keeping Vicente off our backs, and he did whatever the fuck he did on his own or with Mia.

"I already thought of that. If Vicente hand-delivered Amorette, he'd be pissed Matías gave her back to us," I drawled.

"You're sure he didn't touch her? And you're sure she didn't know him before she came to us?"

I snorted. "I'm positive. He didn't have a scratch on him. If he'd tried to touch her, she would have fought like the devil. Funny, she lets Grey get so much of her." I grinned, but it was short-lived. "And no, I don't believe Amorette knew him before us. She's not a plant. Just knowing her is to know she's a diehard for her beliefs. She's *not* a plant. You saw her background check just like I did."

"Just covering all the bases and playing devil's advocate." He tapped his fingers on his cheek. "You think he's taken with her?"

"No. He wouldn't have given her back if he was." Matías was a lot of things, but noble wasn't one of them. If he'd wanted her, he would have fucked her. And kept her.

"We need to—" He stopped speaking as his phone rang. He pulled it out and answered while holding eye contact with me. "Hello?"

His eyes widened a millisecond before he raced from my office toward the main doors. The fucker was fast, but I stayed on his heels. He put his phone away and slammed through the glass door so hard I was surprised it didn't fly off its hinges.

A hummer idled at the curb and when the door opened, a long slender leg stepped out. Just from that leg, I knew precisely who it was. Mia appeared, looking no worse for the fucking wear, except for a bit of light color darkening her eyes like she hadn't slept in days.

Dark red hair tumbled around her head as if she'd just left the spa, and her outfit was chic and crisp without a wrinkle in sight. Where the hell had she fucking been?

Her lips were pinched as her gaze roamed over Parker's face, probably disliking the bruises he'd acquired while we went to get Amorette. Then her gaze snapped to me, and her lips flattened even more.

She threw her arms around Parker in a fierce but quick hug and stepped back. "We need to talk," she said in a low voice. I could only hear it because I was now essentially riding Parker's ass.

"My office," I snapped, then led the way. Their footsteps quickened behind me.

I hadn't wanted Mia to be hurt. Contrary to Amorette's opinion of me, I didn't enjoy hurting and killing people unless it served a purpose. My purpose. Nevertheless, Mia simply waltzing back into our compound like nothing had fucking happened.

It stank of suspicion. For more than a few reasons.

Inside my office, I waited until they filed in, then shut the door behind them. Seething with fury at the unexpected turn of events, I planted my ass against the wall and crossed my arms.

"What the hell happened to you?"

"Back the fuck off," Parker growled. Then he turned to Mia. His gaze didn't soften, even though his tone did. "Where the hell have you been? I was convinced Vicente had you."

She dropped her head until her red hair fell in her face. After a little shake, she turned back to him, cutting her gaze at me every few seconds as if she wasn't sure what I knew. That was right, they'd always had their secrets, but I knew about this suicide mission.

Their secret club was about to gain three new members.

"He knows. I told them what you were doing when I thought Vicente had you and took someone else from us. It's too dangerous for them not to know." Parker flicked his gaze at me, then back to Mia.

It was clear neither one enjoyed my presence here. Well, too fucking bad. Parker's time of running rogue was over—if he wanted to stay with this family. If he didn't...

A burning knife twisted in my chest, but my expression never changed.

If he wanted to leave, that was up to him, but I'd be damned if he took all of us down with him.

"I've been tracing Vicente's childhood and visiting the villages. There's nothing crazy in his past. Nothing that we can blackmail him on." Mia inhaled and slowly let it out. "He was born to Mexican-American parents in Texas but moved to South America when he was ten. Parents died when he was fourteen and he joined the local cartel. The rest is history. I have the full, or as full as I could make it, report on how he climbed to the top then started his own legacy. He did some shady shit, though nothing that wasn't expected or respected with a man taking over the cartel."

"Is there any way Vicente could have known what you were doing?" I asked.

Mia turned to face me. Her face was tense, like she wasn't sure she wanted to share any details with me. "No. I'm absolutely certain that he couldn't have known. I was disguised, went dark, and kept my probing to a delightful minimum."

Delightful. Now she sounded like Parker.

I glanced at Parker. If Vicente didn't know about Mia, then why the hell had he taken Amorette? He must have been thinking the same exact thing I was, because he touched her shoulder.

"Is there anything—anything—you found that was suspicious?"

She hesitated.

"If you have something to say, fucking say it." I was losing my patience with them, fast. This whole time I'd been tiptoeing around Vicente. Maybe Grey was right, and he was just fucking around with us because, like idiots, we flaunted a woman in front of him. Something we'd never done before.

"I wasn't the only one asking about Vicente. There was someone else there before me. I don't know who, and the locals wouldn't share. They were nervous, like they knew exactly who had been there but were too afraid to tell me."

What a clusterfuck. "Thanks, Mia. You can go now." I reached out and opened the door.

She scoffed and glared at me. "Whatever." Mia looked at Parker. "I'll stay with Grey tonight. Then I need to head back home tomorrow."

Parker stood up with her and caught her elbow. "About that..." He tried to contain his shit-eating smirk and failed. "I wouldn't go to Grey's place. You can crash in my spare."

"I always stay at Grey's." Her face twisted up in confusion. "You're a terrible roommate."

That almost made me grin. Parker could be eccentric when he wanted to be.

"We've..." His gaze darted to me for a second as he considered his words, and that caught my attention. Did he not trust Mia? They were childhood best friends. If he didn't trust her, I sure as fuck didn't, either. "We've collected a woman. She's ours now, right, dear brother?"

Mia looked at me, and I raised one brow. What the fuck was he playing at?

"Okay...So you've all finally broken the seal and brought a fuck buddy here. What's that have to do with Grey's guest room? That's where all my stuff is at."

"You see, Mia. Grey's quite smitten with her. I'm sure he's currently busy fucking her into next week. You'd be cramping his style, you understand?" Parker grinned full-out.

"And you're all sharing her?" She glanced between us. *That* shocked her.

"No," I denied.

"Yes."

What the fuck, Parker?

"In a platonic way, of course. We've all taken responsibility for her. She's like our new little sister. Right, Andre?"

Why was he constantly putting this back on me?

"Mia, it's been a pleasure." I ignored Parker and nodded my head toward the door. She huffed but left. When Parker tried to leave on her heels, I shoved him back. "Not you."

He laughed and shrugged, leaning his ass against my desk. "And sit the fuck down. I don't want your ass prints on my desk."

Now that Mia was here, with no news of Vicente's sinister plot, he was acting like his old, devious self. Yet I hadn't forgotten why Mia was gone in the first place.

"What's wrong, Andre? This is great news."

"Are you done? Are you going to leave this ridiculous scheme alone?" I didn't need to elaborate, Parker knew exactly what I was talking about.

The humor dropped from his face. "No."

"Why the fuck not?" I exploded, pushing away from the wall and yanking him to me by his collar. "Do you have any fucking idea how dangerous your games are? We have ourselves to look after. Hell, we have Amorette to look after, because she's a fucking liability! And you're going to continue to put our asses on the line? Abso-fucking-not!" Our noses nearly touched, then I shoved him backward.

He barely budged, straightening his shirt as he scowled at me. "We'd already decided to take Vicente out. You agreed, Andre. You fucking agreed! For us to thrive, he has to go. It's great if he didn't know what Mia was doing. Except the fact remains, he still took Amorette! He still took her, and that's a sign. People are talking. We're not safe, whether I sit with my thumb up my ass or not." He stopped, his chest heaving.

"We don't know that. Vicente has always played his games."

"We do know that, and if you're ignoring the signs, you deserve the death that's coming for you." He tried to push past me, but I stopped him again.

"This family is all I've ever cared about. If you want to continue trying to thwart Vicente no matter the cost, be my guest. But not here." I slowly shook my head.

Shock widened his eyes. "Are you fucking kidding me? You're kicking me out of the compound?" His eyes nearly disappeared under his brows as he glared at me with something close to hate. That twisted the knife a little harder, but I returned his glare.

"If you're going to get us all killed because you can't stop stirring shit up, yes." I grimaced. "You wanted to leave us anyway, so consider this my blessing."

Parker vibrated with so much rage he was about to go off at any moment. "We're supposed to take Vicente down together! I never wanted to leave you fuckers! I wanted to live my own life, and yes, for a moment, the only way I could see to do that was to leave you all behind." He seethed as he walked toward me, hitting my chest with both hands until I stepped back. "Is this truly the life you want? You work yourself to death. You obsess over every little thing Vicente does or doesn't do. Everything is a sign to you, and it has to be fucking exhausting!" He hit me again, and my back hit the wall.

"I'm not going to watch you get yourself killed!" I yelled, balling up my fist, ready to knock some sense into his thick skull. Pain started to gather behind my eyes. My fucking baby brother was trying to give me one hell of a migraine.

He stepped back and composed himself. Barely. When he opened his eyes, fury burned in their depths. "I'm not fucking leaving, and I'm living the life that you want for us. Is that what you want for Lafe? He'll be dead before he's thirty. Is this what you want for Grey? He's finally focusing on something other than fighting his way to the whipping post. What about for sweet Little Love? Regardless of whose bed she's in, she's ours now. We took responsibility for her when we let her live and refused to let her go home. You know Vicente needs to die. I just gave us a head start."

I huffed. "You want to bring Amorette into this? She'd hate the idea of a war. She hates murder. She thinks we're all one step away from evil already. That bitch will either try to run again or turn us over to go home, because she's stupid enough to believe Vicente will let her go."

"She's not," he argued. "If she's learned anything, it's that she can't trust anyone else. Don't worry about Amorette. I'll take care of her."

This time, when he tried to leave, I didn't stop him.

Parker was wrong...but he was also right.

Que chingado. I pulled my chair out from my desk with too much force and it rammed the wall. When I pulled it away, black scuff marks marred the wall. God damn it. I'd clean it off in a minute. Better the wall than my desk.

Firing up my laptop, I started researching and crafting a few messages. No matter what we did, Vicente taking Amorette was a clear fuck you. We were out, and everyone knew it.

We needed to know why.

10

PARKER

Well, well. What a pleasant surprise.

One of Vicente's leading vendors for his smuggling business wanted to have lunch. Not terribly out of the ordinary, considering I ran the thieves. An idea started forming in my mind as I debated how to respond to his text.

"See, this is why I hate staying with you." Mia walked out of the bedroom, dressed in the same clothes she was in yesterday. I guess I could have collected some of her things from Grey's, but I didn't want to disturb the lovebirds.

I also didn't fancy getting sucker-punched again. I doubt the bastard would wait for me to tell him Mia wasn't the reason Vicente took Little Love.

"Why? Because I'm not a dick on tap for you to ride?" I read Snowman's message over again.

Snowman: Dinner at my place?

His estate was practically a museum for the rich pricks of Costa Rica. Right on the coast, in the elite part of the tourism district.

Mia gagged. "I've never wanted your dick. Grey's was

okay. But I find I much prefer the sweeter things in life."
Sometime after her romp with my brother, she decided she
preferred women. I had been waiting for the right time to
taunt Grey about driving her to the other sex, but now
wasn't that time. "What I meant was, you're terrible
company. You're on your phone constantly when I stay with
you."

"Amorette didn't have any complaints when she stayed
here," I murmured.

Park: 7 sharp. I'm bringing a plus one.

"Who? Oh, the adopted sister?" She snickered. "Why is
she even here? You four have never trusted anyone to be in
your collective inner circle. I can't even remember the last
time the four of you were in the same room together." Mia
tapped her bottom lip with her finger. "The others don't
even trust me, and we grew up together."

"Mia," I glanced up with a smirk, "are you jealous?"

"No." She straightened her spine, offended. "I'm just
pointing out that this is strange for you four."

I shrugged. This wasn't for her to understand. Little Love
brought something to the compound that had never been
here. Amusement. She made things interesting with how
Grey lost his head over her, and Lafe was now breaking all
his rules.

She sighed. "Fine, I'll butt out. On to more important
matters, I want to start working on who this mysterious
party is."

Now that caught my attention. "Yes, tell me more about
this mysterious party. Is this a new gang on the street?" Mia
wouldn't have shared all her information in front of Andre.
As much as he didn't trust her, she returned the favor.

"I'm not sure." She twisted her lips to the side. "This

mystery party is no more than a ghost. If it wasn't for my excellent skills at reading people—"

"You're welcome for that."

"—Then I wouldn't have even known something was going on. I'm going to look into it more."

A new player made sense. Why else would a man try and take out Grey? Of course, we could never rule out Vicente as the mastermind. He was too twisted, enjoying how people acted and reacted. Exciting things were happening lately.

"Let me know what you find," I said absently as I went back to my phone.

Park: Where are you?

Grey: My apartment. Going for a workout later.

Mia rolled her eyes when I glanced at her. I was surprised she was still sitting here.

"I'll take that as my cue to go."

I grinned. "Don't let the door hit you on the ass on the way out. And don't go by Grey's. I don't think he'd take it very well if you tried to steal our Little Love."

She shook her head in disbelief. "You all have lost your minds. Absolutely gonzo." Then she tilted her head. "Is she beautiful? It's been a while since I've had a good hookup."

"Sorry, you won't be meeting her. And I'm sure as much as Grey is fond of you, he'd tear out your heart if you made a move." I laughed. Maybe I should take her to meet Amorette. It would be fun.

I headed to my room to take a shower, and by the time I came out, all traces of Mia were gone.

As my best friend, we didn't feel the need to put on false pretenses. We were happy to exist as our authentic selves. And truth be told, as much as I trusted some of my top men,

Mia was the only one I would bet my life on outside of my brothers.

The history was too deep. She would never betray us.

Whistling, I walked down the hallway to Grey's. Knocking on the door, I stepped back and waited. Now that Mia was safe, and Amorette was safe, all was right in the world.

I was just glad to be rid of that dark fucking rain cloud that had been hovering over my head for days.

When no one came, I knocked again. Louder this time. More obnoxious.

"Grey! You can't hide. You already texted me that you're in there!" I called through the door.

Another minute passed, then a flushed Grey answered the door, his dick at attention under his towel.

"Did I interrupt? My apologies." I grinned and stepped through the door as he moved back.

"Motherfucker," he grumbled. After he shut and locked it, he left me standing there as he stalked back through the apartment like hell was on his ass.

Strolling through, because I wasn't in a hurry, I froze when I hit the living room. The kitchen and living room were empty. *Where the hell did he go?*

He did have an erect dick...

Then the rhythmic banging started up. Grey's headboard was having a hell of a time, and look, he left his bedroom door cracked.

Sex had always been a fun recreational activity. And if I could piss someone off while doing it, even better.

The thought of big, bad Grey railing our sweet little love, well, that was too compelling to sit on the couch and wait like a good boy.

I stepped up to the crack, peering in. I could barely make out their calves. So what did I do? I opened the door.

Heat engulfed me from the bottom of my feet to the tips of my fingers, ending with the hair on my scalp. Thank fuck, Grey kept his doors oiled. It hadn't made nary a sound.

I stepped into the room, crossed my arms, and leaned back against the door.

My brothers getting their rocks off had never done it for me. But the size difference between Grey and Amorette, as he had her on all fours in front of him while gripping her petite but round ass while pounding into her...that was a sight to see. The span of his hands nearly swallowed up her entire cheeks. And look, I had the profile view.

Perfect.

Her face was turned away from me, but all that lush dark hair was draped across her slender back. Her skin was just as pink as Grey's face, scattered with little drops of sweat. One drop, in particular, rolled down her spine, and I wanted to lick it.

Her sweet gasps and moans complimented Grey's guttural groans perfectly. I had to give it to my brother, they did sex well together. The tempo of her noises increased as his pace became erratic.

"I want—" She tried to push up, but he slammed a hand on her upper back to keep her pinned to the bed. He gave her ass a smack with his other hand, never faltering for a moment.

"This way," he growled, and it tapered off into a deep grunt.

"Fucking hell, Grey!" She struggled against him, and when he moved his hands over her petite body, his red handprint glowed on her pale ass.

Little Love just managed to turn her head my way, and

her eyes widened. Her mouth then became a perfect little 'o'.

I grinned, biting my lip.

"Park—" she started, but Grey smacked her ass again and grabbed the meat of it to pull her into his thrusts. Her eyes rolled back, and a long, decadent moan filled the air.

My cock throbbed as her hair stuck to her face and her body twitched. A sure sign of a woman well-satisfied. I ached to take mine out and stroke it. It wouldn't take much.

Two pumps. Maybe three.

Then Grey was going so hard, I thought he was going to slam her head into the headboard. Just when I was about to step forward, he followed after her, tossing his head back.

I couldn't keep the absurd grin from splitting my face. I was so glad I decided now was the time to come here. Over the years, I wanted to be the one others watched. There was something thrilling about it, and I thrived on the ecstasy of it.

However, watching them was just as–if not arguably more–hot than anything I'd ever experienced. And that she came when her gaze collided with mine. Mmm.

Little Love opened her eyes, alarm sinking back into their depths. Shit, I hummed out loud. It didn't matter. She knew I was here.

Her gaze dropped to my own massive tent, and somehow, the impossibly wide grin grew even broader. Grey just ignored me as he started to lazily pump inside of her. The bastard was still half hard.

She scrambled forward in a burst of energy, grappling for the sheet to cover herself. Grey stayed still in his shock, and to be fair, I was also frozen.

The glimpse of her beautiful, tiny, yet curvy body was

hell on my erection. It would be up for at least another ten minutes.

Once she was covered, Grey backed off the bed, his half-hard dick swinging.

I balked.

"You took her raw?" We never fucked anyone raw. Ever. The last thing we needed was little minis running around when it took all our energy to keep ourselves out of trouble. Not that Grey or I tried very hard. Trouble was so much more fun.

He barely glanced at me as he reached for the discarded towel on the floor and wiped away the clear cream coating his now softening dick. I didn't really need an answer; it was there for everyone in the room to see.

"What the hell are you doing in here?" Amorette screeched, and I plugged a finger in my ear.

"Ow. I'm glad that's not the pitch of your screams of pleasure. That would have been a turn-off, Little Love."

Grey snickered but didn't respond. He was too busy getting his shorts on for his workout, although it looked like he'd already had a great one.

"Get out!" she screeched again, tossing a pillow at my head.

"If you wanted privacy, you shouldn't have left the door open." I adjusted my pants. Hell, my dick was sensitive, rubbing against the denim like that.

Her anger turned to Grey, who glared at me. "I thought I shut the door, but he wasn't going to stop knocking, and I wasn't going to stop fucking you. Anyway, it's not like you haven't seen him fucking."

"Oh, is that so?" I was fucking delighted. What a fantastic turn to the conversation.

Little Love flushed an even deeper red, then covered her face.

"The club. We were standing at the glass by the conference rooms when you bent the girl over." Now that he was dressed, he walked on his knees to where Amorette was propped against the headboard. He tried to pry the sheet from her face, but she wouldn't budge. He frowned down at her.

"Well, then I feel extra validated for being here." I peeked down at my aching cock. "I came to get you for a job, Little Love. Only it appears I need a cold shower." Then a smile tipped one side of my mouth. "Unless you'd like to help me take care of it?"

Her instant refusals were overshadowed by Grey's swift bark of, "No!"

My smile dropped.

"Be happy you got to see that much," he said, managing to get the sheet down. She was still embarrassed to hell and back, but she looked up at him with a mixture of desire, anger, and frustration.

"Did you invite him on purpose?" she accused.

What an interesting thought.

"No," he answered like that was a ridiculous question. "That was just a taunt to get you hotter, *mamí.*"

And wasn't that curious. I'd have to find out more about that later.

"All right, lovebirds. I need to go take care of this." I waved at my dick. "Thanks for the material. Little Love, I'll return to get you in a couple of hours. Get pretty, we're going to dinner with an associate of mine."

Grey whipped his head my way. "Hell no. Not while Vicente is watching us."

"Not an issue." Not much of an issue, but I also knew he

was plucking away at my men. "Mia's back. Taking Amorette wasn't because of Mia. I'll make sure to take men with me. Nevertheless, on the off chance this was some twisted joke, we need to carry on as usual." I turned toward the door.

"I'm going too."

"Sorry, big brother," I called over my shoulder as I walked through the apartment. "You're not invited. I'm meeting with the Snowman."

He groaned and started speaking to Amorette in a low voice.

Shit, too bad we were at the compound. I really could use some help with this...issue.

11

AMORETTE

Two hours after Parker watched me fall apart, I was still heated. I'd never been watched like that before, and I wasn't sure if it was the shock, surprise, or a newfound kink, but I'd never come that hard.

I needed foundation makeup to cover up the blush if I was going to spend hours with him, and there was none here in my shade. Damn it.

Tossing the mascara into the drawer, I left the guest bedroom. I'd found another wrap dress and paired it with another set of small heels Grey had gotten for me. Except I felt silly walking out of here as red as a grape. It wasn't attractive.

And the closer it got to Parker picking me up, the more flustered I grew. How was I supposed to look him in the eyes?

This was different from the warehouse. Those men seeing me naked, Randal assaulting me, it was all in a different compartment. They were pure evil and my anger at their deeds made the situation different.

The brothers had given me some semblance of normalcy again, and three of the four had seen me naked.

I sucked in a deep breath. This was ridiculous. Things like this didn't matter to me.

But when I glanced down at his body.... he had been turned-on.

That was the issue.

I didn't want Parker. He gave off too many frat boy vibes with a dash of sociopath. But there was something about being in the room with both Grey and Parker as they watched me...

I shivered.

"I don't like this," Grey sighed as he came up behind me and hugged me to his chest. Dropping my head back, I did my best to control my expression. There was, unfortunately, nothing I could do about the constant pink in my face.

"You're sure you didn't invite him in? You threatened it last night."

He sneered, "I didn't threaten. It was the heat of the moment."

"We should have stopped when you let him in." I tried to step away, but he squeezed me tighter.

"Like hell. He's my brother. He's seen people fucking before. It's not a big deal."

"Really?" I narrowed my eyes at him. "So if he would have joined—"

"Fuck no. You're mine, and I don't share." Funny how he defined *share*.

A knock came at the door and Grey went to answer it.

When Parker appeared, he was dressed in a sleek black suit perfectly tailored to his body. Without my permission, my gaze skated down to his pants, then I turned around and closed my eyes. What the hell was wrong with me?

"You look fabulous tonight, Little Love," Parker taunted.

"Fuck off." I flipped the bird over my shoulder as I picked up my clutch off the couch. It was empty except for Chapstick and a paring knife from the kitchen that I'd slipped under the liner. I wanted to be armed in case something went wrong. Again.

"She comes back tonight, and do not fuck her." Grey thought for a minute. "And don't leave her to fuck anyone else because you have blue balls."

Oh God. They were making this worse, talking about me like a blowup doll.

Parker cackled but sobered when I turned around, only a ghost of a smile lingering behind. "I promise, Little Love is safe with me. I'm taking seven of my best men, and they'll canvas the place. They're also all men with families on the island. They know if they fuck up, they can kiss at least one family member goodbye."

My mouth dropped open in shock.

"Why would you threaten that?" I almost yelled.

"Why wouldn't we?" Parker's voice was dead serious, matching Grey's expression. "In our world, people die for less. We don't want to kill anyone, but sometimes, that's the only motivation that ensures they do their jobs."

"The men know us. They know the only way that would happen would be if they betrayed us or fucked up royally. At the end of the day, it's an empty bluff because they're good men."

Good.

Their definition of good was so different from mine.

"Ready?" Parker held out his arm with a ghost of a smile.

At least I could count on that exchange for one thing. I was no longer flustered.

"Ready." I ignored his arm and walked right past him.

Grey caught me around the waist, and when I faced him, he softly kissed my lips. Why did he have to be so sweet when I knew he wasn't? And why did they have to fight with Vicente when it could get them all killed?

"Come on, Little Love. There's no more time for sexcapades. Well, the flight is a few hours." He lightly grabbed the inside of my elbow to steer me away from Grey. When I glanced up at him, he winked at Grey with a smirk.

"I'm warning you, *hermano*."

Parker chuckled under his breath as he let his fingers trail down my arm, linking his fingers through mine. I tugged my hand back. Holding hands with Parker was a big fucking no.

"I don't bite, Little Love." He grinned, keeping his face forward.

I scoffed and followed his lead, keeping my gaze on the path forward.

Outside of a few words as we got in the helicopter, we didn't speak on the way there. The ride was beautiful as the sun was setting, and I took the time just to take it all in.

A smile broke out as I leaned over to see the ocean beneath us. Grace would love this. Maybe one day I could share it with her. Until then, I wouldn't take these moments for granted.

I'd always known life was ugly. I saw it every day in law school, then when I joined the firm. Since I was taken, however, I learned just how ugly life could really be. And these small glimpses of how beautiful the world truly was, suffused warmth in my soul.

We landed on a pad in a private yard. Guards stood alongside it, watching us with severe frowns. I glanced at Parker to make sure nothing was amiss, though he didn't seem worried in the slightest.

One of the men stepped forward, hovering around the door as we climbed out. Immediately, his hands were roving over my body. I guess I should be glad it was clinical and cold. He snatched the clutch from my hand and looked inside. He grunted, probably because he only saw the Chapstick and gave it back. Holy shit, he didn't find the knife. I glanced over to see another man doing the exact same thing to Parker.

The house, which was a very modest term for this monstrosity of a sprawling home, was set maybe a hundred feet away from the pad. As the men were finishing up, another guy walked out onto the porch and watched us with a carefree smile and hands stuffed in his shorts. He was the epitome of an island boy with his pastel button-down short-sleeve shirt and khaki shorts.

At first appearance, he seemed kind as his sandy brown hair lifted in the breeze. Parker placed his hand on the small of my back as his people fanned out around us and we started to move up the pristine boardwalk to the house.

The ocean crashed against the shore, the sound of the waves overshadowing everything else as we approached. Parker waited until we were at the base of the elaborate steps before greeting the host.

"Snow, it's a pleasure. Although I thought you would have saved the frisking for a little more intimate setting," Parker drawled. "I would have appreciated a nice dinner first."

Snow—was that his real name?—chuckled. "My apologies, old friend. These days are strenuous for an old man like me. You can never be too careful."

I tried not to let my skepticism show on my face. This man was forty max. Something was off here, and I didn't know enough about anything to know what it was. Or if I was just being paranoid. I peeked at Parker to see if he felt something too. If he did, he didn't show it.

"Understandable," he shrugged, then nudged me forward. "Snow, this is my friend..." he hesitated like he forgot he might actually have to introduce me to anyone. "Amorette. Amorette, meet Braden Snow. The very best in his field."

I almost asked what his field was, but I didn't. With Snow riveted with our interaction, he would see my question for what it was. Naivety. If Parker hadn't shared what he did, then why was I here? At least, that was what I would be thinking.

Parker winked at me like he knew the exact path my thoughts had taken.

"Come in. Dinner is being served, and there are some things to discuss." Snow pivoted on his heel and led the way inside, all the while keeping his nonchalant composure and never once taking his hands out of his pockets.

The inside of his house was just as mesmerizing as the outside. All cool colors with open windows and ocean-themed abstract art. It was gorgeous and calming. Everything I would have imagined for the vacation home of an oil tycoon or maybe a movie star. Definitely not for someone wrapped up in the Institution.

We passed a baby grand piano in the center of the house, along with many other pieces of art and history that looked priceless. Parker cataloged it all.

I would have thought his friends were safe from his particular business.

Snow rounded a corner, but soft voices floated to us before we made it around ourselves. Parker cursed just as one of the voices sent a trickle of recognition through me.

As we stepped into a formal dining room, there was

already a man and woman seated at the long table. They were right next to each other, the woman smoothing her ring finger over the rim of her wine glass. Her face was severe yet beautiful. Her dark hair was half pulled up into an elegantly messy bun. There was something so familiar about her mild expression; it was like déjà vu.

The black-haired man had his chair facing away from me with one knee propped on his ankle, lazily rocking his foot. I recognized the broad shoulders and tanned neck. Even the subtle movements of his body language. After spending a week with him, how could I not.

Our footsteps caught their attention because both turned to look at us–or me.

My gaze lingered on Matías, trying to read his intentions for being here. It couldn't be a coincidence, could it?

Outside of a few rare moments, his face had been set in a constant state of mild indifference. Which was eerie with how much he watched me. Now was no exception, even when his gaze swept my body and lingered on Parker's closeness.

The woman's face pinched, but when she noticed me looking at her, her expression smoothed into something light and engaging. "Parker, who's this lovely jewel?"

"Amorette, Valentina. Valentina, Amorette," Parker said in a bored tone.

Matías slowly rose from the chair, buttoned his suit jacket that did very little to hide his broad stature, and approached us. He dipped his head while holding Parker's stare. "Amorette. I'd say it was a pleasure seeing you again, but..." He finally dropped his gaze to me, and something softened in his eyes.

"Matías. It's never long enough between our visits." Parker caught my hand in his and brought it up to his mouth, pressing a hot kiss against my knuckles while he glared.

A shiver worked its way down my body, and I was just barely able to suppress it. I narrowed my eyes at Parker.

Seriously? They were having a pissing contest. For what? It certainly didn't seem like it was all about me.

Matías certainly never made a move against me while I was with him the entire week. And he'd called Andre when he could have been his father's son and done unspeakable things because he wanted to.

"Funny, Snow." Parker headed toward the other side of the table, tugging me along behind him. "When you sent the invite, I had no idea you had a death wish."

Snow laughed, but it was forced. He took the head seat, only two spots down from where Parker had planted us. And coincidentally, right across from Matías and the woman.

Then more tension slowly bled into the room until the silent glares being tossed around were so uncomfortable I struggled to keep my calm. Finally, Snow broke. "Inviting you here was risky, but Matías insisted on it." He flicked his gaze to Matías.

Valentina rolled her eyes. "It would have been nice if someone would have shared that with me. This is my one night here before I return to the states."

My heart skipped a beat. What I wouldn't give to go back, even just to hug Grace. But I kept my emotions locked down.

Then Valentina turned to me. "Amorette, how did you come to be with my brother?"

My eyes widened. I couldn't help it. In what seemed like slow motion, I cut my gaze to Parker. He shook his head but answered my unspoken question. "Andre, Lafe, Grey, and I are bastards. You know that. What you might not know," he raised his brows as if asking if any of the brothers had told me, "is that Vicente had a wife. And two perfect babies were a result of that sanctimonious union."

Valentina and Matías were the legitimate children. Holy hell, there were six of them. For a man with an inflated sense of self, it didn't surprise me that he would try to populate the world with his offspring. He probably knew at least a few of them would hate him.

Valentina rolled her eyes, and Matías just watched Parker with an unreadable expression. "So tell me, Amorette, how did you come to be with *him*." The way derision dripped over him had my spine straightening.

I hesitated, waiting for Parker to jump in and say I wasn't with him, but he took a swig out of the wine glass in front of him, watching me with glittering eyes. Just as I was about to open my mouth, Matías beat me to it.

"She's not Parker's. Apparently, she's Grey's."

Valentina has a good snort over that, and it did everything to ruin the beauty of her face. "Please. That savage?" She shook her head and stared back at me. "Honey, these boys," she cut her gaze at Snow, "all boys are a waste of space. If you want to have a real place in our world, let me know. I can read the intelligence in your eyes as easily as I can sniff out a rat. You'd go far with me."

"Go far doing what? Blowing men under tables for favors? That's what you do best for Vicente," Parker drawled as he slouched down in his chair like he was relaxed with old friends. But the hatred that sizzled between brother and sister killed any impressions of that.

So different from his visible dislike of Matías. It was like comparing an annoying gnat to a venomous snake.

Snow knitted his brow as he watched the exchange.

Parker tapped his finger on his glass stem. "Snow, I'm disappointed. I thought you invited me here to discuss a particular piece of merchandise I've had my eye on for ages. I can't say I'm happy about this turn of events. I hate being ambushed." Parker broke his stare with Valentina to quirk an irritated brow at Snow.

"As Snow said, this was my request." Matías crossed his arms and leaned back in his chair. "Vicente knows that I no longer have Amorette." He flicked those cool brown eyes to me, then back to Parker. "You needed to know, and this was neutral ground."

As if without his permission, Matías' gaze landed on me again. It was a living, breathing thing as it swept over my body. Heat built under my skin and I turned to Valentina to give myself a breather, but she was eyeing me speculatively.

"Like you couldn't use a burner to call Andre like before." Suddenly, Parker leaned into my side and used the back of his fingers to move my hair from my neck. "Are you sure you didn't ask us here so you'd have a chance to see Little Love?" He dropped a hot kiss just below my ear, and goosebumps erupted over my skin.

I wanted to punch him in the balls, to kick him away from me, except I couldn't. Sitting at a table with three very dangerous unknowns, I had no idea the best way to play this, and Parker was taking advantage of that. One of his hands slipped down to grip my hip and his fingers tightened, and I knew—I knew he was thinking about Grey fucking me.

Matías glared at Parker like he was two fries short of a meal. "How could I have known you'd bring her." Then he switched to Spanish, and everyone at the table stiffened.

Parker responded, almost spitting at him with his reply, and shoved up from the table. "Thanks, Snow. Let's never do this again." He held his hand out, and I took it, for appearance's sake.

I allowed Parker to usher us out, looking every bit the intimate lovers he wanted us to be, as his hand on my back lowered to my ass just before we were out of sight.

The men who came with us joined us on our walk back to the helicopter. The way they fanned around us out of nowhere made me think they were watching and waiting for this very scenario to happen. It seemed too planned.

Anger burned so hot, my hand itched to rake down his chest and leave bloody welts in their place. How fucking dare he.

Snow's men stood back, watching us with all the energy of docile alligators. Happy for us to leave, but ready to snap if provoked. As soon as we took off and our headsets were in place, Parker glanced back at the men behind us on the benches.

"Did you get it?"

When I glanced back, all the men accompanying us were utterly stone-faced. Until one cracked a smile and pulled an envelope out of his jacket. "Got it."

"What did you do?" I turned to Parker, alarmed that there was so much more going on here than I had initially thought.

"I told you it was a job. I fucking hate Snow. If I had known he was going to pull that shit, I would have had my men grab more stuff." He faced forward and continued our ride back to the compound.

The entire time I stewed, outlining exactly what I would say to Parker as soon as we got back. Everything was too tame. There weren't enough words for me to tell him what a fucking bastard he was for first, watching me with Grey, and second, for acting like he had rights to me when I couldn't do anything about it.

I needed to know the stakes. I needed to understand the rules so I didn't feel so fucking helpless ever again.

We landed, and I yanked off the headset and tossed it on the seat as I climbed out. Parker came around the corner, holding his hands out with a smirk like he intended to pull my hips flush against his.

It was an awkward angle, but I cocked back my fist and let go with everything I had, hitting the underside of his chin. His teeth clicked together, and he cursed as his head popped back.

"Don't you ever—fucking ever—touch me again without my permission. And keep the hell out of my sex life." I shoved at his chest as victory instantly hit me when he stumbled back a few steps.

That was probably more to do with the surprise coating his face than my strength. Regardless, I'd take it.

Lafe was walking toward us, his steps slowing to a near halt. I pointed at him. "Take me the fuck inside. I can't look at him anymore."

I stomped toward him, passing as he stepped aside. Parker didn't follow us, and that was for the best.

My anger was starting to calm, but I already wanted another go at him.

Tomorrow. I'd ask myself if I still felt that way tomorrow.

What a fucking mess.

I scrubbed a hand down my face as I pushed the door open to the commons. That was a stressful forty-eight hours I was ready to put behind me. Marcus was probably one of the most put-together dealers running street teams in the Southeast of the US. He was the only one who didn't actually skim off the top of his product.

An ironic laugh escaped as I grabbed a bottle of water from the commons kitchen. It wasn't lost on me that I was a hypocrite. I couldn't leave the fucking drugs alone either. Not when I left home. Everyone was out to get us, especially now, and I needed to stay sharp.

Except, I was so fatigued walking was a chore and my head felt like fifty pounds. A sure sign that the coming crash was going to be a bitch.

Heading down the residential hall, I slowed as I approached the movie room. The door, which someone had replaced, was open with the light on. I stepped inside enough to see who was in there and stopped.

Amorette was cross-legged on the couch, using a pencil and muttering to herself in...what I thought was supposed to be Spanish.

"Killer?" I said softly, and she jumped.

When she glanced up, a brief look of guilt flashed through her eyes before they settled into determination. "Lafe."

Before she was taken, I would have latched onto her guilt and used it as every reason not to trust her. I would have watched her and tried to lock her away somewhere she couldn't cause us any trouble.

Now? I was alert but amused. At some point, maybe when she admitted she'd asked for me, I saw her as more of a sweet kitten than a devious femme fatale. It was just so hard to let go of my suspicion.

My lips twitched as I walked deeper into the room. It had been hours since my last hit, and I needed to pick a spot to pass out. Outside of my apartment, this was the only place I felt safe. The exhaustion was setting in, and my eyes were getting heavy. But I was intrigued by whatever secret she was trying to keep.

"What are you doing?" I approached cautiously, because even though I trusted her, it was such a small amount and not entirely stable. Since we got her back, she hadn't tried to escape, hadn't tried to slit our throats in our sleep. That had to count for something, didn't it?

She pursed her pink lips and shut the book, hiding it in her lap as I sat beside her. "Nothing."

"Nothing? Are you sure? Deceitfulness doesn't suit you, Killer. Your face gives too much away." I reach forward and pluck the book from her lap. She didn't even put up a fight. Just sighed when I flipped it over. "The Art of War," I translated. Amorette had found a Spanish edition. Although that's not surprising. Everything in the compound was probably written in Spanish.

"Is that what it is?" She flashed a little grin, like it was hilarious she hadn't even known what the book was. We laughed, and I leaned my shoulder against the couch to face her. This felt good. A normal conversation, without thinking she was going to kill me or my brothers as soon as I went to sleep.

Then an unwanted thread of paranoia slithered its way in. Was she just waiting for the right time? Was someone about to ambush us? Why else would Matías have sent her back?

No, I didn't have those thoughts when I was sober. I wouldn't let them crowd my better judgment now. And I damn sure wasn't about to sniff my way into an early grave. I'd–mostly–learned my lesson.

"What are you trying to do?" I held up the book and waved it side to side.

Her hackles rose, and she steeled herself. "I'm trying to teach myself Spanish. I'm tired of being on the outside, not understanding what's going on. I can't stop making stupid decisions if I don't know what's happening around me." She was nearly panting, her chest rising and falling beneath Grey's t-shirt. Did she have anything on underneath it?

I forced my attention back to the book even as my cock twitched.

Damn you, Parker. Putting thoughts in my head. At least I got to see her knock some sense into him a few nights ago. Whatever he'd done, he probably deserved that and more.

"And you're using a very boring, complex piece of literature to achieve that? Why not just ask one of us?" My stomach fluttered and I had no fucking idea why. I never had feelings like that.

Amorette blew out a breath. "Who would I ask? Andre barely tolerates me. Parker's a hell no. And Grey is more interested in teaching me to fight and defend myself. Which is a useful skill but only one of many I need to stay here."

My heart gave an extra heavy thump in my chest. She planned to stay? That could change everything. "What's wrong with me?"

She cast me a sardonic look. "Lafe, you hate being around me too. You nearly overdosed because I stressed you out so much." There was no heat behind her words, no intent to hurt or mock me. Killer said it more or less as fact and maybe a little hurt on her own part.

I clenched my teeth and pressed the heel of my hand into my eye. I needed the drugs, but I hated how they amped up my fear. When she stayed in my apartment, I had been afraid of her. Of what she meant to this farce of a family.

But I didn't want to be the weak brother. The one she always had to tiptoe around. I was a fucking badass outside this compound. The Institution feared me like they feared Andre, or Grey, or Parker.

"I'll help you. But you need something different than this." I tossed the book at the wall, and the sound of it sliding down to the floor signaled my decision. I was doing this. I wouldn't let myself get in my own fucking way.

When I first brought Amorette here, I'd offered her a choice: the Gallery, us, or death. I could do myself a favor and give myself an ultimatum. And I damn sure wasn't going to allow doubts to rule me.

"You need some kind of program, like an app or something..." I had zero experience teaching. Not when it came to this. I could school the dealers. Tell them what to watch out for, how to navigate a sticky situation. But at the end of the day, I hadn't cared if they came out alive.

They knew the risks of working for me. I didn't blackmail people into my business like some of Vicente's other companies. No one ever started dealing with the belief it was like every other nine-to-five. They did it for the thrill and the cash.

I did care if Amorette fucking died. It would be on my shoulders if she did, and I...couldn't fucking take that. Not again.

"An app?" she asked. "Are you going to give me a phone and unlimited access to the internet?"

No, was the immediate thought. I glanced at her, and the hopeful expression closed down. "That's what I thought."

"I'm sorry," I rasped. I had no idea why I was even apologizing. She was here with us, but she was also our captive. "Let me think about how we can do this. I like that you want to learn Spanish." It meant she was putting in an effort to stay with us.

"It's not for you." She destroyed all the small hopes I'd started to pin on her. "I need it for me."

Regardless of the reason, this was good. It was.

"Let's start with the basics. Spanish is a phonetic language. If you can get the sounds down, you can read it. Speak it. It's the memorizing that will get you. And maybe a bit of the grammar." I shrugged, then yawned.

I pointed to myself. "Boy, *chico*." I pointed to her. "Girl, *chica*."

She shook her head. "I know those are probably important words, but I need to know the vocabulary of what's spoken in meetings. What others might say around me. That's going to be the best way I learn to survive."

Nodding, I spread my hand out on the cushion between

us. She wasn't wrong. But how did you teach someone to speak Spanish on a fast track without learning the fundamentals?

"I have an idea." I got up and grabbed the clicker. A blanket too. Back to my spot, I glanced at her, then the arm of the couch. I wanted to lie down. I was minutes away from sleeping off the high of a shitty job.

"What?" she asked.

"I want to lay down, and you're on my favorite couch." I motioned to the length of it. A wicked thought crossed my mind.

Damn you, Parker.

"Here." I motioned for her to get up but caught her arm before she could go to the other couch. "I'm going to lay down, and you're going to lay down with me."

"Lafe—"

"I'm going to put on a *telenovela*. Explain it as best I can, and I don't want to scream at you across the room. I'm exhausted and I've been up for two days."

Biting her lip, she glanced at the couch, then at me, her blue eyes laying all her uncertainty between us. "You've been up since I came back with Parker?"

"Yes, I had a job to do, and I left as soon as I deposited you in Grey's arms."

She rolled her lips. This was a terrible idea, and she knew it. "Grey would flip if I cuddled on the couch with you."

I shrugged. Parker had been right about one thing. She was mine before she was Grey's, even if it wasn't sexual in nature. "I'm about to pass out. I won't take advantage. Remember? I like my women willing. I also like to be conscious myself."

She grinned, then squashed it like it was inconvenient to find humor in a situation that could get us beaten bloody.

"What's your answer?" I asked, shifting from her. I took off my shoes and laid down on my back, arranging the blanket before relaxing back. With my head pillowed against the arm, I lifted the ear of the blanket back as I gazed at her.

Amorette hadn't moved, and my heart started rioting in my chest as she struggled with her answer. I hadn't actually thought she would take me up on it.

Without lowering my arm, I used my other hand to turn on the TV, searching the guide for a *telenovela*. Something not too sappy or romantic. It would be suicide to get a hard-on with her on top of me.

Cursing under her breath, she came over and lifted the blanket back a little more. "This is a terrible idea. Absolutely fucking terrible," she mumbled as she put her knees between my thighs, then gently tucked herself against my chest and pulled the blanket up over her shoulder.

My heart was unstoppable. A stampeding herd of wild horses inside my chest, and with her cheek to my chest, she had to feel it. I curled my arm around her back, and once I put on a show, I brought my other arm up to hug her against me.

I let out a slow breath, trying to calm my shit down. What was a delirious haze edging closer turned into a raging fit of sensation. Her tiny body tucked against me felt nice. Intimate.

This was more intimate than any sex I'd ever had. I never cuddled. Never stuck around. Until this very moment, I hadn't even realized this was something I'd wanted.

I huffed out a laugh.

"What are you laughing at?" She was just as confused as

I was because there was a funeral on the screen.

"I should have just held you like this when you were in my apartment. Then I could have slept without thinking you were going to turn on me."

She stiffened, but I used one hand to rub up and down her back until she relaxed. "I wouldn't hurt you. Or your brothers. I wanted to go home. But I never wanted to hurt anyone."

"I know you did," I cooed. "And I think now, I believe you. You promise you won't do anything to get me or my brothers killed?" I asked. Not because I needed the answer, but because I just wanted to keep her talking to me, and this was the safest topic with her pressed tight against my cock.

Her exhale was loud and slow. "I promise. Just don't... You all better not do anything stupid to put yourselves—including me—in danger."

I grinned, using the remote to turn out the lights. That was like asking for a miracle. Between Parker and Grey, we were bound to have some bloodshed. It just wouldn't be hers. I'd make sure of it.

The scene changed to the reception, with lots of tears and dirty looks. I gave her the highlight of the plot as best as I could gather. I'd never been a telenovela fan. Then I quieted and let her listen to the cadence of the language. Exposure might be the best thing to help her. I'd have to figure out how to turn on the subtitles so she could see what they were saying.

Another time.

My system started settling down, and she felt so good and warm against me.

Her easy breathing slowed as she watched the show, and soon, I crashed into the serene black sea of unconsciousness.

13

AMORETTE

"How is your Spanish coming along?" Blanca asked when she found me wandering the commons.

Since I'd returned, the brothers hadn't locked me up, and I essentially had a free pass to roam. I hadn't gone outside the compound just in case I was mistaken for an intruder or something equally as dangerous...like an escapee.

Men inside left me alone. I still got the random stares that were more than a little curious, but everyone inside the building seemed to know I was off-limits.

"The book you gave me was far too advanced." I glanced at her hand full of cleaning products. "Where are you going?"

"To do some cleaning in the offices. You can come too if you'd like." She nodded toward the wing where Andre and Parker's offices were.

"Do they all have offices here?" I joined her, dipping my head in greeting to the few men we passed. Even though their stares weren't as blatant as in the beginning, they still seemed like my presence was an oddity.

"Some of their men have offices here. But Grey doesn't have an office. Lafe neither. I barely see Parker in this hall. I think he prefers to do his work outside the compound. Andre is the only one who comes here with any regularity."

Parker worked in his office the day Grey and I had made up. My cheeks flushed at the memory.

"Where is everyone?" Grey had been gone when I got up, and I hadn't seen any of the other brothers. Lafe had promised to teach me Spanish, but I hadn't spoken to him after our weird but sweet nap.

The calming sound of his even breathing had put me out like a light, and I hadn't been drowsy at all. Sometime later, I'd woken up with his erection digging into my stomach and his fingers digging into my hips. I had startled, thinking he was trying to fuck me, but when I lifted my head, he was out cold.

I disentangled myself and snuck out like I was doing the walk of shame.

"Amorette?" Blanca asked, touching my arm.

Wow, I'd stopped right in the middle of the hallway.

"Hm?" I tried to play it off. It was rare that I lost my head like that. Fuck, just because I was back here didn't mean I could daydream about things that didn't matter.

"Why are you pink in the cheeks?" She scrunched her brows up in confusion as she glanced between my eyes. "You okay?"

Oh, yeah. I was great, just feeling guilty about napping with one brother while the other brother liked to fuck me. We weren't in a relationship. I didn't sleep with Lafe; this wasn't a boy-next-door situation. Why did I care?

"Yep. All good. Which office are you cleaning first?" I

started walking again and she immediately followed. Her steps quickened because I was apparently speed-walking away from my problems.

"Andre's, then Parker's. After that, I'll get to the others. They're not as important as the boss'." She shot me a crooked grin.

I returned it, even if it felt weak.

"Want me to help?" I stopped at the door to Andre's office, but Blanca fluttered around dusting surfaces. She kept the cleaning supplies in her hands instead of putting them on the desk. "I can hold those." I motioned to her bundle. "Or you can put them on the desk..."

"Oh no. That won't do. Grey would not be happy if you were cleaning."

I raised a brow. Grey wouldn't care if I cleaned, cooked, or butted into the training in the courtyard. Although he'd probably be angry he missed it.

"You just keep me company. I'll be done in two minutes." She smiled over her shoulder, then continued cleaning. She moved onto the windows next.

Her phone rang, and she grabbed it from her pocket. "Hola?" She paused, then several Spanish words fell in quick succession out of her mouth. Blanca hung up in a huff. "I'll be right back. Jorge is here, and he needs help." She rolled her eyes like she didn't believe that for a second.

Blanca raced out of the room and her sweet scent wafted over me. I watched the door for a few seconds, then turned back to Andre's office. I'd been in here once before. When he and Parker were convincing me of all the reasons I needed to work for them, but I hadn't been in a frame of mind to really check out the space.

I moved closer to the desk, keeping my footsteps light in case someone was nearby. A person's office said a lot about them. The disorganized messes of some of my colleagues were a direct reflection of their thought processes. Mine was clean, uncluttered, with a memento or two. A picture of me and Grace, then a picture of us with our brother and mother when we were kids. I smiled.

My office said I was compassionate, family-oriented, and straightforward. At least, that's what I would assume. Andre's office was spotless before Blanca ever stepped foot inside.

No dust anywhere. No smudges on any surfaces, not even oil on the mouse and keyboard. And absolutely no personal items, pictures, or otherwise. This was a standard hotel space yet built for executives.

I stopped dead in my tracks.

A phone.

Next to his computer, pushed back in the corner, was a phone.

My chest started to hurt with the strength of my pounding heart. I snuck a glance at the door. No one was here. No one was coming. Blanca was a heavy walker and I'd hear if she were on her way back.

I crept closer to the desk, reaching out a hand to pick up the receiver.

This was the opportunity that I'd been waiting for. I could call my law firm. I could call Grace. I could go home. Breathing became difficult, and my palms started to sweat. I could do this.

The phone was cool in my hand as I picked it up.

Holy hell—there was a dial tone.

Grey popped up in my thoughts. The possessive way he dominated me and the affectionate way he held me. Then Lafe as he looked at me with his broken spirit in his eyes and how he held onto me like a lifeline in sleep.

Even Parker and Andre pushed to the forefront, but not for any warm and fuzzy reasons other than they'd been as loyal to me as they could while first keeping their loyalty to each other.

If I made the call, I'd put them in danger. They could be jailed or, worse, hunted because they let a traitor into their midst. Could I truly be the catalyst for that?

I squeezed my eyes shut. I wasn't sure. They weren't good men. They didn't do good things. But could I sacrifice them to save myself?

Hell.

Screams built up in my throat as I held my hand suspended. A quick call to Grace wouldn't hurt anything. I'd ask her to keep my location a secret.

I laughed under my breath at the absurdity. Grace would blow the top off their operations so fast I'd get whiplash. If it would save me, she'd do it without the pesky conscience I had.

Me or them.

Me or them?

Was that what this had all come down to? I refused to believe it. They'd tried to bring me into their circle. It was me on the outside, pushing against their grasp on me.

I was the problem.

Shaking my head, I sighed. I was even disgusted with myself.

I put the receiver down and stepped back.

Either I was the biggest coward on the planet or the biggest idiot. Would any of the brothers choose me over saving themselves? I hope I never had to find out.

Tingles swept through my body as the adrenaline slowly seeped out of me. I laughed again. This time the shaky sound hitting my own ears was slightly unhinged. Raking a hand through my hair, I turned toward the door and froze.

"Well, hello there." A tall and slender yet curvy woman greeted me with a slight curl to her lips. Gorgeous red hair fell in loose waves around her shoulders, and her makeup was flawlessly applied. Grace would have a million things to say about her, but I couldn't find a single superficial fault.

Affecting a calm mask, I gave her my professionally bland smile. "Hi. And you are?"

"Mia," she said and grinned. Pushing into the office, her gaze swept my body, leaving an uncomfortable heat behind. The way she looked me over...

"Mia," I repeated slowly. I'd heard that name before. Where the hell had I— "Oh! Your stuff is in Grey's guest room, right?"

Her eyes sparkled. "So you've heard of me. Parker made it sound like you had no idea I existed." She crossed her arms, pushing her breasts up against the tight button-down shirt. The few buttons left open now showed two inches of cleavage.

I slowly twisted my head to the side. "Parker hasn't mentioned you to me."

She waved her hand like that didn't surprise her, then she plopped down in one of the chairs in front of Andre's desk and pulled the other one around to face her. "Here! Sit down. I want to get to know the little bird who caught the attention of my childhood friend and his brothers."

I knew it! When I'd first heard her name, I assumed the relationship was something like this. Why else would her stuff be in the guest room?

"How did you meet Grey?" I asked as I took a seat. The residual excitement left flutters in my stomach, but the longer she didn't try to attack or out me for almost making a call, the more relaxed I became.

"My father is one of Vicente's right-hand men. I was at the mansion often as a child. The brothers all ignored me, except Parker. After I saved his ass from a beating one time, we became fast friends. Thick as thieves." She held up two twined fingers with a smirk.

"Parker?" That was weird. "Your stuff is in Grey's apartment."

Her grin turned into a smirk as she tucked her chin and leaned forward like she was about to deliver a delicious secret. "That's because, for a time, we were lovers. And Parker's a ridiculous roommate." She laughed, tossing her head back. "So, I keep my things in Grey's spare. I'm not here often, but when I am, I usually crash there."

Hot and cold shivers rolled up and down the back of my neck in contradictory waves. Grey wasn't mine. Not really. But sitting here with a gorgeous ex-lover who had a close relationship with at least two of the brothers was still awkward.

"Are..." I started, trying to phrase this in the least revealing way possible, "you still with Grey?"

She winked. "I was never with Grey. We were purely fuck buddies, banging it out when the mood struck. It was fun for a while, and I was young, so the danger Grey gave off was an excellent aphrodisiac. Then I discovered the charms of women." Her gaze did a burning sweep down my body again, pausing on my chest in the loose blouse. "And I have to say, I've never gone back."

I cleared my throat. This woman was hitting on me. My brain was having a tough time wrapping around all the ways this was fucked up. Grey didn't seem bothered at all when he'd mentioned her. He didn't talk about her like the one that got away or like a bitch who had broken his heart. He was nonchalant. Like he talked about the weather.

If the weather was ever something Grey wanted to talk about.

Completely ignoring her comments, I asked another question. "What are you doing here now? Catching up with Parker?"

"Among other things. You're every bit as beautiful as I thought you'd be. Parker didn't really share the details, though I knew you'd be a knockout. How did you get to be with the bastards?"

I bristled. Was that how people referred to them here? As bastards? That sucked. "Lafe," I supplied, and even though I tried to avoid it, a small smile slipped through. Enough time had finally passed that I seemed to find the hilarity in how I came to be here. That, or I was sliding back from a healthy psyche.

"Lafe?" She pulled back with a frown. "How did he bring you into the fold? Do you know his runners in the US or encounter him on a job for Vicente?"

"Something like," I muttered, briefly turning my attention to the window. Would they want this woman to know the truth? Was there danger in sharing it?

Lafe made it sound like this compound was their safe space, and only people they trusted were allowed. Or they locked them in the birdcages. By that logic and Mia roaming freely, it meant that she was trusted.

I faced her again and plastered a smile on. "It's a long story. But Lafe brought me in. Then Grey stole me away." I wouldn't get into how Parker messed with me for giggles or how Andre would no sooner leave me on an ice cap than keep me here.

Although Andre had been one of the ones to come get me. But how hard had he really looked for me before that?

Mia twisted her lips to the side as sharp shrewdness entered her gaze. "I feel like there's more to that story than you're letting on." She thinned her lips. "We'll do drinks soon, and you can tell me all about it."

Not likely.

"It will be a nice break from everything going on with Vicente," she continued, watching me for any visual cues that something was not what it seemed.

It took everything I had not to react, even though the brothers hadn't mentioned Vicente since I'd been back. From Mia's tone, their father hadn't been quietly waiting for them to screw up again.

"Oh!"

I turned to see Blanca backpedaling out of the office, her face now flushed in embarrassment.

"I'm so sorry! Your rooms are ready! I just helped Jorge clear out the ones you wanted." Blanca dipped her head. She wasn't acting like Mia was a criminal or an enemy; she was showing more deference to her than I'd seen Blanca exhibit toward anyone.

Why was that?

"Perfect!" Mia smiled, putting her blinding white teeth on display. She rose and dropped a gentle touch to my shoulder.

I glanced up and immediately regretted the disadvantage of being so far beneath her.

"Well, Amorette. It's been a pleasure, and I can't wait until I can steal you away myself." She slid her fingers toward the back of my neck, then she was gone with an exaggerated sway to her hips.

"Amorette!" Blanca ran in and took the other chair and scooted closer. "What the hell! Why were you with Mia?"

I tugged my hands free of hers. "Should I not have indulged her in conversation?" Blanca was being incredibly suspicious, and a knot of worry formed in my stomach.

"No! It's fine. She's probably the only visitor they'd trust you with. But it's all so sordid! I've always thought Parker had some unrequited love for her. Then Grey with his history! And now she's trying to pick you up!" Blanca's strange excitement bled through every facet of her face and body. "This is better than any telenovela I've ever watched!"

I sighed. Speaking of telenovelas...

"Come on. I have a show I'm watching to try to pick up the language. You can explain the plot to me."

She squealed and hopped up. "Okay! Let me finish cleaning the offices, then we can go."

I waited patiently for her, keeping my seat in Andre's office. All the while, I stared at the phone.

Had I made the right decision?

14

GREY

Wrapping up my workout, I tore the tape off my hands, kicked the trembling soldier out, and turned off the stereo. We did need to find a stronger crop for sparring partners. Or grow one.

There was barely any blood during today's session. I looked over at the bare gray mats. Tomorrow I'd get one of my brothers in here with me. I grinned. That was exactly what I needed to work off some steam. I'd grab Parker.

Every time I thought about how Amorette was almost killed because of him, my knuckles itched. He argued that she had been perfectly safe with Matías, but we hadn't known that. And it was pure luck that Vicente wanted to fuck with us enough by giving her to the legitimate son. The heir.

Like, we gave a fuck about that.

We'd always been perfectly happy in our own world, away from the devious plays of the mansion. It was fun to rile Vicente when I felt like it, but I enjoyed my place in the Institution too much.

Matías was a puppet and a slave. He knew it and couldn't do a damn thing about it. Vicente had always pulled him into meetings and made him attend events that we were excluded from. He probably thought that hurt our feelings, but none of us wanted to spend any more time with him than we had to.

The door to the hallway slammed against the wall, and footsteps padded toward the gym. Lafe appeared in a muscle tee and gym shorts. I snorted. He never worked out unless I forced him to.

"Why are you here?"

He glared and walked over to a treadmill. "A run. I have too much energy, and I slept like shit last night. If I wear myself out, I'll be able to sleep better." He grumbled the last bit, like he was trying to force himself to believe it.

I grabbed the tape off the metal chair and tossed it back in the bin. "What's up your ass? When I saw you the other day, you were sleeping like a baby."

Out of the corner of my eye, Lafe tensed, then slowly glanced over his shoulder. "When did you see me?"

"In the movie room after your trip." Some of the blood fled his face. "What the hell is your deal? You're suspicious and creepy on the best days, but right now, you're extra paranoid. You sniff today?"

I leaned my ass against the wall and crossed my arms.

"Nah." He left it at that as he went through the program options.

Walking over, I gripped the side of the treadmill and took a good, long look at him. Lafe was a little sweaty, but otherwise, he had good color in his face. His hands weren't shaky. He was telling the truth. "You're following your rules?"

He flicked an irritated gaze at me. "Yes. Why the sudden interest?" He hit the start button, starting a slow walk, then quickly picking up into a jog.

I narrowed my eyes at him. This seemed like an avoidance tactic. But I couldn't fault his question. Why did I care? We didn't have this type of relationship. We didn't shoot the shit for fun. We didn't even have fun together.

Everything was a means to an end.

"Just checking. I'd hate to see you die from your own stupidity."

He scoffed and faced forward. At least the view outside was nice and sunny today.

I turned away, but he stopped me with a comment.

"I'm going to start teaching Amorette how to read and speak Spanish." His voice was normal, except for the slight pant between a few words.

"Okay..." Why the fuck did I care about that? I didn't have the patience for it. I'd try to fuck her the minute she pursed her plush pink lips. It was better she worked with someone else, although Parker would have been my first choice if he wasn't such as asshole.

"I'll be spending time with her," he threw down like a challenge, his chin tipping up.

Canting my head, I slowly walked back to the treadmill, bracing my arms against the front so we were face to face. "Are you trying to tell me something?"

He studied me for a long minute but didn't say anything. Eventually, he let out a long breath and shook his head. "You've never had a woman in your bed like this. How territorial are you going to be?" He pressed the speed button a few times and slowed down to a more manageable level to have a conversation.

I quirked an eyebrow. "Do I need to worry about you

fucking her?" I asked drily. "If it were going to happen, it would have before I ever caught sight of her. You had her to yourself for a week, and she hated you. Then you had another shot when she was in your apartment, and you fucking blew that too. Why should I worry about you?"

He snarled, cursing a blue streak, and I laughed.

"Turn the lights off when you leave!" I yelled over my shoulder as I left. It was more of a Parker move to point out his shortcomings like that, but they were the truth. If it were going to happen with them, it would have already. Lafe was the one to blame. He let his fears and past get in the way of taking what he wanted.

One day he'd learn. It just wouldn't be today.

Or tomorrow.

I'd just made it to my door when my phone rang. Enrique. My manager at the Venezuela hotel.

"Enrique."

"Mr. Morozov, there's a problem," Enrique said.

I sighed. Fighting was the one business where there were hardly any issues. Men, and sometimes women showed up. They fought, and money was paid out. I didn't even run the books. Not directly. I liked the low angst of the business.

"What's wrong?"

"The Nogueira team is threatening to pull out. I spoke to the booker. There's more than five hundred mil on this fight tonight, not including the openers. If they pull out, someone will die." And it wouldn't be Nogueira is what he'd meant.

Scratching the back of my head, I let myself into the apartment with my other hand, then brought the phone back up to my ear. "What about the Olesteens? They're good?"

"They're good. Hungover from a night at the strip club,

but they're good." Then they were solid. Enrique wasn't one to split hairs.

"What's the issue with Nogueira?" I headed to the bedroom to get showered and dressed. I'd have to be on-site to fix this. These arrogant assholes never changed their minds over a phone call. They'd need an in-person reminder of why you didn't fuck with Grey Morozov.

"Not sure. They came in fine, but over the last hour, they became belligerent."

"Fine, I'll be there in a few hours. Keep them in their suite if they can't mind their fucking manners." I ended the call and did a quick rinse.

Amorette wasn't here, and I had no fucking clue where she was. I understood why Andre wouldn't give her a phone, but being unable to pin her down was a nightmare now that we'd given her freedom to roam the compound.

I paused—we could always put a tracking device on her. That would solve so many of our problems. If Vicente ever took her again, we'd have her back before Vicente even got home.

Grinning at my reflection in the mirror, I chuckled. I'd mention it to Andre. He'd go for it. Maybe even Parker too.

THE CLUB WAS ALREADY open for business as I walked through the main floor. Music blared from the speakers and sweaty gyrating bodies moved on the floor. The bar was five people deep on all sides, and the fight girls down by the ring were emptying their trays before they even took a handful of steps.

A good night for business. The fun in sin was never slow.

There were always assholes willing to party and women willing to fuck to find their next target. The fights and bets were just icing on the cake.

And the club revenue? Outside the books for the fights, the club and hotel were all mine.

One glass-eyed woman appeared in my path, pulling her top down with a finger and sending a sultry smile. I looked right past her and bumped her shoulder when I walked by. She was lucky she moved, because I would have fucking bowled her over. I moved for no one in my fucking club.

"*Cabrón!*" she screeched behind me.

"Boss," Enrique drawled from my left.

I glanced at him and grinned. The bastard was amused, he just didn't want to show it. "You give these thirsty bitches an inch, and they take a mile. She's new, or she'd know better than to approach me. Hopefully, that little display will be enough to discourage other women from trying something similar."

He nodded like he was pacifying me. "I'm sure someone will set her straight that you'd do much worse if she offended you."

I grunted. "You say that like I like to hurt women."

Shaking his head, his lips twitched. "You don't seek to hurt women, and the only thing you have ever hurt on a woman is her pride. But to these bitches," he shook his head again and lowered his voice as we entered the hallway away from the bumping club music, "stomping on their pride is the worst offense there is. They'd just as soon have you kill their sister and fuck their mother than have you disrespect them in public like that."

Enrique was on point like he always was, the clever bastard. But he wasn't telling me anything I didn't know.

The rest of the walk to the suite Nogueira's team occupied was silent. I smoothed my hand down my dress shirt and adjusted the tie. I hated these fucking suits. They choked the hell out of me, but I'd found when dealing with belligerent assholes like this, money talked. Well, pain spoke, and flashing more cash than he'd ever hoped to make just firmly solidified me as superior in their heads.

I didn't knock. I didn't use a keycard. No, I kicked that motherfucker in.

We had a maintenance team on hand to fix it before we'd need it again, and I wanted to set the record straight. Palacio de Hielo was my fucking domain, and I owned everything in it while it was in the building. That included their sniveling little asses.

And it helped to send the message, *I'll damage my own property. What will I do to you?*

Nogueira, a built man in his thirties with a full head of dark hair and skin glistening as if his team had already oiled him up, jumped to his feet.

"What the fuck! You can't barge in here." His face turned red and spit flew from his mouth. His manager and two of his crew surrounded his back. Nogueira was the only one of the bunch that was maybe a threat. The others were aging, balding and pudgy, living the high life off his earnings.

I gripped his neck and shoved him back until Nogueira had his manager pinned between him and the wall, then I pressed my body up against him and grinned. Neither man was going anywhere unless I allowed it.

Squeezing my thumb and fingers into his windpipe, I grinned wider when he started to gasp.

"This is my club. My hotel. My fucking kingdom. You don't want to fight? That's fine, but you're going to pay the penalty. Enrique? Tell this asswipe the penalty for backing out hours before the fight."

Enrique kept his voice smooth as he scared the shit out of Nogueira and his team. "First, we take a finger from each member of the team. Including the fighter. Then if we're not satisfied, we take the cocks. Mr. Morozov is a master blade maker and has some of the best-serrated knives for punishment."

Blood drained from both Nogueira's and the manager's faces, from what I could see past Nogueira's shoulder, anyway. That was impressive since Nogueira's face resembled a hot pepper a minute ago.

"I don't care why you're upset. I don't give a fuck if you feel slighted. You fight, or you lose your fucking cock. Then there'll be no fucking in your future or for any member of your crew. Are you going to argue?"

He couldn't speak but tried to shake his head against my grip.

"Nogueira will fight. There isn't an issue. We were only —" one of the men tried to speak up, but another member punched him.

"Shut the fuck up!" the other man hissed.

I twisted my head. Now that was interesting. "I changed my mind. I am interested in the reason you're all being asswipes today. Talk fast though, because Nogueira has about a minute before he passes out, and two before he dies." I gave a hard shove, pulling a grunt from the manager to emphasize my point.

The man, barely scraping five-foot, the one currently struggling for breath after being punched in the throat, held a hand up. "Please, *senōr*! Please! We mean no harm! This was not our intention! You—"

"I said shut the fuck up!" I think the other guy's name was Smith—said. He pulled out a gun and shot his friend in the temple.

"Enrique, restrain him." I loosened my grip so Nogueira had enough space to talk. "Another thing you need to learn —no one bloodies the suites except for me. Now, you have two seconds to talk before I take matters into my own hands."

Nogueira coughed and reached up to wipe the sweat on his brow. "Vicente sends his regards—" he didn't get the rest out. His other hand whipped something from his shorts, and I jumped backward just in time to catch his wrist. A nice little boy scout knife in his hand.

"Are you trying to kill me with that ridiculous thing?" I asked quietly, squeezing the bones in his hand together until he dropped the knife. When I glanced up, his mouth was slack and his eyes were squinted, hopefully in fear. "You'd need a longer blade to do any fatal damage from that angle."

He stared back at me like he couldn't understand anything I was saying. That was fine. Now that I knew Vicente had set this up, I no longer needed his explanations. Strengthening my hold on his throat, I reared back and hit his nose. Blood sprayed everywhere, and I grinned once again.

I repeatedly punched him in his eyes, cheeks, nose, and mouth. A great example of Chinese water torture. The same spots over and over until the pain was so excruciating he screamed.

And screamed and screamed.

The manager pinned behind him grunted and cried with every hit that fell on Nogueira. By the time I was done, the warm smatter of blood decorated my skin and Nogueira's face was a bloody concaved mess.

"Enrique, call in the Carver. He'll take on Nogueira's fights and he's more brutal anyway. The bookies will allow changes to bets until the fights start. Spread the word."

Looks like I got my bloodshed today after all.

15

AMORETTE

"*El pequeño gato se sentó,*" I muttered as I walked around Grey's apartment. Lafe had gotten me a few children's books from someone outside their compound, and I had spent the last two hours reading and repeating the words.

I doubted small cats would ever come up in conversation, but Lafe was right. I needed a foundation if I was genuinely going to master the language. At least it was a phonetic language, and everything sounded like it looked.

"*El pequeño gato,*" I repeated, enjoying the foreign way my mouth moved to make the sounds.

"Mm...." Grey slid his hands around my waist and nuzzled my hair. "I'm going to spar in the courtyard. Come watch."

"I can't." I placed my hand over his forearm. "I need to speak the language. I can't stay here if I'm unable to understand anything happening around me." What secrets would I learn when people assumed I couldn't speak it? The thought of having the upper hand sparked excitement in my chest.

Grey groaned, pulling his face away. "You can bring the book with you." He pulled the flap over so he could see what it was. "The kid's story will be just as nice in the sun as it is here. Don't you miss being around me?" He flexed his hips, digging his growing erection into the small of my back.

"It's not about missing you. Or having sex with you, or anything else. This is about me and giving myself a tool to succeed. You four fought so hard to keep me here. Andre and Lafe brought me back. Let me help myself. Unless you want to help me." I turned in his arms and raised my brows.

"I think about you and your sweet pussy all day long. When we're together, I fantasize about stuffing you with my cum, shoving a tracking device under your skin in a place where you can't tear it out. I'd fuck you non-stop if I could. You're telling me that I'm giving you an opportunity to be around me while still doing what you want to do, and you're refusing?" He gripped my waist, his face a mask of incredulity.

Taking a step back, I pressed the hand with the book against his stomach. "What is your problem? We see each other every day. Every night. At least most of the time. This is something I want to do for me, and it has zero to do with you. If it's such a big deal, why don't you stay here while I work on learning these words!" I raised the book and shook it at him. This wasn't a big deal, except the way he was treating me like a brainless Stepford hole was insulting, damn it.

"Fuck that. I have to stay sharp for what I do. For the life I live. Hell, you should be out there training too." He pointed toward the courtyard.

"You're right, I do," I agreed, and some of the bluster left him.

"Then—"

"Just not now. This is as important as protecting myself. If I get taken again—"

"That's not going to happen," he growled.

"It's not fucking up to you!" I heaved a breath and turned to the side. All of the possible outcomes with their father were on my mind every day. They were trying to...I didn't know, shelter me from it? Or just didn't care to keep me in the loop. But it was building and building until I felt like I constantly needed to be on alert and working to give myself every advantage conceivable. "What's going on with Vicente?"

"What?" His face scrunched in confusion, and I turned back and took a step toward him.

"What's going on with Vicente? Did you all make up? Is he still after you? Is he doing sneak attacks or about to storm the gates?"

His lips twitched and I wanted to claw his face for not taking this seriously.

"This isn't funny!" I snapped, throwing the book on the couch. "These are things on my mind, and you all are ignoring me or keeping me in the dark on purpose. Is this the life you wanted me to have?"

Grey started to respond, but a knock came at the door. He just left me standing in the middle of the floor to go answer it. The bastard.

When he came back, a smirking Parker followed in his wake, and the joy on his face increased as he glanced between Grey and me.

"Tell me this is about to be a repeat, dear brother." He rubbed his hands together and locked his gaze on my rapidly rising and falling chest.

"Don't." I pointed at him, a flush creeping up my chest at the memory of the last time we were all in this apartment.

"But, Little Love, that was downright the highlight of my week." He started to walk toward me, but Grey gripped his shirt and pulled him back. Twisting, Parker shoved Grey away. "If you wanted to spar, say so. I'm not a fucking kid you can sling around."

"I do want to spar. And *mami* just gave me a hell of a motivation to beat the shit out of someone. That might as well be you." He nodded toward the door for Parker to follow him, only Parker didn't go anywhere.

"Sorry, can't. I actually came here for Little Love. She owes me some work." He kept his attention riveted to my face like he was waiting.

Did this mean I was going to be able to use the internet? That traitorous pounding started in my chest again. Even knowing I wouldn't jeopardize what they had here to save myself, any crumb of freedom was intoxicating.

"The items you wanted me to research," I breathed. "Let me grab my shoes."

"Hold on a fucking minute. You're stopping with the Spanish to go work with fucking Parker?" His voice pitched in tone as he stalked forward. He growled under his breath as he yanked me to him. "It's unacceptable that this is one-sided, *mami*," he whispered and crashed his mouth against mine. Dipping down, he cupped his hands just under my ass cheeks and loose shorts to pick me up against him.

Lost in the familiar sensation of his drugging kisses, I opened my mouth to let his tongue slip in. Then he pulled back and bit my lip, hard.

"Ouch!" I yelped. The bastard used one hand to smack my ass.

"Mm. The recoil," Parker murmured. I couldn't even look at him, leaving my focus on Grey's brilliant green eyes that seemed to brighten with his anger. Holding me almost to the point of pain, Grey leaned forward and pressed a soft kiss on my lips. I didn't return it, merely glaring at him.

"Remember when she's with you that my bite mark is on her lip, and handprint is on her ass," he said quietly, holding my gaze. He lowered me back to my feet and stormed out the front door, leaving a shit-eating grin on Parker's face.

"Trouble in paradise?" He chuckled.

I almost lost it on all the ways Grey was showing his crazy, but I stopped myself. Parker wasn't my friend. We weren't buddies, or even allies. He only tolerated my presence because it amused him to watch his brothers lose their goddamn minds, and because at least Grey would kick his ass if he sent me away.

"Where do you want me to do my research?" When in doubt of how to react in a situation, pretend there wasn't one.

He smirked as if he had my number and was happy to play along, for now. "At my place. Come on, Little Love. I'll give you a lift if you're scared to walk in the hallway barefoot."

I scoffed. "It's fine. Let's go." I led the way to the door when it was clear he wasn't going to go first, but I dead-stopped at his next words.

"The imprint is half under your shorts, and half on the cheek that's exposed, in case you wanted to know."

Closing my eyes, I counted to ten. When I first came here, Parker was a wild card. He stirred up trouble to get a rise out of people. He was doing the same thing now, except everything out of his mouth was sexual. If I ignored him and his comments, he'd leave me the hell alone.

And that was what I did. I ignored him all the way to his apartment.

Inside, Parker already had his laptop sitting out on the

coffee table. He hit the mousepad and turned it on, then entered a short password that was too fast for me to catch. "This laptop is monitored and restricted. You can Google search. However, any submissions, emails, or communications are prohibited. You can thank parental locks for that." He smiled at the screen. "And when you're done, a detailed report of every click will be delivered to my own personal email. Andre's too. We're trusting you just a little. Don't make us regret it."

He snickered, softening the sharp angles of his face. "Not that you can really do much, but you have to crawl before you can walk, right, Little Love?" The soothing tone of his voice was almost mesmerizing if it wasn't for the insulting connotation of his words.

"Fuck you, Parker," I said as I stepped around him to take a seat on his couch. But it lacked the heat I'd had with Grey. I expected this nastiness and distrust from Parker. From Grey, because I'd shared my body with him, it felt like he should trust me or at least give me the information I needed to stay alive.

"I'd love to," he grinned. "Though something tells me you'd be too much work with my brothers clamoring after your delightful charms."

"Brothers?" That feeling that I'd done something wrong reared its ugly head.

"Come on. Like you don't know." He leaned toward me, his black eyes sparking with glee. "Grey's eating out of the palm of your hand. Lafe, too, except he's so afraid of his shadow, he'd never act on it. Don't you find it odd that *that* particular brother who never goes against anyone for anything was the one who took you?"

Dropping my gaze, I pulled a pillow on my lap, then placed the laptop on it. I didn't like this kind of chat. My

poker face was damn good. Usually. There was just something about Parker that made me believe he'd know everything that happened to me as I would think it, especially if
he was looking into my eyes.

"That's not nice to talk about him that way. With Gr—" I
sucked in a sharp breath. "With Grace, I'd never say
anything so mean and condescending to her or about her to
strangers."

He leaned back, placing his elbow on the back of his
couch and two fingers against the side of his head. When he
smiled, there was nothing nice about it. "Let's discuss this. I
would wager you and your darling sister had a perfect
childhood?"

"Of course not," I scoffed. We'd lost a sibling and our
mother. That wasn't perfect in anyone's most desperate
dreams.

He rolled his eyes. "Not that bad things didn't happen.
I'm sure they did. You're human, and you experienced life.
Life is a fickle bitch who can be cruel just as much as she
can be gracious. Most of the time, she's both. To be fair, for
the majority of the population, they mostly experience her
graciousness."

I pressed my lips together. He wasn't wrong, and I
wanted him to be so very badly.

"What's the worst thing that happened to you as a
child? Skinned knee? Grandmother died too young? Your
dog was killed by poison?" The words sounded crass.
Harsh. Like he was being sarcastic. But the look on his
face was riveting, like he truly wanted to know this
answer.

Hesitating, I chewed on my bottom lip. It'd been years
since I spoke about Louis. Only to Grace. I wanted to tell
Parker about him, almost desperately. But I doubted he'd

care. I wasn't convinced Parker felt emotions like that. If this was Lafe, I didn't think I'd have the same struggle.

"Come on, Little Love. Don't leave me hanging. What was the most traumatizing thing that happened in your childhood?" He nudged my knee with his.

Twisting my lips to the side, I went for it. If this blew up in my face or Parker tried to use this against me somehow in the future, I'd probably cry. But in the end, I couldn't be mad at myself for wanting to keep my loved ones alive.

"We had a brother. Louis Pissaro Black. He was a teenager when we were just little kids. He passed away from cancer, and it was probably the single most devastating event of my childhood." Losing our mother was heartbreaking too, but I was at least older and better equipped to handle such a loss.

I gripped my shirt over my heart. What was Grace going through knowing that I was missing, unsure if I even still lived?

Parker shifted his weight and leaned forward as if he needed to be just a bit closer. "That's fascinating, you know?"

"What is?" I stiffened. Where was he going with this? If he said a bad word against my brother, I'd leave. I couldn't trust my actions if I were to stay.

"That the worst thing that happened to you was watching someone you loved get taken by a natural act of life, and that you never once referred to him as yours. But ours. For you and your twin." He reached out a hand and grazed his thumb over my collarbone. "So much goodness inside you and yet you still let Grey put his hands all over you. Does he make you feel dirty?"

I wanted to slap him, but he was being one hundred percent serious. The man was dying of morbid curiosity.

"No." I tried to think of how to put this to him without... sounding like a psycho or naive idiot. "The four of you aren't so bad. Not as bad as I originally thought. You have a code, and you've done the best you could with a shitty life. I understand that, at least on the surface level. Sometimes, I feel like I still would have done the right thing, or ended up where I was if I'd grown up in the same life, although it's impossible to know that for sure. In fact, sometimes, I think I'd be just as violent and brutal as you four."

One side of his mouth tipped up. "You do like us. That's good, Little Love. Considering we'll never let you go."

Ice sunk in my stomach even as he kept going, before I had the time to think about what that actually meant.

"You want to know the most traumatizing event in my childhood?" He dipped his head like he was about to whisper a delicious secret in my ear. Maybe he was.

I nodded.

His nose brushed the shell of my ear. "I watched... we all watched Vicente murder Grey's mother in cold blood. And you want to know the funny thing?"

There was nothing funny about that. Nothing at all. The hairs on the back of my neck stood up as he continued.

"She was his favorite." He pulled back so he could see me again. "Does it surprise you that he'd go after his own bastard sons?" This time when he grinned, it was full of the sarcastic humor I had expected earlier.

"It doesn't matter to you that he's a terrible man? Or that he's trying to hurt you all?" That was something I think I'd known for a while, but sitting here with Parker right now, it was coming across loud and startlingly clear.

"Why would it?" He furrowed his brow. "He was never a father to us. He whipped us more than he praised us. Pitted us against each other for sport and treated us little better than servant boys. He still treats us that way when he's not trying to take us down."

"But this is new, right? He's never publicly opposed you all as a group before?" I'd seen the marks on Grey's back. I knew there was a whipping post and Grey was no stranger to it, yet that was very different from attempting to murder your own children.

The skin around Parker's eyes pinched as if I'd hit a nerve. "Vicente is your definition of evil. The institution that he's built is only so strong because it's soaked in the blood of the innocent and steeped in the fear of those who serve him. The people love him as much as they hate him. And they'll carry out any of his wishes in just a whisper of a promise to gain his favor. Our lives—my life—are miserable. We're stuck in a birdcage just like you were when you first came here. Only ours is a little bigger, and we understand the bars that hold us like the jailer that keeps us. He has to die."

I sat up. "But what if you die in the process? Or Lafe? Or Andre? Grey? Are you really going to risk everything you love?" My blood pressure started to soar as we touched on the sensitive topic that had been plaguing me for days.

He looked at me out of the corner of his eyes. "What kind of relationship do you think my brothers and I have? We can barely stand each other." He laughed. "I know they can barely stand me, for various reasons. We are only as close as we are because we know, without a doubt, we will never betray each other. We don't have to like each other for that."

"No, that can't be right." I wanted to argue with him. The brothers did love each other. I knew it. "Love is not about liking someone. It's about valuing them as a person. Knowing you'd do anything, *be anything*, to keep them alive." My words were hypocritical to my own ears. I'd always placed right and wrong above everything else.

But more and more, I believed I'd just been lucky to never have been in a situation where I needed to choose.

"Mm. And you think I'd do anything for my brothers?" He lifted an eyebrow as if I saw too much good in him.

I blew out a breath. "I don't know you. Not really. So it's possible you could throw them to the wolves to further your own agenda. But...from the outside looking in, it appears that the four of you have already done so much to stay together. You would have jumped ship before now if that's what suited you."

"Would I? Little Love, it's amazing how you see the best in all situations." He smiled sardonically.

I snorted. "Hardly. I see the worst in people. In my line of work, everyone is suspicious, at least the men. And I've thought plenty bad about you four, but this is the one obser-vation I've made and it's not a bad one." I shrugged and turned to the computer.

Parker bent forward and grabbed a folder off the coffee table. As soon as he handed it to me, I recognized it. It was the same one from lunch that day, with all the details of the art he wanted to acquire.

"Your faction is thieves," I murmured, remembering Mia's wording as I flipped the pages, reacquainting myself with the items and detailed information.

"You could say that. However, running a heist operation sounds much better than common thievery. A successful heist requires research, preparation, coordination." He fingered the corner of the folder.

"You run an operation of convicts," I deadpanned. Men who stole for the fun of it. Men who were good at it.

He laughed, tipping his head back. "If you knew how

many of my men had actually been to prison, you'd find that funny."

"What does that mean?" I peered at him, but he shook his head.

"Nothing. We're a bunch of regular convicts. Now, let's review these pieces." He tapped the page in front of me. "And we'll see how long it takes my dear brother to come collect you out of raving jealousy."

16

AMORETTE

Having a laptop at my disposal did wonders for my confidence with the brothers. I was no longer a prisoner, although I'm not sure if that was how the men who worked for them viewed me in the first place.

Laughing, I tucked my chin as I walked down the hallway toward the offices. Of course, the men thought I was a prisoner. Maybe not in the same sense as the warehouse, but I was a glorified live-in girlfriend. Nope, that was probably too generous a word.

Either way, I was sure they viewed me as Grey's property, and maybe the brothers' too to a certain extent. And for them, that was normal. The men never even batted an eye when I traipsed around the compound.

Regardless, with a laptop under my arm, I felt like I was contributing—a real person with value instead of a thing that was only good for sex.

I approached Andre's office and stopped in the doorway. Andre had his phone on speaker as he sat back in his chair with his hands clasped under his chin. The chair continuously rocked back with his weight. I gave a short, low knock on the door, and he twisted toward me.

There was no smile, no greeting, just a cursory glance down to my feet and back up to my eyes. Then he waved a hand at the chair in front of the desk.

"We've been trying to work this out for years, Andre. You know how long I've been on this particular case. It would make my career if I were able to secure this information with informants." The man on the phone was definitely no spring chicken. His voice was raspy, like he'd partied hard for too many years. If I had to gamble on his age, I'd place him at least in his mid-fifties, but most likely mid-sixties.

He also carried a note of desperation.

"What information I give and when–is up to me, not you, Lescheva." Andre's voice was cold and hard, like Lescheva had been trying this precise conversation longer than just today.

Andre said his name? In front of me? I glanced back at the open door. It was more shocking he was having this conversation with the door open. It seemed like it wasn't strictly kosher.

"You reached out to me. I didn't initiate this call. If you've got a problem with someone and want to take them down a peg or two, I can get behind it. But you can't dictate the rules," Lescheva huffed. "Don't you see? This would make my career and make your life so much easier with that father of yours."

"This is a big risk the men would be taking. What can you promise them?" Andre spun until only his profile was in view. The light behind his desk highlighted the straight, proud line of his nose and his plump lips. Not too full but very defined.

"They'd get immunity. That's more than most men in their line of work would get in any other situation."

Not true. Criminals got immunity all the time when they were in a position to help take down a bigger fish.

This wasn't my typical area of law, yet something about Lescheva's words sounded off to me. I could be reading this entire situation wrong, but I didn't think so. Motioning to get Andre's attention, I mouthed 'mute' when he looked at me.

"Who is this man?" I asked once the mute button was engaged.

Andre studied me. His gaze was heavy, like he was weighing my intentions and my trustworthiness. When he finally answered, I felt one of the many knots I'd been carrying around in my chest loosen. "A consultant for the FBI. He works with them on several cases."

"You're offering up men to take down Vicente?" That was the only logical reason he'd be having this conversation.

"Andre?" Lescheva called, but we remained on mute.

"Maybe at the most basic, although it's more complicated than that. My men are not the ones on the table."

I pointed at the phone. "Then this man can't promise your people's immunity. He's a consultant. That could come only from the FBI. He's not actually employed with them, right? He's like a contractor?"

As he unmuted the phone, he kept his amber-brown gaze locked on mine. "Lescheva. How can you promise immunity? My understanding is that it's outside of your wheelhouse," Andre said lightly.

Lescheva blustered for a few seconds. "I'm a consultant. I've worked with the FBI on multiple occasions, and with *you*, I'll remind you. This has never been an issue."

A small smile tipped one side of Andre's mouth. "I was

never playing chess before, and certainly not with people who weren't throwaways. Everyone I tossed you in the past we wanted gone."

"Listen, I understand this is the big leagues you're trying to get into, but if you want to pull off a series of operations as delicate as this, we'd need to be careful. Head players can afford big lawyers who know their way around the law."

I motioned for him to hit mute again.

"Are you trying to catch Vicente in the act with informants?"

Andre gave me a single, almost imperceptible nod. "Long game."

"There's a fine line between the legality of using informants and entrapment. Maybe that won't matter if you're in South America, but it's something to consider."

Now Andre was grinning, his perfect white teeth on display. He hit unmute. "Lescheva, I'm getting an urgent call. Let's pick this up later." Then he ended it without a second glance at the phone.

The itch to fidget hit me as I sat under his intense stare. Then horror started to wash over me as I realized exactly how I'd just fucked up.

"Shit," I groaned and dropped my head into my hands. I'd begged them not to use me for anything that dealt with the law. That's not what I wanted to do in this new life. Yet here I was at the first opportunity to help take down Vicente, and I was spilling my minimal knowledge of criminal law.

"That was impressive. I should have consulted you before I called Lescheva."

When I picked my head up, there was nothing except respect and maybe a glimmer of admiration shining on

Andre's face. His black hair was swept away from his face, except for one wavy lock falling over his forehead.

I decided to focus on that instead of what I'd just done. "I've been working on research for Parker, and I had a couple of questions for you," I said, then coughed to clear my throat. I could see the wheels turning behind his eyes.

"Let me tell you what I think would have happened if you hadn't walked in...." He reached back and gripped the top of his chair, stretching his shirt across a toned body. The movement didn't appear to be a trick to distract me. Andre didn't operate that way, as far as I knew. "I've worked with Lescheva and a few other agents over the last few years. Mostly when Vicente wanted to ruin someone in a different way. I turned them in. Set them up. Sometimes even coordinated for them to be sent to a prison with their rivals so they'd meet an untimely death. It's a quick and easy way to eliminate someone without dirtying Vicente's hands or reputation.

"But now Vicente has called a war on us, and I need his key players removed from the board. Lescheva was going to help me do that. These men have a party they'll attend in the US in a little over a month." He paused, giving me time to digest the information he was throwing at me.

I heard him, but suddenly white noise filled my ears. Until now, I hadn't known what Andre's role was in the Institution. I knew Grey's, Lafe's, and Parker's, but Andre's had been a mystery I hadn't particularly cared about solving.

Now though? He was an informant for the FBI. Or close enough if he turned people over. They'd never cared about holding me hostage here, because they had connections. What was one girl to the FBI when they had an open tap to take down many other, bigger and more attractive fish?

I'd encountered enough of the agents in DC to know they only cared about making a name for themselves.

"It was never an issue about me being here with you against my will, was it?" I cut Andre off mid-sentence. I had no idea what he was saying.

He canted his head and narrowed his eyes. "Where's this coming from?"

I laughed, even as the sound was wet and disgusting. These fucking emotions rearing their heads out of the blue without warning were pissing me off. "Nothing. I just realized how connected you are. I'm not trying to escape. I haven't for a while. But I'm realizing just how impossible my situation would have been if I had gotten away. It would have been short-lived." I swiped at my eyes, ecstatic that my fingers had come away dry.

The respect that had been shining in his eyes moments ago dimmed as his top lip curled. I got it. This was terrible. I'd have never made two days in the law office like this.

"Sorry, keep going. What would have happened if I hadn't walked in?" I set the laptop on his desk and his eyes sparked as he tracked the movement.

"I was saying, the men I would have used would have been arrested or at least taken into custody. There are a fuck ton of problems we could have faced if Lescheva wouldn't have been able to follow through. But that wouldn't have mattered to him. He's a stone-cold bastard, and the only thing he would care about is the notoriety of taking down some of the players in the biggest cartel in existence today. And he would have pressured for more informants if he couldn't get Vicente's top men."

He was a good sport in pretending I wasn't melting in front of him. Yet he still watched me as if waiting for me to come apart at the seams. And I was, but I had also locked it down on the surface.

Straightening in my chair, I opened the laptop. "I'm glad I was able to help. Lescheva seems like an arrogant ass. Now, about these jobs for Parker—"

"What about them?" He hit the call button on the phone and cut it off again once he had the dial tone. I guess even sophisticated men in crime aren't exempt from paranoia.

"There's one particular job that I don't think he should take." I pulled up the notes I'd compiled on the Qing Dynasty vase. He tapped my arm when I turned the computer around to face him.

"Why are you coming to me with this? Parker runs this side of the business." I glanced up and got caught in his stare. He looked so much like Matías. Or maybe Matías looked like Andre. I wasn't sure, but it was in my best interest not to point it out.

"I already shared this with Parker, and he's determined to go after it even harder now. But I think it's a terrible idea."

"Go on," he said, skimming at my notes on the screen.

Pointing to a picture in the corner, I laid out my argument. "This vase is from the Qing Dynasty. Worth about two million. Last known possessor was a man named Joseph Gates, otherwise known as the Curator." I stopped there, watching for any sign of recognition. "He was a man who collected children, both boys and girls, for clients. A pedophilia ring." I took in a shuddering breath.

"Was? He's no longer alive?"

"No." I shook my head. "Death unknown, although it appears to have been murder."

A divot appeared between Andre's brows as he moved his gaze between me and the screen. "What's the problem, then?"

He didn't find it as abhorrent as I did or even displayed satisfaction in the man's death. That seemed to twist a bitter knife in my chest. "He had a group of boys in his own..." I gulped. "Collection. They were saved twelve years ago. I think one of them has the vase or even other artifacts Joseph owned."

"Amorette," Andre was losing his patience. We weren't the same, and our minds were thousands of miles apart in wavelengths. "Get to the point."

"They were placed into the foster system, but somewhere along the way, they were discovered. Or at least a couple of them. They're the hottest items in male fashion right now." I had actually met Isaac Kim. He'd done a photo shoot with Grace a few years ago. He was so smooth and pleasant; I had no idea of his background. I wanted to throw up just thinking about the articles I'd read. "They're successful, but they live an insanely lavish life. Too much for what they'd have made as models. I want you all to leave them alone. Don't steal from them..." When he didn't say anything, I continued. "They've paid enough. Let them keep this."

No change in Andre's expression. No clues to give me an inkling of what he was thinking.

"What did Parker say?" he finally asked.

"He said that the world wasn't fair, and if he could steal it, they weren't protecting it well enough. He seemed almost giddy at the prospect of going himself."

Andre rubbed a hand over his jaw, the rasp of his stubble filling the space between us. "Parker would. He thrives on chaos and misfortune."

Yeah, I knew that. But these were victims. They'd been molested for years and never returned to their families. From what I read about them, they weren't bad people—no public tendencies for violence or anything like that. At least on the surface, they were breaking the cycle. They deserved a bit of happiness, even if it wasn't necessarily the justice I usually fought for.

We stared at each other. Me putting all my heart into my eyes, and him watching me with an unreadable expression. Sometimes I felt like I could settle in here. Then others, like now, I felt like the divide between who we were as people was so vast we'd never be able to bridge it.

"Nevermind." I snapped the laptop closed and pushed to my feet.

"Amorette." I paused in the doorway and glanced over my shoulder. "Thank you. We would have been in a bad way if you hadn't set me straight."

I nodded, because what else was there to fucking do?

As soon as Amorette's footsteps were no longer audible, I stood up and shut my office door. I should have closed it earlier, but the constant video monitoring and threats of violence to the men not to come down this hall unless invited made me lax. The one man who actually had an office here never used it unless we were away and everything was locked up tight.

A stupid mistake on my part, considering what Grey had shared.

I dialed Lescheva back and took my seat, smoothing the wrinkles out of my button-down shirt. Even in the office of the compound I wore suits almost exclusively. It gave the severe impression I needed to make on the men, on video calls, or anyone who happened to see me.

"Andre. Glad to see you've come to your senses."

"What is Vicente paying you?" I asked. It was a long shot, and I'd dealt with him for years in some capacity. Lescheva was a straight shooter, for the most part, and absolutely self-serving. He usually wasn't one to make promises he couldn't keep, but he'd also never pushed so hard for a job.

"What the hell is this?" He blustered.

"You're salivating for this job. Even better if I come on my own. And you lied about what you could promise my men. What's he paying you?"

"You're mistaken, son."

I laughed. "I'm not your son. And I don't take kindly to manipulation. Don't forget, if I can go after my own father, what would I do to *you*?"

Lescheva didn't like that. I smiled. Fucking with him was so much more fun than dealing with Vicente. That was a beast I hated where every move and word had to be analyzed. Lescheva wasn't so smart.

"Whatever you think is happening, it's not. I can promise your men immunity for their part. We just need to make sure there's enough evidence to take his officials into custody. I'm a consultant but a veteran with the team and they listen when I ask for something."

"So, you're already saying that you haven't gotten their explicit approval to offer immunity?"

"Hey, that's not what I'm saying," he backpedaled. "We'd have to work out several layers before the big day. You'd get your guarantee before then."

Suddenly, this wasn't the path I wanted to take. Not even close. As a rule, we didn't trust anyone, but we had fragile truces where it suited us. This wasn't suiting me anymore. It stank like a trap.

"What's in this for you? Say you're not getting paid by Vicente. What's in this for you?"

He huffed out a laugh. "Even without Vicente, this would be the takedown of the century. I don't need to explain the glory that comes along with that."

"I thought you never allowed your picture or information to be printed on the news."

He hawed. "That's for the public. I want the glory in the Bureau. It racks up tons of clout and favors that go a long way to get me what I want."

"Which is?"

The only sound was his breathing. Lescheva wouldn't have slipped up. He wasn't so careless. But he also wasn't sure how to answer.

"We all have enemies. I do just like you do, and I want to see my own brand of justice served." Was that supposed to make me like him more? He was trying and failing to relate to me.

"For now, this is tabled. I won't be supplying men for your operation, and I won't be contacting you any time soon. And Lescheva..." I waited until I knew with certainty he was listening. "If I find out that you accepted payment from Vicente to fuck me over, I will hunt you down and skin you alive. Then I'll let Parker play with you."

I hit the end button, effectively hanging up on him twice today.

Sending a text to my brothers, I told them to meet me at my place. We needed to have a meeting. This entire situation was getting out of hand.

At my place, I cracked open the bourbon and grabbed four glasses, arranging the tray on the sleek black table. My place differed from the others. It was all black, with the exception of a few silver statement pieces. Everything was buffed until it was pristine and glossy, just as I liked it.

The order kept me calm.

"What's this about?" Grey knocked the door open as he came in, his face like thunder. Someone was in a fucking bad mood.

"What's up your ass?" I poured two fingers in each glass.

"Nothing." He tossed the drink back and slammed it on the tray. The glasses shook, and some of the bourbons sloshed onto the tray. I gritted my teeth, holding my words. We didn't need a fight right now.

Lafe came in, more alert and present than I'd seen him in a while, although he had dark circles under his eyes. Then Parker brought up the rear, locking the door behind him.

"Look at this, a family reunion. Does anyone else think this directly results from our sweet little love?" He picked up his own glass and perched on the cabinet to face us. Everyone else was on the couches and he had to make a fucking statement.

Grey glared at him while motioning for me to top his glass off.

"I'm not drinking. You can have mine."

We all turned to look at Lafe. His ears started to darken as he scowled at us.

"That's fine. I wanted to get you all here to discuss what we're doing with Vicente." I tapped my fingers on my knee.

"Yes, brother? Enlighten us on how you've decided we would proceed," Parker snarked.

I glared at him. "This isn't about me making decisions for us. It's about you not throwing us into a bloody battle-field because it fucking amuses you or fits your plans for yourself."

He held my stare, but I didn't care. I wasn't backing down. Not when I didn't know if he would stay with us or suddenly be gone one day without a fucking word.

"I think we're going too fast," I said, still daring Parker to fuck up. I wanted him to. I needed to let go of some steam, and a good sparring session with my brothers sounded like an excellent way to release it. "I've been focusing on taking players off Vicente's board to ultimately take down Vicente, but I'm moving too fast. There's too much room for Vicente to fuck us over." I finally looked at Lafe, then Grey. "I'm almost certain I would have walked my men into a trap if Amorette hadn't decided to pay me a surprise visit."

Lafe's eyebrows shot up. "Why did she come to see you?"

Of course, he'd be confused. I held a gun under her chin and would again if she double-crossed us. But something Lafe didn't seem to understand, but Amorette did–It wasn't personal. For now, she served a purpose; more than that, she was slowly becoming an asset.

We'd have to see how that would play out in due time.

"Because Parker wants to steal from people she deems victims. She's disgusted." I cut my gaze back to him, and Parker, the bastard, gives us a close-lipped grin, fucking ecstatic with himself. "Care to tell us what that's about."

"Not yet," he said and swung his feet, lightly kicking the cabinet like a child.

"Parker," I growled. "No more of this stuff. You either bring us all in on the plan, or you don't fucking do it."

Grey and Lafe both shot him heated looks.

"If you put us in danger again, I'll kill you," Grey shared without an ounce of hesitation. "Brother or not, that boat only goes so far as being able to trust you. If I don't trust you, you're not my brother."

Lafe didn't say anything, he just watched Parker with more than a little hurt in his clear blue gaze.

Parker lost his shit-eating grin and hopped off the counter. "You bastards are acting like I'm selling you out for the hell of it." Heat hit his cheeks and bled down his neck. "You assholes," he spat.

I stood up and faced him. "What is your issue with this

vase? Are you stealing it anyway? Are you just fucking with her for fun?" A few minutes ago, he had that look about him that he always got before he planned something big. I never paid that much attention because it hadn't affected us.

That was before he started trying to take down Vicente on his own. Or gain enough leverage to escape on his own, leaving the rest of us to endure Vicente's twisted ire.

He wanted to argue. I could see the scathing words on the tip of his tongue, but he glanced between the three of us. For the first time, maybe ever, we were united against Parker, and that bothered him. Perhaps not like it would most people, but it did. He grunted and swiped a hand over his head in irritation.

"Whether I stay or not, whether Vicente means to take us out or not, we have to beat him to it. The men Amorette is referring to were the personal collection of the Curator. She thinks they have or had the vase I'm looking for, as well as several other of his artifacts. I'm inclined to believe her." He paused, waiting for Grey or Lafe to pipe in with questions. When they didn't, he continued. "Their life is too lavish for what they've made even with their success, and she thinks they deserve to keep whatever they've gotten as payment for such a shitty childhood." His top lip raised. "I wonder what Little Love thinks we deserve?"

"Are you going after the vase?" I urged. He was getting lost in his thoughts and I had shit to do.

"Not in the way Amorette believes I am," he reluctantly answered. "I have a plan, but I need to work out some details. It won't jeopardize us with Vicente, not any more than we already are."

"Vicente isn't playing this time," Lafe interjected, shaking his head. "He tried to kill Grey. He's slowly hitting us where he can. I think he hasn't gone after the rest of us more directly because we haven't left the compound."

"This doesn't make sense," Grey added. "You said Mia wasn't caught. What else has happened to push him over the edge?" He kept his gaze on me, completely ignoring Parker.

We exchanged glances, because none of us had any idea.

"It could be that Vicente doesn't have a reason. Which is more motivation for us to take him out," Parker argued, taking a few steps closer to their chairs.

I didn't disagree with him, not with the erratic way Vicente was trying to get to us, but hell, this whole mess was starting to give me another migraine. My right temple throbbed as I tried to lay the plans out in my mind. "Then we need a plan. A solid, well-thought-out plan. Otherwise, we'll just end up fucking ourselves in the ass." I loosened my tie, pulled it off, and tossed it in the corner. "I think Lescheva was setting us up."

"He's been one of your contacts for years." Lafe scooted forward in his seat and clasped his hands between his thighs. "He's never fucked you over."

"What's the number one rule?" I smiled sardonically.

"No one can be trusted forever," they all parroted. And I flicked a brief glance at Parker. He ground his teeth and looked away. Luckily, he kept his mouth shut, as I couldn't be responsible for my actions if he pissed me off.

"Right. Everyone has a price, and it's fluid depending on their life situation and circumstances. Amorette happened to be in my office at the tail end of our conversation, and she pointed out some critical flaws on his side. He couldn't promise immunity like he said he could—"

"Hasn't he promised that before?" Grey asked, slouching down in his own seat.

I shook my head. "No, not like this. My dealings are usually turning over rats or men we don't want the responsibility for. A clean death. This would have been an operation to set up Vicente's top advisors. A completely different operation. And anything close to this in the past was run through Special Agent Morgan." I rolled my lips together. "Another thing Amorette warned of... She said we'd have to be careful that our plan wouldn't be seen as entrapment. And I have to say we'd be flirting with the line. I ended the call with Lescheva."

We were all quiet, me for an entirely different set of reasons I was sure.

When I glanced up, Grey was smug, and Parker had a dirty little smile on his face. "What are you two so fucking happy about?"

Grey raised an eyebrow. "I knew Amorette would fit in here."

"I knew Little Love would be useful." Parker smirked.

Then there was Lafe. He looked at them like he wanted to believe in Amorette as much as they did but didn't know how. I was partly to blame for that, but there was nothing I could do about it now. Paranoia was a better tool for him than trust. He'd live longer because he wasn't cruel or detached like the rest of us.

"So, how are we supposed to protect ourselves?" Lafe turned to me.

That was the million-dollar question, and one I didn't have the answer to. "The only thing I know for now is we can't rush anything. We can't leave the compound without a clear plan and contingency plan. And we can't trust anyone."

"And Killer? Can we trust her?"

Could we?

AMORETTE

"*Refrigerador*." I pointed to the fridge.

"*Bueno*." Lafe nodded while he chopped up lettuce and tomato.

"*Estufa*." I pointed at the stove.

Lafe nodded with a smile.

"*Cuchillo*," I said with a grin, nodding to the knife in his hand.

"*Muy bien*," he returned.

I gave out an embarrassing but low squeal and hopped. Damn, that was ridiculous, but I couldn't hold in my excitement. Every day I was committing more and more words to memory. I still couldn't understand the conversations that happened around me. Everyone here spoke much too fast for that, but I might be able to pick out a few words here and there soon.

It was all progress, and I'd take it.

"What's all the excitement in here?"

I turned to face Parker, losing a bit of my joy. No, that wasn't fair. It wasn't that I hated him. I certainly didn't trust him, but I didn't trust very many people here, anyway. The greater issue was that every time I saw him, I saw his face shrouded with desire and the massive erection in his pants while I fell apart beneath Grey.

Lafe gave me a weird look before answering Parker. "We're making lunch and working on Spanish. Killer's decided it's a tool she needs to survive us."

"Not survive *you* specifically," I pointed out, but maybe I spoke too soon. I was thrown into this life because of them. I was trying to come to terms with who they were and who I was coming to be, so loosely, I did want to survive them.

"You want to learn Spanish?" Parker perked up. "Little Love, languages are my thing. I can have you fluent in no time." He stepped closer, and I took a small step back. His brow furrowed, and one side of his mouth tipped up in a barely there smile. "What's this? You're not afraid of me, are you, Little Love? Not after that one afternoon."

I stepped forward, but was jerked back into Lafe's chest. He wrapped an arm around me for just a second, long enough to shift me to the other side of him.

"You're making her uncomfortable." Lafe went back to cutting up the veggies. He'd made bacon again, which seemed like his go-to meal. I wasn't complaining. A good BLT went a long way to temporarily elevating my happiness.

Parker released a high, amused laugh. "Oh, brother, you have no idea. You weren't there that day bu—"

"Shut up!" I snapped, and he grinned like he was just waiting for me to blow all along.

He grabbed a shiny red apple from the counter and took a bite. The crunch of his chewing almost blocked out the sound of Lafe finishing up on the cutting board.

Lafe ignored him, arranging the tomato and lettuce on a plate beside the bacon. Parker glanced between us and grinned even wider.

"Lafe, why didn't you send her to me when she wanted to learn Spanish?"

He grunted. "Why would I? You torment everyone."

"But I'm efficient and brilliant." Parker pointed at Lafe with the hand holding the apple. "I'm the best man for this particular job...Unless you—"

"Fuck you," Lafe said as he started assembling sandwiches. "Like last time?" He glanced at me without stopping the bacon layering.

"Yeah, it was perfect last time." A ghost of a smile coasted across his face, then he twisted back to the sandwiches.

Parker opened his phone and typed out a few words as he continued to snack on his apple. "We're going after the painting this week. I have two groups of men on standby. One team is a decoy. The other is the real deal," he informed me, and some of the pressure surrounding my heart relaxed. Good. He was leaving the men alone. This could all be a game to him, and he'd go after them later, but I was focusing on the small mercies for now. I didn't think he was heartless, and stupidly, I was waiting for him to prove it to me.

Someone hollered for Parker down the hallway. He glanced over his shoulder and sighed. "Here. Text Rod the location you gave me. I'll be right back," he said, sliding his phone across the counter.

It was open on Rod's name, and a string of cryptic texts was already in the chat. I peeked at Lafe, but he was absorbed in making the sandwiches. A wave of tingles rushed over my body, just like the day I'd been left alone in Andre's office. Would the adrenaline rush ever die down?

I'd already decided I wouldn't run; I was going to see this through the best I could. At least as long as they kept their word and didn't hurt women and children. Yet, every time an opportunity presented itself, my naive heart thought it was the opportunity to escape.

I typed up the information I'd given Parker and hit send, then pushed it back over to where he had been standing. Even though I'd decided, I didn't want to risk temptation. In a weak moment, I might break down and call Grace. As much as I wanted to hear her voice again, I wanted her in this world like I wanted to saw off my own foot.

"Do you think you'd miss your brothers if you couldn't see them anymore?" I asked, rubbing a hand over my heart. When I caught myself, I forced it back down.

Lafe had finished the sandwiches, and his eyes were glued to my chest, where I'd been rubbing seconds ago. When he lifted his gaze, the skin around his eyes had softened. He watched me, or maybe he was trying to determine the answer. I wasn't sure.

"Let's eat." He nodded to the table in the corner of the commons kitchen. It was a large, wooden round table with ten chairs around it. Perfect for large families, yet I'd never seen anyone sitting here. He set out plates side by side while I'd already placed the water pitcher with glasses on the table earlier.

I sat down, trying to forget about Grace. It hurt to think about her. It was a physical pain embedded in my body. I'd never lose the feeling completely. But just like every other time she crossed my mind, a warmth so sweet it almost brought tears to my eyes burned inside me. This, missing her, was the epitome of conflicting emotions. I loved to remember her, just as much as I hated it.

"I don't know," Lafe started, picking up half of his cut sandwich. "Some days, I think I would be lost without them. Then other times, I hate them." His jaw worked as he stared at his sandwich.

"Why do you hate them?" I whispered as I nudged my own plate. I wanted to know these answers like I wanted to talk to Grace. Well, maybe not quite that much, but it was close. If I understood them, why they stuck together even when they didn't like each other. Maybe I would want to stay too.

He rolled his lips together and brought the sandwich closer to his face. Then he closed his eyes and just stopped. "I don't hate them. Not all of them. I just want to."

Lafe took a bite of the sandwich, and the crunch of the bacon and lettuce rang between us like that was the end of the conversation.

For now, I'd accept that, but this wasn't the end. I had too many questions. Part of me also ached for them to confide in me, just a little. Not so much to know their secrets but to feel like I was part of their circle and not a prisoner. Not even a pampered one.

"What are you doing after this?" I asked before I took my own bite. The salty flavor burst over my tongue and I hummed my enjoyment.

"Nothing," he rushed out and stuffed another bite in his mouth.

I slowed down my chewing because, one, that was weird. And two, I wasn't sure why he was acting weird.

"I'm on season two of that show you hooked me on. Do you want to watch a couple of episodes with me?"

He set his sandwich down and looked me square in the eyes. The light blue more electric than I'd ever seen before. Clearing his throat, he adjusted his seat. "No, I can't today. I'm happy to help you continue learning Spanish. I wasn't lying, Parker's a bastard who likes to torment everyone. But I don't think we should watch any more shows together."

Instantly, the sharp sting of embarrassment and rejection slid over me. I knew why he was turning me down. It was because of the cuddling we'd done. But that wasn't what I was offering.

"You can sit on one couch, and I can sit on the other." I raised a brow as if he was being ridiculous. More guilt heaped onto me for that too.

"I think it's better if we don't." He finished off his sandwich in short order while I sat there staring at him. When he was done, he picked up his dishes and carried them to the sink. "We'll work on weapons next," he said as he exited the room.

With much less enthusiasm, I continued eating my sandwich. It wasn't long before Parker popped back in. He looked at me, then searched the kitchen for his phone. After collecting it from the counter, he pulled a chair across from me and crossed his arms.

"You could have used my phone to call for help." He wasn't smiling. There wasn't even a hint of one anywhere on his face.

"I could. I also could have called for help when I was alone in Andre's office. I didn't." I pushed my plate away.

Was this it? Was this the moment I became the actual accomplice, in heart if not in action? We both knew I'd already crossed that bridge a while ago.

The weight of his stare peeled back the layers of my intentions, or so it seemed. There was an intelligence about Parker that I wouldn't say was missing in the other brothers, but something about his eyes made him seem.... Sharper. Perhaps it was what made him cruel.

"What's changed, Little Love?" Seriousness dripped from his tone.

I blew out a breath. What *had* changed? I wasn't even sure myself. "I don't know."

"That's not a soothing answer."

"That's the only one I have." I shrugged, like he could take it or leave it.

This time, he did crack. Mirth returned to his eyes, and they sparkled as the corners of his lips slowly turned up into a Joker-esque smile. This was the smile that made him look the part of the villain. And he was undoubtedly someone's villain. I was sure of it.

He just wasn't mine.

"Fair enough." He tilted his head as he regarded me. There was so much working behind his eyes, and I couldn't help but ask what I should have questioned Lafe about.

"Am I trusted now? Not the enemy anymore?"

He stretched his arm out on the table as he leaned back, a flirty grin twisting his lips. "You were never the enemy. We don't allow our enemies in our compound, and we certainly don't sleep with them." He raised his eyebrows.

"Don't you?" I wanted to kick myself. That sounded suggestive, teasing. When I had only wanted to point out that the brothers seemed like the kind of men to sleep with who they wanted to, alliances and any other pesky issues be damned.

"Are you insinuating that I myself sleep with the enemy, or that Grey does?" His face lit up like he was enjoying this conversation far too much.

I coughed and dropped my gaze. "Neither. I just meant... I've seen you with women." My face was on fire, and I could feel Parker's gaze eating me up. "It's not like you're interviewing them before you bend them over."

He laughed a high, hyena-type laugh and slapped the table. "Little Love. Is that your kink? You like to watch? Tell me... how many women have you seen me with? There couldn't have been that many opportunities."

Like a siren's call, I lifted my gaze to his. Exactly as I thought, delight was stamped over his entire body, and he was pressing against the table like he regretted sitting on the far side.

"A few," I whispered, hating the way it came out strangled.

Before he had time to respond, Lafe walked back in. He grabbed a bottle of water from the fridge and stopped by the table, his blue gaze bouncing between Parker and me.

"Why does Amorette look like you're embarrassing her?"

Parker straightened up and grinned at Lafe. "Little Love was just telling me about the women she's seen me with."

Lafe chuckled as a devious glint entered his eye. He snaked a quick glance at me before turning back to Parker. "You mean the women who are eerily similar to Killer?" He untwisted the cap and took a swig of water as his comment settled between us.

I sucked in a short breath as Parker glared.

"Nothing to say?" Lafe screwed the cap back on and faced him with an expression that said he was over Parker's games.

"Why would I need poor imitations when I can watch the real thing? Amorette's so pretty when she comes. Did you know that?" Parker's gaze was cold on Lafe.

My heart dropped into my stomach as Lafe squeezed the bottle, the crinkling plastic cutting through the sudden oppressive silence.

"I didn't know you were there!" I pushed myself away from the table and stood up.

"Grey did. Does that bother you, Little Love?" The playful tone was absent in his voice now as he slowly rose to his feet. "Maybe my brother isn't as possessive about you as you think he is. Do you want that? Do you want to be in the middle of us? Do you thrive on us fighting over you? Or maybe you just want us to share you?" He directed his attention to Lafe on the last question, who had completely bristled.

I walked around the table, my hands trembling and my head buzzing with too many out-of-control emotions. Parker's gaze softened when I stopped directly in front of him. He had just raised his hands to touch my hips when I smacked his cheek as hard as I could.

"You're an asshole, Parker," I said through clenched teeth.

Without giving either of them another opportunity to anger me anymore, I stormed out.

Yet, I couldn't forget Parker's words. Grey had known Parker was there. Was this what he wanted, or was Parker just trying to fuck with my head?

19

GREY

"Come on." I opened the bathroom door where Amorette had been hiding for the last ten minutes.

She hopped up from the toilet, screeching. "Close the damn door! I'm peeing!" She bent over to hide herself from me.

"It's a piss. I've seen, touched, kissed, fucked your pussy in every way imaginable. Seeing you take a piss shouldn't bother you." I walked further into the room to prove my point.

"Well, it does!" she squawked, wiping quickly and pulling up her shorts.

"Whatever." I set the clothes on the sink for her. "Get ready. We're doing a fighting lesson today." Then I left without giving her time to argue. I was done with her brushing me off to do other things. Protecting herself was just as important as learning to speak Spanish. Protecting herself was more important than any fucking research she did for Parker.

I grabbed the box I'd left on the counter. Andre had thrown a fit when he found out, but I didn't give a fuck. Her skills were abysmal. If she took him out with it, it was his own damn fault.

Amorette came storming out of the bedroom in under five minutes, spitting mad. She'd been angry for two fucking days. I tried to fuck it out of her, and it had worked for about twenty minutes, then she'd tense up again.

I grinned. I'd give it another shot after today. She didn't even know we'd be going to another fight tonight. I was overseeing this one, so I could keep her with me the entire time. Hell, I'd sit her in my lap and keep my hand up her dress. Everyone in the club would know she was mine.

Andre could fuck right the hell off. Now that Vicente was being a bitch about it, there was no reason not to show her off. It was safer for her if everyone understood she was mine.

Ours to protect. Mine to fuck.

Amorette was past escaping, but it was never a bad idea to let others know it would be their death on the line if they tried to help her.

"What's that?" She stopped in front of me, her gaze locked on the small black box in my hand.

"A present," I grinned. "But you have to wait until we get to the gym to open it." I placed my arm around her shoulder and guided us toward the door.

She sighed and wrapped her arm around my waist as we walked. Her fingers brushed against the residual bruising from my fight with Bruno, but I didn't care. It was just pain. It wouldn't last.

"Something tells me it's not jewelry."

I laughed. "No. Andre is the only one of us who would

give out something useless like that. Parker would give his fuck buddies priceless art and laugh about it. If he ever kept a girl around that long."

"And Lafe? What would he give?" She glanced up.

That took some thought. I didn't actually know what Lafe would give a woman. "I have no fucking clue. But he's the bleeding heart. He'd probably watch a tear-jerker or a rom-com in that movie room he loves so much." I almost snorted.

Her body tightened up under my arm.

"Is that your thing? Are you a snuggler, *mamí*?"

"No," she answered too quickly. Wicked Love was lying. "Is this session just going to be us?"

I shrugged. "The gym is for family only, but occasionally, we'll invite some of our men in."

There were more questions on her tongue, but she held it.

Inside the gym, we weren't alone. Andre was running on the treadmill in just his gym shorts and no shirt. Sweat glistened on his chest and back, so he'd probably be winding down soon.

I scowled when Amorette peeked over at him. She was suddenly too interested in all my brothers. Even if it was cautious or suspicious attention, attention was attention. At least he didn't give one fuck that we joined him. He was too lost in his own workout.

"Okay, *mamí*. Now it's yours." I handed her the box as I opened the rest of the gym. There were enormous windows, but I still liked to have the lights and music on.

"Wow," she whispered as she pulled the top off. The knife blade was about four inches long, with a slight curve. The shorter side was serrated with a sharp tip. On the other end, the obsidian handle was also worked into a sharp point.

Any way that she hit an attacker with this knife, it would do damage. Front swipe, back swipe, blunt handle hit. This was a lethal weapon in a tiny package. Like my wicked love.

"Your lesson today will be on how to use that. Because tonight, I have a fight to attend and you're coming with me." I pulled a dummy knife out of my pocket and gently swapped them in her hand.

The treadmill slowed down, and Andre pulled his earbuds out. "Like hell, you'll go tonight."

I guess he was listening. "The fight is in my hotel. I'll be damned if one of Vicente's men tries to show up to run the fights."

He grabbed his towel off the arm of the treadmill and wiped his face and the back of his neck. Even with his black hair plastered to his body, he put off the same controlling air. "Vicente has declared war on us, Grey. The fights are his business. You manage it, but considering how he's doling out his attacks, I would consider you fired."

I sneered. The fights were mine. I'd worked them from the ground up. They were as successful as they were today because of me. That also didn't change the fact that the hotel was mine.

"Hell to the *fuck* no," I said at the same time Amorette asked, "What attacks?"

"The fights are mine, Andre. If we're on the outs, they stay mine. The profits are mine," I growled. I'd already started redirecting a lot of the profits to my own shell corporation.

"You think this is some divorce where we split the assets?" Andre shouted, slinging the hand holding the towel toward me. "You know it's fucking not, Grey! You stay here and kick the fights out of your hotel!"

I got in his face and shoved him backward. "Vicente is going to do whatever the fuck he wants. But he's not taking away the one thing I've loved all these years. Not after my mother. This is my life, Andre. I *am* the fights. They're mine!"

Amorette wedged herself between us and shoved at our chests. We didn't budge. Instead, we now just had a spitting kitten stuck between us.

"And what about taking Amorette to the fights? We just fucking discussed this! It's too dangerous! You want her to get stolen again? The next time Vicente might not take her to Matías, but Maikel."

"You think I haven't thought of that!" I roared and pulled Amorette to my chest and away from Andre. "One, I'm taking men with me. Two, I ordered a fucking tracker. Two of them! One to wear and one to inject under the skin."

"What the fuck!" Amorette struggled in my grip even though I refused to let her go.

"Then there's the knife. It's so sharp it will cut through skin and muscle like butter. I'm giving her all the tools she needs, so she doesn't have to stay in a cage. What are you doing, Andre? You fucking coward. You talk about Lafe, but *you're* the fucking coward. You'd happily sit your ass here and wait it out until we can take Vicente out from afar, or he kicks the fucking bucket." I spat on the ground at his feet. "I'm not living like that. And neither is she."

I turned us away and moved back over to the mat. I placed the knife in her box, caught her hand holding the dummy knife and brought it up between us.

"This conversation isn't done, Grey." Andre pressed closer.

Yes, the fuck it was. He didn't exist for us right now. "There are three ways you can strike someone with this knife. But any way you hit the skin with it, it will do damage."

Amorette watched me with a mixture of worry and concern. "Grey, we have to talk about this. I need to know what's going on." A thread of frustration wove through her strained words.

"After the lesson, I'll tell you what you want to know, but this is important. As much as Andre's an ass," the man himself growled his fury at my side, "he's not wrong about it being dangerous."

"I'm not getting a tracker under my skin," she asserted, shaking her head. "That's barbaric."

"Not now. We'll talk about that soon. This very second, we're going over how you can use this to maim or kill someone." I rotate her wrist to show her the different ways to strike someone. "Go for the eyes if you can reach them. A quick jab to the eye with the handle end will incapacitate them for several minutes, and that eye will be useless. Otherwise, go for the throat. The main artery is on the left side." I showed her where to hit on my own neck.

"You're fucking ridiculous, Grey. Fine. Fucking fine. I'll be ready at the chopper. If you're going, I'm going too. Someone has to keep your psycho ass alive and watch Amorette if Vicente pulls any shit and distracts you." He stomped out of the gym.

"Hit me." I motioned for her to start.

"No." She shook her head and glanced down at the wooden dummy.

"Yes," I countered. "I'm better than any punching bag. You won't hurt me." I paused, then a smirk started to touch my mouth. "Just think about me holding you down and having the doctor inject a tracker next to your shoulder blade where you can't get it out." I lowered my voice as I leaned my head toward her.

She swung her arm, and I had to jerk back to avoid being clipped. "Good girl," I murmured through a grin. She didn't hear me, however. Every step I took back, she took one forward, jabbing, swiping, and stabbing.

"Tuck your thumb just like when you punch. Good. Longer arcs if you're trying to slash a neck." I kept giving instructions, but she was grunting with fury, her teeth bared. I had no idea if she was even hearing me, although she did make subtle changes to her form when I told her to.

Her motions started to lose steam.

"Just think, my wicked little love. I'll be able to track you anywhere. You'll never escape me," I whispered in her ear as I gripped her arms. The anger burned a little brighter, and she renewed her attack.

I loved this side of her. The savagery. The ferocity of my tiny love. I blocked each of her moves effortlessly, but I was expecting them. Someone else wouldn't have a fucking clue there was this much pent-up aggression inside her small body.

Then she clipped me in the temple with the handle. "Fuck," I grunted. "Remember, go for the eyes with the handle. The side is good too, if you're struggling for range. The neck is the best. It will kill them almost instantly."

We went round and round for twenty minutes. Both of us were sweaty messes by the time she dropped the wooden knife. My leftover injuries were aflame, but I thrived on that.

Every cell in my body was on fire, and my swollen cock ached from each brush of her body against mine.

"Fuck," she gasped and tossed the wooden knife to the

ground. She raised her arm to wipe her forehead, but I caught it and trapped her against my chest. "What are you doing?"

"Giving you what you asked for." I pushed her shorts and panties down, then lifted her onto the counter where the stereo was. "Perfect." I nudged her with my cock through my shorts. I loved when we found surfaces that were just the right height.

I dropped to my knees and shoved my nose against her clit, then licked a long swath from her ass up. Her musk was more pronounced after the workout, and I couldn't get enough of it. Hell, I might have to fight with her every time to get this smell in my nose. My dick twitched as I started to tongue fuck her, scooping up all her cream while rubbing soft circles with my thumb.

She moaned and dropped her head back against the wall. Her pussy started to clench around my tongue, and I stood up, shucking my shorts as I went, and thrust all the way to the hilt. I groaned, and she gasped, her face turning red from the sudden invasion.

God, I loved the way this girl looked when she was getting fucked.

I grabbed the hem of her shirt and pulled it over her head, locking her arms behind her back. Using it to grip her to me, I powered into her. Barely three strokes in, and she clamped around me.

"Fuck, yes," I grunted, pushing as hard as I could against her, only to pull back and do it all over again.

Her eyes closed, but as soon as my thrusts started to stagger, she opened them and drank in my expression.

Let her watch. Let her see what she did to me. If this was another way to tie her to me, I was happy for it.

My balls drew up tight and I used her arms behind her to force her chest against mine—her softness to my muscle.

"Fuck," I muttered, losing the speed as I emptied myself inside her. I squeezed her arms, then released them to grip her waist.

When I opened my eyes, hers were glassy pools, the ice blue nearly blotted out by her blown-out pupils. She pulsed gently around me, pulling a soft groan from my lips.

"I love watching you," she whispered, tracing her thumb over the corner of my mouth.

I wanted to grin, but I was still high off the release. Then clapping started behind me.

"We have to stop meeting like this." Parker laughed. I turned with a snarl to find him standing there with his shirt hanging over his shoulder and a fucking hard-on in his shorts.

"Fuck off," I barked, tightening my grip.

"Fuck in a bedroom," he returned. "Invite me there, too." His beaming smile turned devilish as he took in Amorette's delicate form. He walked closer, gaze drinking in every inch of pink, sweaty skin.

She started struggling against my hold, but I was too focused on glaring at Parker to notice.

"Stop fucking looking at me," she griped, trying to twist away from him. All she did was make her tits bounce. His smile turned into his shit-eating grin as he walked up to my side.

I stepped back and my cock slid out, making Amorette whimper, and Parker groaned.

"Fuck you and your cream pies. This is so fucking hot." He extended his hand as if he was going to catch some of my cum on her thighs, but I finally snapped out of it and released Amorette, at the same time punching him in the shoulder to get him to back up.

"Get the fuck away, you *pendejo*." I grabbed my shorts and pulled them up, sucking in a breath as the material slid over my glistening dick.

Amorette hopped off the counter and dressed with quick efficiency while keeping her back to Parker.

"Remember what I said, Little Love?" he taunted.

"What the fuck did you say?" I stepped between them, so he had to look at me instead.

"I told her you might not be as possessive of her as she thinks you are. That maybe the best thing for her is for us to share her."

Parker always knew how to push my fucking buttons. I swung, but he dodged me, laughing. He ambled over to the treadmills along the wall. "Get mad all you want, dear brother. But how would you have reacted if I had been Anton?"

I vibrated in rage. Just the thought of him seeing her like this lit my fuse.

"And consider this. What better way to make sure your precious *mamí* was protected than if she was truly *ours*." He smirked over his shoulder as he set the program and turned the treadmill on. "What better way than to ensure we're all out for the same goal?"

That bastard. I stepped forward with clenched fists, but Amorette was suddenly in front of me, hugging my waist.

"You'd have a better chance at this if I were Andre. He's the one that doesn't trust you." I linked my hand with hers, grabbed the knife, and left the gym. The sound of his feet pounding against the belt behind us.

As soon as we were back at my apartment, she rounded on me. "What the hell is going on? Do you *want* to share me?" Anger burned in her eyes, and fuck it, but my dick twitched.

"Fuck no," I yelled, tossing the box on the couch.

"Don't throw that!" She raced to pick it up, saving it from falling onto the floor. Like it would have broken. It wouldn't have. My weapons were of the highest quality; she just didn't know that. "Then why do you constantly let him watch us? Let him *see* me?" A frantic note colored her voice and her movements.

"Twice, *mamí*. Both times I didn't invite him." He was right too. It was my fault today for fucking her in the shared gym.

"But you didn't let me go to cover myself either! You gave him a front-seat fucking view! He almost touched me." She turned to the side and took a deep breath to control her breathing. Twisting back around, she still had a fire in her eyes, so fucking far away from the calm in her words. "Do you want to share me? Is that what you're trying to do?"

I kicked the chair next to me and watched it slide across the floor. "How many times do I have to tell you, no!"

"Then why did you let him look at me!" she screamed.

"I don't fucking know!"

Jesus Christo, I had no idea. I wouldn't admit this to her, but Parker was right. I would have reacted much differently with one of the men. As she stormed off, I yelled behind her, "We leave in two fucking hours. Be ready!"

She flipped me off right before slamming my own goddamn bedroom door, leaving me with my thoughts.

I imagined Lafe walking in. Or Andre. I didn't want to share her. I fucking didn't. But I also didn't have the same violent reaction as I would with Anton, or Jorge, or even Enrique.

"Fuck," I muttered, kicking the chair one more time.

Parker and his crazy schemes. We all knew he wanted to fuck her and was playing head games to get his way.

Was he spewing this same shit to Andre and Lafe? I dropped onto the couch and groaned. I'd end up fighting all my brothers before the week's end.

Fucking Parker.

20

AMORETTE

I didn't know if the silence between Grey and me, as we walked toward Andre's apartment, was concerning or gratifying. He hadn't even tried talking to me when he entered the bedroom to get ready.

He'd been broody, and every time I glanced at him, he had the same pinched expression and seemed a thousand miles away. I was the one who was angry as hell. He had held me in place as Parker got closer. Yet he was the one who ignored me and stomped around like he'd been wronged.

I desperately wanted to know what ran through their heads. Except right then, I didn't even believe Grey knew what he was thinking. Or he was just simply confused by it.

Did he want to share me, and this was some fucked up plan the brothers had cooked up for giggles? Or was he shocked that Parker pointed out his own reactions to him?

I doubted it. He seemed genuinely caught off guard at Parker's accusations. At the same time, his actions pointed to everything Parker wanted me to believe. The thought of them passing me around...

At Andre's door, Grey pounded with the side of his fist. He didn't make us wait long. When he opened the door, he looked every bit the billionaire CEO from his crisp all-black suit, gold cuffs, and wavy, inky hair brushed back away from his face.

Grey looked sharp in his suit too, but anyone with an eye could tell that Andre's cost triple what Grey's did. The only difference was that Andre seemed to care about the status his suit gave, and Grey seemed as if wearing one was a chore.

Grace could have told me the designer, collection, and year released on both.

But the rest of the population wouldn't be able to discern the quality based on how they carried themselves. They were both attractive, confident men who wore brutality like a second skin. The air constantly buzzed around them, making the hairs on my arms stand up.

Andre's gaze swept down my body, taking in my dark royal blue dress and short black heels. "You look stunning," he murmured, causing Grey to stiffen beside me. Andre shot him a questioning look, but he let it go when Grey didn't say anything.

"We're taking the plane," Andre said as he moved past us. "Twenty men are coming with us. Parker and Lafe have a list of every one and the leverage we have over them, if needed. I also have a few men on the ground willing to help if it comes to that. If we die, Grey, I will haunt you from the fucking grave." Andre spoke all this while strolling at a brisk pace toward the commons.

It was eerily empty, but I found out why when we stepped outside. Men were decked out in their simple black uniforms with some type of rifle gun strapped over their backs along with one in their hands. They patrolled the top of the wall, inside of the wall, and several were perched strategically around the roof.

"Are you expecting an attack?" I twisted my neck to peer up.

"After Vicente tried to take out Grey the last time he left the compound, I'm not taking any chances."

I glared at Grey, who ignored me. During our...whatever that was when we got back to the apartment, I'd completely forgotten to ask. Parker appearing out of thin air while I came again rattled me.

Partly because I was shocked and mainly because his words wouldn't leave me alone. Whether or not Grey admitted it, some part of him did want to share me. Otherwise, he would've flipped out at Parker watching us.

Unless... I peeked over at him. Had they shared before? I had never asked, although maybe that was the reason for his mild reaction. There was nothing about Grey that didn't scream jealous or possessive asshole in every situation, unless it involved his brothers.

In the plane, Grey and Andre took the cockpit. They hung up their suit jackets, then started running checks on everything. I stood in the entrance, glancing between them and the back area where their men were already seated.

"Get your ass in here," Andre said as he flipped buttons and hit others.

"There are two seats," I pointed out, even though deep down, I was relieved. As much as their men didn't scare me, I didn't want to spend a few hours with them by myself.

A flight attendant shut the door to the cockpit with a smile, leaving me standing behind their seats. Grey grabbed my hand and tugged me down in his lap. His hold was loose and comfortable, yet there was still something off about him.

"What was the attack from Vicente?" I asked, as I looped an arm around his shoulders.

His eyes widened a fraction, as if surprised. "I had to go clean up a mess with one of the fighters. It was a trap to draw me in. He tried to stab me, but I was better." He shrugged nonchalantly.

"What happens when they catch you off guard?" My temper started to rise. Grey and possibly Parker thought they were untouchable. Invincible. They weren't.

"He tried." Grey gave me a devil's grin.

"What about next time? Or the time after that? You've requested me to stay, to forget everything I've ever known. The cost for that is you take some care with your fucking life."

Andre grunted in agreement, and Grey glowered at him.

"What else has he done? Since I was taken," I demanded, looking to Andre because getting information from Grey was next to impossible. If it were easy, I would have had it by now.

"I'm surprised no one has told you." He glanced at me then back to the dashboard. "Not much. The attack on Grey was the most forward, but he targeted both Parker's and Lafe's people on jobs. I'm fairly certain he tried to set my people up. However, thanks to you, I terminated that mission." He raised a brow and gave me a brief smile.

I used the bottom joint of my thumb to rub my eye. "I don't get it." Vicente seemed to be playing hot and cold, but I had nothing to compare it to.

"Join the club," Andre muttered as he steered the plane toward the runway.

Even though I still had more questions, I held my tongue. There was so much I didn't know, and I wanted more information and background before I was able to make any assumptions. I at least knew Vicente was dangerous and we were all at risk by venturing out. I shivered.

This was like playing Russian Roulette. And these men lived this life every day. How were they not crazy or prematurely gray?

I smiled. That explained why Grey was the way he was. Parker fit the crazy bill. They were literally a product of this fucked up world because they grew up in it. Everything Vicente did to them or around them shaped them into the dysfunctional men they were today.

Back home, I never would have given them a second thought. Or a second look. But here, where I was trying so hard to let go of everything I thought I knew, they were growing on me even as I wanted to strangle them.

It wasn't long before we were up in the air. Andre was doing most of the piloting while we just took in the beautiful view of the oncoming sunset. Grey's vibe was still off. Glancing at him, I met his stare before my gaze drifted to the furrow between his brows. He was thinking hard, and I had a good idea about what.

A terrible, devious plan came to mind. My heart thumped erratically in my chest just thinking about it, although this was the perfect opportunity to know where Grey stood. Part of me felt it was cruel to force the issue, but the rules I'd lived with most of my life didn't apply here.

These men responded best to actions that skated the line between bold and crude. The more cutthroat, the happier they were.

Andre suddenly sat back, grabbing the headrest and relaxing. "Now's the easy part."

Moving my gaze from Andre to Grey, something must

have shown on my face because his arms tightened around my waist.

I peeled his hands back, and he reluctantly let me go. His gaze burned my skin as I stood up. Oh, Grey was not happy with me.

Andre didn't realize anything was happening until I slid into his lap. He jumped but kept his arms above his head.

"Grey, your lover is in my lap," Andre deadpanned.

I leaned forward, brushing my nose along his jaw, feeling at least a little vindicated when he stopped breathing. Then I pulled my head back and narrowed my eyes on Grey. His fingers gripped the armrest so hard they'd lost all their blood. He ground his jaw but didn't move a muscle otherwise.

"Is this what you want?" I asked.

"Is this what *you* want?" he returned.

I shook my head. "Since I've been with your family, it's never been about what I want." I glanced up at Andre's hooded eyes and gripped his jaw. Bringing his face down the tiniest amount, I bit his bottom lip before soothing it with my tongue.

His cock twitched under my ass, and as much as I hated it, color hit my face.

"Does this make you angry or horny?" I turned back to Grey.

Grey didn't answer, but his gaze swirled with both fury and desire. "Do you want to see my hands on him?" I stroked his chest, going down toward his stomach. His muscles flexed under my hand. What had been a growing erection was now a full-blown pipe underneath me.

I turned to straddle his lap, swallowing hard because what the fuck was I doing? My dress rode up, the material bunching against my waist as I spread my legs wider and pushed my clit against him.

Grinding against his cock, I groaned. Andre was a predator at this moment as he watched me with dark, slitted eyes. A deep rouge colored the top of his cheeks, giving his tanned skin a flushed, sexy appearance. He was completely in control. I didn't doubt for a minute that he would and could take over if he wanted to. But he was content to see what I would do. I'd shocked him too much. Leaning forward, I slid my hands up his biceps and down his forearms to cover his hands as I pressed my lips to his. They were pillowy soft, and not demanding, as I took what I wanted.

I rolled my hips again, this time earning a tortured sound from Andre. With more willpower than I thought I possessed, I laid my head on his shoulder where I could see Grey. Molded together, I could feel the pounding of his heart against mine.

"Is this what you want?" I whispered, dropping my hands to Andre's shoulder. "You want to see me ride your brother?" I rocked, using Andre's cock to hit my most sensitive spot. The heat built so much faster than expected.

Andre started slowly thrusting from below, dropping his hands to cup my ass to help me along.

"Do you like this?" I whispered, but it came out strangled. I was so close. So fucking close.

Grey's green eyes were a livid storm as he watched us together. But he never stopped me. Never got up. This was as much an experiment for him as it was for me. At least with Andre, I knew there were no feelings there. Lafe was tender, so I risked hurting him.

And no fucking way would I try this with Parker. Over my dead body he'd touch me like this.

Then I imagined him here with Grey, watching like he loved to do.

I broke apart. It was sudden, blinding, and empty. Stars danced behind my lids as I clawed at Andre's shoulders and squeezed my eyes shut. Andre was still rocking me against him when I pushed back from his chest and climbed off.

Without a look at him or Grey, I stomped for the door. I needed to get out of here. Cold water and fresh air were the only things that could get my head back on straight.

What the fuck had I just done?

Andre hadn't come, and I couldn't finish him off. I'd already pushed my limits by forcing Grey to watch that. It was a bitch move, but if I didn't get out of there right then, I'd break apart in a very different, less pleasant way. And I didn't want either brother to see that.

"I hope you have your answer." I tried to growl at Grey, to show my anger, but the words tumbled out breathlessly. Fuck.

Andre muttered something like 'cocktease' under his breath, but I didn't stick around to find out.

21

AMORETTE

I ended up taking the extra seat with the flight attendant for the rest of the ride. She was discreet and minded her own business enough that I wanted to hug her.

When I went into the bathroom, which thankfully was larger than standard commercial airplane bathrooms, I was a hot mess. My hair was slightly ruffled, and I didn't even know how that happened. My cheeks were on fire and my eyes were glassy and bright. The light blue dominated the gray so much they practically glowed.

Anyone who saw me–like the flight attendant–would know I'd been fucked.

I dropped my head in my hands and groaned. She probably thought they doubled-teamed me in the cockpit. And what actually happened wasn't much better. We were descending already. Another ten minutes and they'd be opening the door, and I'd have to face my bad decisions.

Parker always made terrible decisions and laughed like it was the highlight of his year. Except, I was sure he didn't actually view his decisions as bad.

I wasn't like him.

We stopped all too soon, and the flight attendant went to the back to take care of the men, leaving me sitting in the fold-out chair facing the cockpit door.

Here they came, and I felt like I was about to burst out of my skin in the long seconds it took for the door to open and one of the brothers to appear. Grey was first, and he didn't even look at me. He unlocked the main door while talking to someone on the radio. Probably to make sure they were hooked up to a tunnel or something.

Nope, he got the door opened as the stairs had been rolled up to the door.

Andre slid his jacket on as he appeared, and it seemed like he couldn't take his gaze off me. I dropped mine first and swiftly unbuckled. Then I glanced at his crotch against my will, like my brain needed to know if he was still hard.

He wasn't. Of course, he wasn't.

I stepped up behind Grey and waited for him to move down the stairs. The hairs on the back of my neck stood up, and I could swear Andre's breath rustled the hair on the top of my head.

It was dark outside, with the exception of a few lights in the distance. A group of men also greeted us with a handful of golf carts behind them. Wherever we were, we were farther away from the hotel than the last time we were here.

A noise caught my attention, and when I looked to my left, men were filing out of the plane on a second set of steps. They immediately fanned out to surround the men and us. No one skipped a beat, as if this was standard.

Where were all these men going to go? Golf carts carried six people max.

Then the sounds of a bus met my ears before it pulled around the side. That explained it.

Grey spoke to the men as Andre stepped up behind me. I almost jumped when he placed a hand on my hip. It would be weird normally for him to touch me. Although now, after what I'd done, his touch electrified the small amount of skin.

I could swear his thumb moved gently back and forth, but it was so slight I couldn't be sure. It had to be my imagination. I'd never done something so reckless or without thought. I'd never had to face the consequences of my own actions, and I guess, in some ways, I still wasn't.

But with Grey's avid avoidance and Andre's strange yet calm behavior, I could feel it building like an electrical storm about to lay waste between us.

No one else seemed to notice, which made me even more twitchy.

"Couldn't keep your hands to yourself, could you?" Grey growled under his breath as he swept past us toward the cart.

With a gentle nudge from Andre, I followed behind him and climbed into the middle. Andre slid in after me, putting me right in the middle.

"I told you I was coming here to watch her. What did you do as soon as we got off the fucking plane? Turned your back to talk to your men," Andre said in disgust.

Grey's hands tightened on the steering wheel, but he said nothing. The tension between them crackled and I tried to pull into myself. I'd been the cause of it. Maybe not for everything. This family had so much bad history; I'd be naive and self-centered to think I was the sole cause. But for most of it—tonight? This was on me.

Shit.

I'd let my intrusive thoughts win and what did I get? A

heaping pile of guilt and anxiety as I waited for their reactions to come to a head.

Turning my mind away from my own issues, I cataloged the area. Our cart was leading the way on a narrow path. The hotel was maybe a hundred yards away, and while there weren't any buildings directly around the path, they weren't far off. How convenient to have a landing strip so close.

The closer we got, the more men appeared to be patrolling the streets. They weren't even trying to be subtle about it. The other people, who were probably out for dates or on vacation, didn't seem to pay them any attention. Was this really how life was here?

If this happened anywhere in the US, people would freak out and act like the mafia had taken over. I almost laughed. The mafia had taken over here.

Grey pulled up to the curb at the hotel. This was still a guest entrance but probably less flashy than the front. Although, I was making a lot of assumptions based on my life in the US. I'd never been to Venezuela before them, so who knew if I was right or entirely off the mark.

"Come on," Grey said softly as he held out his hand. His gaze finally landed on me, but it was distant rather than the relief I thought I'd feel. Like he was going through the motions because he thought he needed to. That almost made me laugh too.

Grey didn't do anything because he needed to. So why did it feel like that? Maybe because he wasn't backing into my space and declaring his possession like he'd done every other time. Before he'd touched me the first time, there had been a sizzling possessiveness between us that was missing now.

I didn't like it, and I was the cause.

What if I'd been wrong? What if he didn't want to share

me, and he just wasn't well-adjusted enough to stop Parker from getting close? I briefly closed my eyes as we waited for Andre to join us.

If Grey did see this as something else, and I killed it because I misunderstood him...

"Why are you laughing like that?" Grey whispered in my ear as he slid an arm around my waist. Relief swarmed me as I sank back into his touch. He was training me. That was the only explanation I could find for why it would hurt so much when he stopped but felt like heaven when he gave it back.

"Like what?" I opened my eyes to see Andre standing right in front of me. Close. So, so close.

Grey pressed closer into my back as he whispered, "Like your world is falling apart, and you can't do anything about it but laugh. It's very sad, *mamí.*"

I tipped my head back and Andre blotted out everything in the night sky.

"Isn't it?"

"*Señor* Morozov!" a man called from the hotel, then followed it up with Spanish. Both Andre and Grey stiffened and slowly turned their heads toward the door.

"No," Andre spoke, shaking his head. "We're going back." He took my arm, but Grey stopped him by shoving his shoulder.

"Over my dead fucking body. You run back to the compound like the scared little boy you are. Take Amorette with you if you want, but I'm not going anywhere. This hotel is *mine.*" Grey's chest pressed into my shoulders and the back of my head as he leaned over me.

"Grey, be serious. You can't believe this is a good idea. This is what he wants, and you're going to play right into his hands!" Andre tried and failed to keep his voice down.

"Who?" I asked, even though I didn't need to. I knew. Just with their reaction, I knew Vicente was here.

Andre grabbed his hair as his suit jacket flared out. He whirled around and grunted, almost like wishing he could yell, but didn't want to draw any more attention to us.

When he turned around, his eyes were wild with emotion as he bared his teeth at Grey. "No. If you're staying here, I'm staying here. I don't know if it's a good thing or a bad thing that you don't have a whipping post in the hotel." He caught my hand, gentler than I would have imagined he could be in the moment, and started toward the door.

Grey rushed to catch up and took my other hand. It was awkward when we reached the door, but Andre took the lead and pulled me behind him.

"Are you really doing this?" Grey nodded to where Andre still clasped me. Andre merely rolled his eyes like he didn't have time for Grey's antics.

"The best way to make sure she isn't stolen again is to hold onto her. Did you put a tracker on her before we left?" Andre raised a brow, but he knew the answer. Grey growled then we all faced forward.

This hall was almost identical to the one we came in before. Except this elevator ride was maybe two floors down instead of many. Several of his men piled in the elevator while the rest ran past us and pushed on the doors to the stairs.

Andre, Grey, and I were shuffled to the back of the elevator. The air was almost stifling. Did all these men know about the war Vicente had called against them? They had to, right? For their sake and the brothers'.

As soon as the doors opened, the all-consuming music roared into the elevator. The two men in front went to the sides of the elevator, and the other three stayed in front of us with their weapons drawn as we exited.

Tonight, the place was packed and the crowd seemed rowdier than the last time. I wouldn't have thought that was possible, but the talking and screaming almost competed with the music. The roving neon lights lit on us a few times, and unlike on the street, the crowd here seemed to be attuned to our every move.

Their gazes tracked us as we moved deeper into the club. We stayed on the outskirts close to the bars, never going toward the ring already set up in the middle.

Then we passed the section where Grey had sat me last time. It wasn't roped off. I glanced up at Grey, even as his gaze was trained ahead and his jaw was clenched tight. When I looked at Andre, his head was straight, yet his gaze constantly scanned over the room. Both men had death grips on my hands and with each step, they seemed to box me in tighter.

We headed right for the corner, where a platform stood behind a glass wall. This hadn't been here the last time. I twisted to take in the glass from where I'd stood before, and I would have noticed this if it had been here.

As we approached, the guard blocking the entrance moved to the side and unlatched the rope.

Inside the small box, there were six chairs. Directly behind the last two chairs was a door almost hidden in the corner. Anyone not inside would undoubtedly presume it was part of the wall.

Two men joined us inside, as the other three placed themselves at the entrance and in front of us on the floor. It was strange. When we'd traveled in the past, men had come with us, but it wasn't so militant as this. Everyone seemed on edge, like they were all waiting for Vicente to blow up the building or shoot us down.

Grey took one seat closest to the glass and tugged me down in his lap. It was rough, nothing like how he was with me at their compound.

"What the hell is this?" Andre sat down in the seat next to us. "Do you enjoy being a sitting duck?"

Grey dropped one hand on my knee and placed the other on my lower back. "This is bulletproof glass. There's an exit behind us. This is my way to keep Amorette from the masses while ensuring they have a front-row seat to see that she's mine."

I expected Andre to respond back with some sarcastic quip, but he didn't. Instead, we watched the floor. The fights started, and the sound came through to us on a speaker in the corner. The first two seemed like amateur fights. The crowd loved it, but they were also only half paying attention. People weren't pressed to the ring or even navigating toward it.

Grey's phone would go off periodically, and he'd bark orders to whoever was on the other line. At least, that was what it seemed like. Everything he said had been too fast for me to understand.

"If Vicente is here, where is he?" I asked, glancing between Grey and Andre.

"Don't know, don't give a shit." Grey pressed his nose into the side of my head as he moved his hand a little higher on the inside of my thigh. I almost stopped him. Only there was no sexual intent in his touch. This was for show.

"You better, because he's heading this way right now," Andre said lightly. When I turned to him, he hadn't moved a muscle, yet everything about him seemed strung tight.

I followed his gaze. There was Vicente, with another

man, walking right toward us. He had his own small entourage, though nothing like the men we had surrounding us. I'd seen Vicente before from afar. Never up close, not when I was completely sound of mind. When I was taken, his face swam in and out of my head through curtains of darkness while he carried me. I couldn't have recognized him on the street. Except...

My breath stuttered in my chest as I got a good look at him. Andre and Matías were almost carbon copies of him. He could never deny them.

Grey pulled me closer against his chest as he sat up straighter, yet he didn't stand up. Our men outside the box closed in, blocking his entrance. Vicente flicked his hand, but none of the men moved.

He gave an order in Spanish, and the men responded in kind, but still, they barred his way.

When he looked up, he met my stare with cold eyes. Chills erupted down my arms. I'd thought Parker's were cold, but they were nothing like this man. He was a true psychopath.

"Andre, Grey. Tell your guards to stand down, or they'll not live to take another breath." He pulled a gun out of his suit jacket. The people closest to him shoved others in the crowd to get away.

I started forward, but Grey locked his arm around my waist.

"Let him in," Andre called to the men as he slouched down a little more and kept his arms crossed. They moved, and he and his companion strolled up the steps, ignoring how the club quieted.

The angry rock club beats still vibrated the glass, but the people were all turning toward our platform to watch the show.

"I didn't expect you boys to actually come tonight," Vicente said as he motioned for his friend to grab a chair. He did, and set it right in the space between us and the glass. There wasn't much, and it was cramped, but Vicente made it work.

The man with him was unassuming, with brown hair and a mousy expression on his face. He wasn't even particularly big. There was just something about him...

"Care to tell us why you're targeting us? You all but declared war on us in a very public way," Andre said as he reached for his glass. The ice clinked together as he lifted it to his lips and took a sip. It wasn't alcoholic, but Vicente wouldn't know that.

Out of the corner of my eyes, I could see the delight seeping out of Vicente. I kept my attention on the other man. I could have sworn I'd seen him before.

"All but?" He laughed good-naturedly. "Just by taking your slut, I've let everyone know you're worth less alive than dead. That you're still here at all is actually quite amazing." Then he made a sound of revulsion. "Pathetic is more like it."

"Why?" Andre pushed, leaning forward to brace his elbows on his knees. "We've always done everything you asked." He was as good as emotionless as he pressed Vicente for an answer. I wasn't sure it mattered. Vicente was obviously crazy and narcissistic. The kind of person he was, he made decisions because they pleased him, not because any logic was involved.

The way Andre was so nonchalant pulled my gaze back to him. His face was passive even though this had to be eating at him. A lock of dark hair fell in his face and he brushed it aside.

I glanced up at Grey to find him glaring at Vicente. He, at least, had a lot of pent-up anger.

"Like you really expect me to believe that. You four have always had your rebellions. Even the small ones. But it suited me to let you live and let everything play out as it would." He rose to his feet and motioned to his friend.

I'd seen him before...

He met my gaze and winked.

I gasped as they started toward the door.

"Why are you here tonight?" Andre asked, not bothering to contradict him.

That man, he was at the back of the courtroom when I left that day...

"Curiosity, really." Vicente walked to the door. "Don't think this visit places you on my good side. There's no going back now."

I shifted on Grey's lap and something dropped to the floor. The man with Vicente stepped forward and picked it up. As he handed it to me, his lips curved up into a slight grin.

Drunk snaps of memory flashed in my head. Being carried, being lifted from a car. A face above mine—a face exactly like the one standing over me now.

"A pleasure to see you again," he whispered as he tipped an imaginary hat. Then he followed Vicente down the steps of the box.

The rest of the club came alive like life as they knew it wasn't about to end.

"That man..." I said, following them through the club. People parted for Vicente just like with Grey. Maybe even more so.

"What about him?" Andre asked as he tossed back the remaining contents of his drink.

"He was the man who took me." In a flash, I was deposited in Andre's lap and Grey was gone.

"Fuck," Andre cursed as he bundled me against his chest and stood up. He dropped me to my feet and caught my arm. Then we were rushing out of the box too. "Tony's barely more than a gnat, but Vicente takes a slight to everything he didn't explicitly approve of."

We rushed through the crowd, which wasn't hard. They were still separated from where Grey ran through. At the other side of the club, right in a hallway, Grey had the man smashed up against the wall. Vicente was nowhere to be found. I breathed a sigh of relief.

The last thing we needed was an all-out fight with Vicente in the club.

Grey whispered against the man's ear, but he didn't say anything. How could he when Grey had his forearm pressed against his neck. When the man sputtered without any coherent words, Grey cracked his fist into his face.

Again and again.

Each time his flesh met the man's, I jolted.

This was just like the last time. Grey was going to kill him. There was no doubt in my mind that this man had minutes left of his life, if that. The only difference was that this time, Andre wrapped his arms around me.

Whether to comfort me or hold me back, I wasn't sure. No matter what the case, I was glad for it. I gripped his hands over my stomach as Grey laid waste to the man who ruined my life.

There was another difference.

Every spray of blood, every grunt of pain, I reveled in it. I was glad Grey was the bloodthirsty man he was. At least today.

Because of this man, I lost the life I'd built for myself. I lost my sister.

Nothing else mattered at this moment as much as knowing the man who took it all away couldn't destroy anyone else.

When the man took his last breath, Grey wiped his bloodied hands on the inside of his suit jacket. Then, chest heaving from exertion, he came right to me with his arms open. Andre let me go, and I stepped into his warm, bloody embrace.

22

LAFE

I spun back and forth in my living room chair as I clicked through the channels. I'd already gone through them a hundred times, but I went through them again. I wasn't in the mood to watch anything; I just needed something to do.

My place felt empty, and the sounds from the teasers did little to fill it up. Amorette had filled this place up with her energy, and at the time, I had thought it was ominous. Whenever I closed my eyes, I expected her to sneak up on me, slash my throat from behind, or even–hell, I had no idea. I was half delirious from the drugs. It had just been necessary.

It was pathetic how much she had scared me.

Now she was staying with Grey, and her absence left a hole. I wasn't sure how to fill it. If I could fill it. Being sober put an entirely different spin on the experience I hadn't been able to understand before.

"Thank you for saving me."

If she'd said that in the beginning in the birdcage, everything could have been different.

Who was I kidding? I would have still thought she was our downfall. Whether she meant to be, or not. It practically took her risking her life and her freedom to chill my ass out where she was concerned.

And what did I do? I fell asleep with her on the couch. I wanted it. Practically salivated for it.

Even though I'd kept off the powder, I wasn't sleeping well. Every night was a restless fight. I woke up reaching for her. *Wanting* her. And where was she? In my brother's fucking bed.

Fuck, if Parker wasn't right. It was my fault Grey had caught her.

"How much does it kill you to know Grey fucked her before you?"

I threw the remote against the wall. The plastic cracking into two pieces was slightly vindicating. I watched TV in the movie room when I wanted to relax, so what the fuck did this remote matter?

It did kill me that she was with Grey. I just didn't know it at the time.

My phone buzzed, and I leaned over to see Andre's name. I clicked the screen to find his message in the group chat.

Andre: We landed. Grey had another fit. V also showed up. Watch your backs.

Grey killed someone else, he meant. And where did he want us to watch our backs? Parker and I were both here, waiting for them to return.

Without hesitation, I shot up and raced toward our airfield. Like a bad withdrawal, I needed to see that Killer was all right with my own eyes. She struggled with the harsher side of our life, and neither Andre nor Grey would understand how that felt.

I understood her the best out of my brothers.

Parker met me in the hall. "Headed out to greet them, too?" He grinned.

Grunting, I walked faster. I wouldn't let him bait me, which was exactly what his cruel ass wanted.

The compound was fairly empty inside. Most of our men had been put on rotation around the property, and the ones not on duty were getting sleep for their shift. Outside, a few of the men nodded, and most went about their work.

In the distance, the plane was already being deboarded. The men were whooping and chatting animatedly. That was a good sign. Our men didn't get excited for no reason.

"I imagine the trip went well," Parker said drily as we approached. He tried to play off his interest, but his eyes were too alight at the commotion.

I was too concerned with the door opening at the front of the plane to answer him. The fumes and heat were barely noticeable as the door pushed open and Grey appeared. His suit jacket was draped over his shoulder, and he held Amorette's hand as she trailed behind him.

Faint blood smears stained her dress, probably a transfer from Grey. It was hard to tell though, because my brothers had always learned to wear dark colors when leaving the compound. There was always a chance of blood, and though we didn't have to hide who we were in most places, we didn't want to flaunt our crimes either.

She seemed okay. Happy even.

That wasn't right. The last time she'd seen Grey pummel someone to death, it had torn her up for days. She'd locked herself in the birdcage. We'd had a brief but deep conversation about it in the movie room.

Killer sure hadn't worn a serene smile on her face then as she toddled behind the best killer out of the four of us.

"You're staring very hard there, *hermano*. You might want to blink," Parker whispered in my ear.

I shot him a glare and started walking toward them again. At some point, I'd stopped, and Parker had to by default. Grey flicked his gaze to me and met me halfway. He used his hold on her to bring her closer to his body, until he wound his arm around her back and clutched her to his side.

She allowed it.

I saw nothing had changed since I'd seen her last.

"Let's go to my place." Andre stopped next to Grey, letting his fingers trail over Amorette's shoulders.

Furrowing my brow, I gauged all their reactions. Grey either didn't notice or didn't care. I thought Amorette may have tensed, but if she did, her poker face was legit. No discomfort marred the sweet expression she was toting.

They started ambling as a cohesive unit, Andre even putting his hand on the small of Amorette's back. I wished this was Andre taunting Grey, riling him up because he was so possessive. But...They didn't even seem to notice each other.

As they left us standing in the middle of the men unloading the plane, I felt more like an outsider than ever. When did this happen?

How had this happened?

"That's an interesting turn of events, don't you think?" Parker clapped me on the back, but when I looked at him, he lost his typical shit-stirrer smile.

He was just as confused and disappointed by this new change as I was.

We followed behind them like kicked puppies until we reached Andre's apartment. Inside, Grey and Amorette had already taken possession of the couch, and Andre was pouring everyone a drink. Amorette took a glass and sipped. Both Parker and I declined when Andre tipped the bottle our way in question.

"No one important died if you're all this jolly on the return." Parker perched on the arm of one chair, and I sat in the other.

That left the third spot on the couch or leaning against the wall. It wasn't by design, except now that we were spread out like this, we needed to see where Andre went. Where did he feel he had a right to go?

Andre had never been a fan of Killer's. He'd also never hidden it from her. What the hell could have happened for him to be so tactile with her?

My heart thumped harder in my chest as he took his glass and settled next to Amorette. He didn't touch her, didn't close the space between them. I let out a slow breath. There was a chance I'd imagined their exchange outside. I could be seeing more than was really there. I'd done it with Amorette previously. I could be doing it with the three of them now.

I wanted her so fucking much my teeth ached, and it wouldn't surprise me if my brain was trying to self-sabotage me.

She released a stunned laugh as she leaned forward to place her mostly full glass on the coffee table. "The opposite, actually. The man who took me from the parking garage was there tonight. Grey killed him." Amorette looked up at Grey with a dreamy smile tipping her lips, and I almost scoffed.

Why was she rewarding Grey for his usual deadly behavior? Grey would kill almost anyone for fun.

"How do you know he was the one who took you? I thought you didn't remember anything about your abduction?" Parker asked pensively, rubbing his hand over his jaw.

"I didn't. At least, not until I saw him. The man who came with Vicente must have been following me. I'd seen him both inside the courtroom and when I'd left that last night. When he stood over me, I remembered seeing flashes of his face as I was carried somewhere. I would say it was a coincidence, but him being there with Vicente was too obvious."

"What if you're wrong? What if that man wasn't the one who took you?" I asked. I didn't want to make her second guess herself, but this was a complete one-eighty from her previous hang-ups.

Grey glared at me, but I kept mine locked on Amorette.

She shook her head like she wouldn't even consider that. "I know my mind. I've seen him before, drugged or not. And if he's with Vicente, then he's no good. I don't feel bad for his death." Tipping her head slightly, she locked her jaw and met my stare head-on.

One side of Andre's mouth tipped up into a self-deprecating smile. "Amorette, you do realize that we're all with Vicente, even if we're currently not in his favor?"

Shaking her head more firmly this time, she turned to Andre, her knees brushing against his thigh. Grey kept his arm looped around her waist but loosened his hold to allow her movement.

"That's not the same. From the beginning, I could tell none of you reveled in the lives you've been given. My hang-up was more that I..." her breath caught, "I was stuck in what right and wrong meant when I lived in a world that allowed me to be whoever I wanted to be. I know you four didn't have a choice. I know you aren't any happier about growing up under a psychopath like Vicente. But you've made the best of it. That man could have taken ten more girls since he took me. A hundred. Who knows? If death is part of this life, I won't feel guilty for the deaths that save the innocents. And I won't think poorly of any of you for delivering it."

A weight I hadn't been aware of slowly slipped off my shoulders, and a relief spread warmth through my limbs to my fingers and toes. Killer wasn't addressing me. She might not be talking about me specifically; she sure as hell had never seen me kill. Yet to know she was starting to understand we weren't inherently evil just because of the family we were born into, put something back together inside me.

"Very touching," Parker said with a smirk. When he started to continue, Andre got a call.

He glanced at the phone then picked it up. After a few curt words, he hung up and glanced at us. "Matías is here."

He rarely came here. Only when he absolutely had to.

We'd grown up at the mansion together, but with the amount of time we'd spent together, we may as well had been on different continents. He was in a special family wing with his mother, while we were in another less flashy part.

When we did interact, he always regarded us as lesser. Staring at us with cold eyes that were exact replicas of Vicente's. It didn't help that Valentina and Matías were always Vicente's pride and joy. They were doted on and spoiled very publicly while we were ignored. We weren't orphans, not for most of our childhoods, but we might as well have been.

Any time our mothers tried to show us any type of love, Vicente would punish them. He said it would make us weak. That it was a danger to us to believe in anything even close to love.

The only one who got away with it at all was Pilar. But she was his favored concubine. She was also sneakier than most. She showed us as much motherly affection as she could, but at the same time, it was apparent Andre was the only one who meant anything to her.

"Tell him to fuck off. He's appearing way too much lately," Grey said as he dropped his head back against the couch.

"Let him through." Parker grinned. "Let's see what he has to say. After he made an appearance at the dinner party, I think he's up to something. We'll never figure out what it is if we don't let him in."

Andre studied Parker, then nodded. I almost fell over. Andre never took Parker's advice. Where Parker was risky and reckless, Andre was thoughtful and cautious.

He sent a quick text, then dropped his phone in his lap. "They're searching him. He has two guards, and they'll stay with his chopper."

Then we waited. Our men were efficient; even with an escort, he made it to Andre's door in record time. When he knocked, I got up to answer it. I hadn't seen Matías since we took Amorette back. I wouldn't share with my brothers, but I wanted to know why he was here too. I couldn't help but think it had something to do with a small, dark-haired vigilante killer.

"Matías." I bared my teeth at him, affecting the persona I wore so well outside the compound. Here, I let my guard down. I relaxed. Out there, among the snakes and con artists, I was a threat to be taken seriously. And sometimes an instigator.

"Lafe," he dipped his head, the corners of his lips turning down.

He didn't say anything else, and after a few seconds, I

stepped back so he could come inside. Matías closed the door, twisting the lock. We walked side by side back into the living room. I didn't feel comfortable with him at my back, and already I was itching for the canister I'd dropped in my kitchen drawer. I also wanted to see his face when he saw our brothers and Amorette.

I doubted I'd be able to discern any tells. He was a master at masking his emotions—if he felt them at all. But I wanted the chance regardless.

With barely any subtlety, I turned my head toward him as we entered. I knew what he'd see. His brothers, all having a nightcap with the girl we'd taken under our wing. It was cozy. Familiar.

And he was very much on the outside. Not that he'd ever cared.

His gaze swept over the room, and when he landed on Amorette, his mouth softened just a hair. Fuck...

Matías dipped his head in greeting and stared directly at Andre.

Andre had always set himself up as the leader of us, and sometimes it rankled that others viewed him as such. Especially when he'd made decisions in the past that he had no right to make.

My thoughts threatened to spiral, but I forced them down.

The here and now were important. Whatever Matías was up to was important.

The past could fuck the hell off.

"Vicente just found out about Tony," he said in almost a monotone voice as his gaze briefly touched on Grey.

Tony... He was Maikel's man, although he occasionally dabbled for Vicente and my legitimate siblings. No wonder Grey didn't question it when Amorette said he'd taken her.

It made so much sense. But there were still missing pieces. If Amorette had seen Tony outside the courtroom, he'd have known who she was. He'd have known she was an up-and-coming attorney. She wasn't anywhere close to the typical steals Maikel usually made.

Grey smirked, not giving one fuck about Tony. "And?"

Matías didn't seem too fucked up over it, either. "He could have let the slight go if you'd taken care of him privately, but you beat him to death in your club, on the main floor." The disapproval dripping from Matías' words had no effect on my brothers or me.

Amorette didn't even seem to mind, but I was still concerned. She could say she was happy all she wanted, but death wasn't a part of her life. This would hit her at some point.

"I think you're overstepping, Matías." Andre stood up, setting his glass on the table. They faced each other in a ridiculous posturing contest.

"I'm not the enemy," Matías fired off.

"You're not family either," Andre returned.

Amorette watched with a confused expression as she moved back and forth between Andre and Matías. I wished I would have asked her about her time with him now. I hadn't wanted to know before, but with them in the room together, she wasn't projecting the hate for him the way she had for us in the beginning.

Why?

"I'm trying to help you, damn it," Matías snapped. "I have information you need. Or are you going to kick me out to spite yourself?"

"I don't hear you spouting off useful intel, Matías," Parker said slowly as he raised a foot and braced it on the coffee table. He rested his forearm on his knee as he regarded Matías like a bug under a microscope. "All I hear is accusations on how stupid Grey was."

Grey growled.

"I'm trying," Matías gritted out and stepped closer to the group. I stepped with him. His face contorted into disbelief as he watched me.

He was a threat here. There was no way around it. We let him in to see what he would do. That was all. He had to know that.

"Fine. Vicente is livid. He can't let it go that you killed the man he brought to the fights. He's going to come at you all hard and fast. I'm warning you so you can get ahead of it."

"You aren't telling us anything we didn't know." Andre cracked his neck on one side then the other. "In fact, you've always been so far up Vicente's ass. You could be here on his orders. As a decoy."

"Like hell! I've tried to survive the same as you four." His tight composure started to crack as his voice rose and his accent thickened. Then he looked at Amorette. We all tensed, preparing to move if he threatened her. "Tell them, Amorette. I'm not the villain here."

She glanced at Matías, then at each of us. The wheels were turning so fast in her head, I was surprised her eyes weren't shaking. When she brought her attention solely back to Matías, she shook her head slightly. "What I say doesn't matter here. There's a history between you all that's none of my business."

Matías stiffened then straightened to his full height, which was an inch taller than me. "I helped you get back to them, did I not? I kept you safe, and I didn't touch you. I fed you and gave you free run of the house."

Amorette's top lip curled. "I also asked to call them every

day. Any of them. And you refused. You taking care of me was never about *me*." She met each of our stares. "I'm starting to think it was about them."

"Hardly," Matías shot back, even as his lips pressed into a thin white line.

"I think we're done here," Parker said too happily as he stood up and clapped his hands together. "If you have any actual information that would be helpful, give us a ring. Otherwise, you can sit on your thumb and spin. I take it you know the way back to your chopper?"

So much blood rushed to Matías' face that I expected it to explode. He eventually nodded and stiffly dipped his head. "Fine. I'll see myself out."

He left without any issues, even closing the door softly.

"Shouldn't someone walk him to his helicopter?" Amorette asked.

"The guard that brought him here is still in the hall," Andre answered her as he poured a little more liquor into his glass. He was the only one drinking at this point. I wasn't sure why he even bothered. He wasn't much of a drinker, anyway.

Our conversation dwindled, and it wasn't long until we all parted to head to our own apartments. Amorette going with Grey.

"You're still staring," Parker whispered as he passed me. I shoved his shoulder and he cackled while righting himself.

"Fuck off," I warned, then opened my own door.

It would be another restless night, and once again, my thoughts were consumed with Amorette.

She took our side. I hadn't expected her to take Matías', but I also hadn't expected her to so clearly draw a line in the sand either.

Had she really asked to talk to me when she was with

him? I needed to know, and I didn't think I'd sleep until then.

I laid down anyway. Tomorrow, I'd corner her. I'd find out all the answers I hadn't wanted to know before.

Tomorrow.

23

PARKER

Each of the paintings were timeless, effortless beauties. They weren't even signed. They were created in the early 1900s by a now-famous artist who enjoyed the secret side of the art world.

I smiled as I spread them out over the spare bedroom. The Olsen twins had a similar thought with their fashion. Only someone who knew what to look for would recognize these paintings for the masterpieces they were.

It was a way for the disgustingly rich to tell each other apart from the less wealthy masses without flaunting their wealth in the face of society.

Would Little Love recognize these? I bet her sister would. Wouldn't that be fun to deck out our feisty little captive with the best art, the finest jewelry, and the most unassuming but high fashion? When we were in a place where they could have a happy family reunion, Grace would be so envious of her sister, who wouldn't even understand the worth surrounding her.

I loved that. Little Love found importance in other

things. But I secretly found a thrill in setting up such a scenario.

Setting aside two of my favorite paintings, I'd slip them on her walls later when we decided where she was going to settle. Grey's place wouldn't work out long-term. Not with Lafe trailing after her like a lost puppy. Andre was beginning to change his tune as well.

A ferocious pounding attacked my front door.

"My, my. Who could that be?" It could be one of two brothers. Andre or Grey. I couldn't wait.

Closing and locking my guest room, I damn near skipped to the front door. Something had happened yesterday between Amorette, Grey, and Andre, and I was dying to know what it was. Those fuckers hadn't been in a place where I could have needled the truth out of them last night.

I wouldn't while Lafe was there. I wanted the truth. The whole truth, and Lafe was too emotional to let them finish whatever sordid tale they had.

Andre stood on the other side of the door with a grim expression.

"Why, hello. What brings you to my neck of the woods?" I grinned and stepped back so he could come in. He headed straight for the kitchen while I shut the door and locked us in.

"I put on a front for Matías, but Vicente is planning something. There are too many rumblings in the Institution. My own network in the mansion is practically pissing their pants from the tension in the air."

"That's...not unexpected." I sighed. This was important, to be sure. Nevertheless, I wanted the dirt. Why was Andre suddenly so touchy with our little love, and why did Grey allow it? If I had tried half as much, he would have gutted me. Or at least tried to make me think he would have.

Grey must have thought over my words.

"Stop smirking. Fuck, this isn't fun and games anymore, Park," Andre snarled.

"Sorry. Rogue thoughts." I smothered the smirk and leaned against the island facing him. "Before we talk strategy, and don't worry, I have ideas—"

"You always have ideas," Andre deadpanned as he grabbed the counter behind him and leaned his ass against it.

Oh, I saw how it was. No one was allowed to touch your shiny surfaces but you could put your greasy paws all over mine.

I almost snorted. I didn't give a fuck about smudges. Andre didn't either if he really dug into it. He was just a control freak.

"Of course I do." I rolled my eyes. "Shoving it up people's asses—metaphorically—is how I passed through the years without killing myself...or you. Back to what I was saying. We can discuss this to your heart's content after you answer a few of my questions."

He raised his brows, giving me a get the fuck on with it look.

My traitorous lips twitched before I could even get the first question out. "What happened with Amorette yesterday?"

He didn't react at all. The bastard was expecting me to question him about it.

"What makes you think something happened?"

"Oh, come on!" I slapped a hand against the granite counter. "I was with Grey and Amorette yesterday. They fucked in the gym before they got ready for his fights."

Andre's eyes widened. "You didn't know that, did you? You were in the gym before I was." Absolutely no way he would not recognize the good fucking stamped over Amorette if he'd been there.

Although I one hundred percent believed he would have fled as soon as they started.

"So you're a voyeur now?"

I grinned. "Don't change the subject. I'll play ball with this one, in any case. Yes, when it comes to Little Love, I admit, I'm quite the voyeur. The few times I've seen her come have only mildly quenched my thirst for her."

Another shock whipped across his face before he flattened his expression.

"Is that why you've only selected women eerily similar to Amorette when we've gone out?"

"Fuck off," I growled. Did they all think they had something to hold over my head because of that absurd piece of information? I hadn't even realized I'd been doing it, although looking back, I couldn't see how I missed it. I'd never admit it to these bastards, though. That I was trying to slide into Amorette's panties was enough of an admission. "You're avoiding the question. How about I recount the conversation I had with Grey yesterday?"

When he seemed like he'd object, I continued. "I'll even paraphrase it for you. That way you don't have to worry about it going over your head."

His eye twitched and his hands clenched on the edge of the counter. Big brother didn't like that at all. He'd punch me right now if he thought it wouldn't hurt his chances of talking out his issues with Vicente.

"I'll take that as your permission to go on." I paused, then went on when he didn't object. "Little Love is a curious little thing, don't you think?"

Andre was undoubtedly starting to lose his patience with my storytelling. Well, too fucking bad.

"Not in the intellectual sense, although she is that too. I mean in the very essence of her presence here. We were all heading in our own directions. We were never close, but before Little Love appeared? We were already miles apart and getting farther and farther every day."

"You don't have to remind me of that, asshole." Andre sneered but hurt flashed in his eyes.

"I'm not trying to piss you off. It's the truth. Who knows how long we would have stayed together. Or even been alive. How long do you really think you could keep Grey from underneath Vicente's blade? Or Lafe from overdosing?"

He ground his teeth and looked away. Andre knew everything I was saying with perfect clarity. He just didn't want to admit it.

"Yes, I wanted to leave," I said softly. "Maybe I still might. Although every day that Little Love is here, that future seems more and more distant." I knocked two knuckles against the counter and shifted my weight to the other leg. "We've talked more lately. We've had each other's backs more presently. Why do you think that is?"

"You act like she's the answer to all our problems." He shook his head.

I laughed. "No. She brings more problems than she solves. And big ones. Especially that pesky little moral compass she loves so much." At that, he smiled a little. "Nonetheless, think about it. We all have different tastes in women, yet we all want her."

I waited for him to contradict me, but he didn't. And that was a beautiful thing.

"You have trouble believing I'm in this for the right reasons, or that I'll stick around. What better than to have a woman between us who we can all share? All protect. She'll tie us together in a way we weren't before. Isn't that what you want, big brother? For us all to be one big happy family," I said sarcastically.

He huffed a disgruntled laugh. "Like families are forever. Who's to say she even wants all of us?"

"She does." I was sure of it.

"Then who's to say we all want her for more than just a fuck?" Andre really believed that. It was written all over his stony expression.

"We do. Otherwise, we wouldn't lose our goddamn minds over her on the regular." I grinned, and he returned it. But his died quickly.

"I still haven't heard about your conversation with Grey. Even if she wanted us, and even if we wanted her, I'm not sure Grey would actually share."

"He'll share."

"You're so sure." He cut his eyes at me in a way that said he suspected there was more to my answer than just speculation. There wasn't. Not really. I just knew Grey, and body language was a beaming tell.

"Twice, I've been in the room while Grey sexed up Amorette. Twice, he didn't kill me. I won't go into the fun details...unless you'd like to trade stories." I grinned, but he didn't bite on that one. Damn. "But Grey has a fascinating reaction when it's us over anyone else. If I were one of the soldiers, he'd have gutted me and continued his thrusting like nothing was wrong. He might think he wants her to himself, but he's turned-on by the idea of us sharing her. I just pointed that out to him. Gave him some...food for thought."

Andre dropped his gaze to the floor. He was unquestionably remembering what had happened between them. I wanted to know what that was. I was curious, but I also needed validation that I was right.

We entered a stare down. My big brother was working out how much he wanted to share and how much he didn't.

Just give me a little crumb, Andre.

That was all it would take. I didn't ask for much. Then I could share with you the plans I had for Vicente. The plans I'd been working on for years. The plans I'd already put in motion.

Mia digging up dirt on Vicente was just the tip of the iceberg.

He rolled his lips and leaned forward—then his phone rang.

Sighing, he pulled it out of his pocket to check it. Our burners weren't the most sophisticated, but they did everything we needed with the maximum discretion.

His brows pinched, and he shot me an irritated look.

"I don't know what you think I did, but I've been a good boy. I swear it," I deadpanned.

"Mia's here."

The words were like ice water onto my scheming mind. "What do you mean Mia's here?" The last time we spoke, she was going to her father's.

"How much do you trust Mia?" Andre was deadly serious.

Given the situation with Vicente and that she wasn't made while on her job for me, I gave it serious consideration. She was my best friend. My oldest friend. But in this life, in the Institution, allegiances changed with the seasons, and friendships were something of a myth.

The life had banded us together because of the cutthroat jungle we were stuck in daily. If I had to wager on it, I'd throw in my most prized possessions or even my fight for freedom before I believed she was out to stab us in the back.

Still, a naive man was often a dead one.

"With my life. Why are you asking?"

"Because she's come to compound barely more than a few times in the last three years. Why is she suddenly popping up without alerting us? It's suspicious, and I don't deal with suspicion well." His nostrils flared as he typed out a message on his phone before shoving it back in his pocket.

Andre started for the door, and I followed.

"I was never here. Why would she come to the compound once she was done fucking with Grey?" I grunted out.

He returned the disgruntled gesture. I locked the door behind us and we wasted no time toward the commons.

"If I thought there was a modicum of a chance she was against us, I would slit her throat and be done with it."

The long side-eyed glance he sent me questioned every word that fell from my mouth. "Could you? Would you be able to kill your brothers so easily too?"

Letting out chuffing laughter, I shook my head. "I value the things that are mine. But I also can't stand betrayal. There's a line, and Mia knows never to cross it."

He didn't believe me but left it alone as we moved through the commons.

"Where is she?" A Hummer was at the curb, but there was no sign of Mia.

"I'm not sure. The guard at the wall just wanted to let me know she was here so I wouldn't be surprised."

There weren't any of our men in the commons either, but there was some small commotion coming from the professional wing. Andre was on the same page because we simultaneously pivoted to that hallway.

Some dishes were banging around, and Mia's distinct giggle filled the air. It wasn't her usual laugh. It was the giggle she took on when she was on a job. Pins instantly prickled the nape of my neck as I rounded the corner.

Little Love was washing dishes in the sink, and Mia was sidled right up to her side, tracing a finger down her bare arm. This was not mutual. This wasn't even playful. Mia was being so aggressive while Little Love's back was rigid and her head was snapped up straight.

I stalked forward and gripped Mia's arm. "What are you doing?" My tone was light, but she knew better. We'd had this discussion when she'd stayed with me last time.

She grinned and rolled her eyes while trying to twist her arm out of my grip. "What's your problem, Parker? I was just trying to get to know Amorette."

"By making her hate your fucking guts?" I growled.

Mia paused, then glanced at Little Love, taking in the angry set to her mouth and her fiery stare. Ah, yes. Little Love was a tiny hurricane, and we were in the eye of the storm. I knew Mia preferred women, and Amorette fit at least one of the types Mia went for. Although she was an equal opportunity fucker, so it didn't matter.

What did matter was why I heard that grating fucking laugh she only used on jobs. Either Andre was succeeding in bringing me over to his cautious suspicion, or something was niggling in the back of my head. I just didn't know what it was that bothered me so much outside the obvious.

My best friend since childhood sighed and deflated. "Look, Amorette. I don't mean to scare you—"

"You don't scare me," Little Love snapped back and I grinned.

I loved her fire, even if it wasn't hot enough to burn anyone.

Mia pursed her lips, probably fighting a smile too. "Regardless. You're in the boys' lives for good. I can see that. We should be friends." She tried to crowd Little Love, but I gave her a harsh shake. "I can be a very good friend to have."

"That's enough," Andre barked, pulling Little Love to his chest. She didn't go willingly, but she wasn't fighting it, either. I was riveted by how they bent toward each other so easily. Andre would tell me what happened. Or Grey would.

One way or another, Little Love would be the glue that held us together while Vicente tried to bury us six feet under.

Mia audibly pouted, snapping me out of my trance. "Let's go." I pushed her in front of me and kept shoving her all the way down the hallway until we reached my office.

"What the hell was that?" I asked as I shut the door and parked my ass against it.

"What? Like you all aren't salivating to stick your dick in it." She laughed and gracefully fell into one of the chairs in front of my desk. My office was less pristine than Andre's, but I hardly worked here, anyway. I preferred to do my research in my apartment or in a hotel close to the job.

"It doesn't matter what we want to do. She's not yours to touch."

She gave me a bland look. "I've been underneath all of your feet since I could walk. I'm practically the only one allowed in your circle of brotherhood. Why is she fair game for the four of you but not for me?"

I ground my teeth and placed one foot on the door. "For starters, she doesn't like you."

"She likes me just fine." She smirked.

"Amorette doesn't like women. Second, you may be my closest friend, but you don't get to waltz in and make demands or throw prissy fits. You're only allowed here because my brothers and I allow it. And I have to say, Mia, I'm not thrilled with the way you've been popping up. Not with Vicente trying to close in on us."

An unflattering mauve stained her entire face as she shot to her feet. "What are you insinuating? I have never— not ever—been a puppet for anyone. My friendship and loyalty are to you, and your brothers by default. Are you calling me a rat?" She scoffed, the thick, grating sound stuck in her throat.

"No. But I'm inferring that you're acting out of character. I don't like it," I drawled, keeping my cool in the face of her rising anger. She had always been like this as a kid. Mia was calm and level-headed in most cases, but when her fuse lit, it lit quick.

"Fine. If that's the way our friendship is heading, I'll see myself out." She stormed toward me, stopping when I didn't move. "I would never betray you. Any of them. We've seen exactly how fucked up life can be and how quickly we can be snuffed out. If you think for one minute I would throw you all to the wolves to cut every trusted ally away from me... That doesn't make sense." She shook her head and shoved my shoulder.

I stepped to the side and twisted the knob, not quite ready to open it. "You are my best friend, Mia. I hope that's always the case, but you can't deny that your behavior is strange. More than anyone else, you know how to read a situation. Don't betray my trust, and we'll be fine." I opened the door but stuck my leg out to stop her exit. "And Amorette is off-limits to you. You can be her friend if—and only if—she wants to approach you for friendship. Nothing else. Start with that, and we'll be good."

Pulling back my leg, I nodded toward the door when she

didn't immediately leave. She simply stared me down like she couldn't believe what I was saying.

"Fuck you," she muttered.

When I turned toward the door, Andre was there with Grey at his back.

"Lafe is with Amorette. To pick back up the conversation I tried to have earlier, we need to devise a plan on how to deal with Vicente."

I only let my gaze wander past them briefly before smiling at my dear brother. "I'm glad you're finally coming to your senses. Let's chat."

24

AMORETTE

I looked at the closed door. I'd really just been deposited inside Lafe's apartment, so Andre could go do whatever the hell it was that he needed to do, grabbing Grey as he was coming out of his apartment to accompany him.

For weeks I'd been given free rein, yet suddenly, staring at the door two feet in front of my face, I felt suffocated again.

"Killer?" Lafe asked as he stepped up behind me.

Andre had texted him when we were on our way, and when we reached his door, Lafe had just opened it. His light blond hair was a mess. He'd just woken up and was greeting us shirtless in only a pair of pajama pants.

"Why am I here?" I literally couldn't pull my gaze away from the door like I could gain answers with my willpower alone.

"Andre said he needed to talk to Parker and that Mia was making you uncomfortable." A scratching sound was close to my ear, like Lafe was rubbing his jaw. His voice was rough, confirming he'd woken up recently.

"I can handle myself. She's Parker's childhood friend. So she's not a threat, right?" I turned.

I couldn't decide if Andre was trying to protect me—misguidedly, or if something happened to kill his trust in me. After the plane, when I'd lost my mind on his lap...

Hell, maybe he didn't trust me now. He could view me like a woman trying to come between them rather than a woman trying to make the best of a terrible life situation.

Turning around, Lafe was much closer than I had anticipated. My breasts skimmed his stomach, but he didn't pay attention to that. Instead, he gazed at me in concern, his blue eyes clouded by the remnants of his sleep.

"I think when Vicente is on the warpath, everyone is a threat." He gently cupped my elbows, his thumbs making slow circles on my skin. Was this an apology? An admission?

"Even me?" I whispered, dropping my gaze to his chest and trying—failing—to ignore the tingles his touch brought to life.

Fucking Grey. I couldn't even blame him. Not really, but I was, because that was better than blaming myself for letting these men twist me up the way they did.

They were bad men—no way around it. I had learned in a short span of time there was more than one type of bad person, and these men sat firmly in the gray and ventured into the black area of the law.

"Most especially you," he returned in a soft voice. But instead of being an insult, one side of his mouth kicked up in a tease.

He stepped back, dropping one hand but using the other to move me deeper into his apartment. I hadn't been back here since he'd nearly overdosed. I swallowed as regret washed over me. I wasn't someone who dwelled on the past. There was no time for thoughts like that.

But I could admit to myself...I could have handled my time with Lafe better.

I should have handled my abduction better...

Wait...I shook my head. That was a bit like victim-blaming, wasn't it? Except I was the victim.

Letting out a slow breath, I gathered my thoughts. I acted in a way that was authentic to me. I struggled with my doubts, with what I saw, felt, and said. But none of that meant I was to blame in any situation. And that made me human.

"Are you hungry?" He asked as he moved us to the couch. His laptop was open on the table like he'd been messing around between the time Andre texted and when we reached his door.

"No. I already ate before Andre carted me away." I sounded just as sour to my own ears as I was sure I sounded to him.

He didn't say anything as he let go of me and claimed the end seat and picked up his laptop.

I took the other end. Looking at me, he grabbed the remote and tossed it to me.

"Put on whatever you want."

"What are you doing?" I leaned to the right to see what he was working on.

My first thought was that he would try and shield his screen, but he didn't. Instead, he rotated it toward me so I could get a better look. Graphs and numbers took up the entire space. I wasn't sure what to make of it.

I knew Lafe managed the drug side of Vicente's business. I also knew he used them. That was the extent of my knowledge.

Honestly, I'd done my best to put the rest out of my head. As much as I was coming to know them, and sometimes even like them, I forced the worst of them as far away from thought as possible. Shame burned inside my chest while logic warred inside my mind.

When you accepted someone, you accepted all of them, not just the parts you wanted to see.

Then again, I should never forget who these men were. They were shaped by their family. By the experiences that were forced on them. But that didn't change who they were.

They were unapologetically themselves. No excuses. No shame.

"I don't know what any of that is." Although, I had an idea.

"My part of the business is managing the fuckups. The men hooked on the product or the men chasing money and power in the streets. I spend too much of my time weeding out the ones taking advantage, skimming off the top of profits, or trying to rat us out. I also have to manage the suppliers. I decide what products are pushed. The ratios of drugs in the pills. The shipping."

I twisted my ear to my shoulder to crack my neck, and then repeated the action on the other side. All to give me time to formulate a response.

My initial reaction?

Horror. Lafe literally ran a company more sophisticated than anything I could have ever imagined that led to so many deaths on the street.

I couldn't tell him that. We'd come so far I didn't want to backtrack. I didn't want to go back into my own head or to the birdcage. That sounded like an even worse hell than this reality.

When I met his sad blue eyes, he must have known what I was thinking, or at least had a damn good idea. "I'm sorry, Lafe," I whispered, offering a wince in apology.

The smile that twisted his lips was as mocking as it was vicious. It didn't look right on Lafe. Outside of how he was at the warehouse where I was first taken, he was the vulnerable one of the four. The one who I felt the most kindred with. If anyone had any idea how it felt to be trapped here, it was him.

He wasn't the evil mask he presented me with.

"You're never going to change, are you?"

His words scored my chest, leaving deep, scarring gouges behind. "That's not fair." Why was I even arguing? I didn't want to be like them. The gray area was not where I wanted to be.

Yet, that was where I was.

After killing that man...After relishing in Grey killing the man who abducted me.

I couldn't argue that I had changed. Not for the better.

It wasn't the life-altering change I thought it would be. I still felt the same, except also so vastly different.

"Isn't it? You'll always think I'm scum because of the business I manage. I run drugs. I have thousands of men who push and peddle throughout North and South America. Are you sorry you laid in my arms as you went to sleep?"

"Stop." I put a hand on his arm and squeezed, hard. "I don't think you're scum," I said with as much conviction as I could muster in such a few words. "I think you do bad things. That might not ever change. But I also think you're just as much a victim as I am. Just a different kind."

He laughed bitterly and turned the computer back to face him. "I'm no victim. I'm exactly who I'm supposed to be. And of the four, I run the most despicable business. At least in your eyes. Parker might come close, but he steals from the wealthy and doesn't kill addicts in droves."

I jerked back. "I said stop. I don't want to hear this."

'White knight' Amorette, meet 'head in the sand' Amorette.

"You don't want to hear how this is such a sophisticated business that I have the best coke, the most potent weed, the trippiest X. And our margins are through the roof. A quarter of our product is stolen by the runners every year, sometimes more, yet I still have the highest margins of any of my brothers. Hell, Andre doesn't even have margins."

My only thought was to shut him up, so I didn't have all this shit thrown in my face.

When I said nothing, he threw his laptop onto the coffee table and it skidded over the wooden surface. Then he was on me, hands gripping my waist, bending me backward over the arm of the couch.

His chest pressed against mine, and his breath fanned over my lips. The normally shocking blue of his eyes was so cold I shivered.

"Does it bother you to know that the hands of a murderer are touching you? Do you lie to yourself and say you don't like it?"

I pushed against his chest. What had gotten into him?

"Lafe!"

"My hands are stained in blood, drugs, and filth. Does this turn you on, Killer? Grey's hands have traveled your body so many times. Does the blood on his hands bother you? Or does it make you hot to know you're sleeping with a man who will kill for you?" He tugged me down the couch until I was flat on my back and he covered me.

I twisted my head to the side, because I couldn't let him see the truth. I did love that Grey killed Tony. Sometimes, I fantasized about it.

If Lafe saw the truth in my eyes, he'd think I was crazy. I wasn't.

I *wasn't*.

He grabbed the sides of my face and forced me to turn toward him. I squeezed my eyes shut, but he shook me.

"Could you fuck me, Amorette? Could you let me kiss and worship your body, knowing I don't give a damn about my life or the millions of others who've died because of me? Do you blame me for their deaths?"

"No!" I screamed, kicking out my legs, but he had me effectively trapped beneath him.

"Would you let me fuck you like Grey?"

I pulled back my hand and slapped Lafe across the face. The loud, resounding crack echoed between us. With his face turned to the side, our breathing took up all the space between us. The rapid beating of his heart touched mine.

How could two hearts beat in sync but be so at odds?

"You're an asshole, Lafe." Tears pricked my eyes and when I shoved this time, he let me go. I stumbled to my feet and reached the hallway before I turned around. Words touched the tip of my tongue, but I couldn't say any of them.

They didn't make sense. The accusations I wanted to hurl rang false with how short I'd known him.

Yet, I was hurt. He'd hurt me when I'd been telling myself these men were bad from the very beginning. My heart was only a heart, though. It didn't see the logic, and it didn't count evil deeds. My heart only saw how he looked at me, or his brothers, and the way he made me feel.

This wasn't him. I *knew* it.

How could Lafe make me feel safe and not alone one second, then a fool the next?

Lafe pushed himself to his knees and swiped a hand through his hair. "I'm sorry, I—" he choked on his words and glanced down my body then at the laptop.

Shaking my head, I took one step back, then another.

"I thought you were different," I whispered. "I know you,

Grey, Parker, and Andre all do bad things. I'm not blind. But you're not cruel. Or are you, and you just haven't shown me this side of you yet?"

The skin around his eyes crinkled in a tortured expression. "I am cruel. But not to you. I'm sorry," he repeated and slapped his head. "Argh! I'm such a fuck up."

Did I reassure him that he wasn't? Tell him he wasn't all bad and was a product of his environment? What kind of comfort could I really give him?

I'd tried that, and he'd accosted me on the couch. Burn me once.

Steeling myself for the pain I was about to cause to my own heart, I turned on my heel and quietly left the apartment. There was no stomping, no slamming doors.

I was not the fool.

I would not be burned twice.

25

PARKER

I t had been a week since Andre, Grey, and I had holed up in my office for two full days. We reviewed the plans I had in place, and where I thought the weak spots were in Vicente's armor.

All in all, it had been a great bonding experience.

How many other brothers could say they got closer while plotting their father's murder?

I laughed. Not many. Maybe not even a few.

Now all we had to do was sit back and reap the rewards of all my hard work.

"Let's go out today." I pushed the rope down on the ring where Andre and Grey were having a pleasant sparring session.

I'd already had my turn. With Andre, thank fuck. For all the progress we made in my office, Grey still harbored ill feelings. He enjoyed my pain whenever he got the chance.

Currently, in the ring, Andre got a kidney shot in on Grey and yelled his triumph. Grey grunted and followed up with a hit right to the chin.

I winced as Andre's eyes rolled back in his head.

Ouch. Grey had a punch like steel.

"Out." Andre tapped Grey's shoulder with a taped hand. "I'm out for now." He panted and rubbed his chin. "Where?" He glanced at me. It wasn't the shining endorsement I wanted, but I'd take heedful possibilities over a flat-out no.

"Let's go to the mainland. Or even Chile. The sky's the limit..." I bounced the rope in faux thoughtfulness. "Or we could go to Vicente's city."

"Hell fucking no," Grey growled, slipping between the ropes. He tossed Andre a water bottle and opened his own.

"Not going to happen. There are too many things that could go wrong." Andre shot my dreams down like the bastard that he was.

"We've been working for an entire week to implement these plans. *I've* been gathering this intel for years. I deserve to see it play out." I pulled the rope out and let go. It recoiled from the force while Andre and Grey stared at me.

"And do what? We all go on a merry fucking family outing?" Andre snapped. "Take Amorette and Lafe too?"

Lafe had been an ass. I had only seen him twice, but each time he had deep circles under his eyes and foul words on his lips. I take that back. He was just foul. He also smelled like he hadn't showered in a few days.

"Maybe. Or if you're concerned it's dangerous, the three of us could go. Hell, I could go. But I'm trying out this new brotherly concept where we do things together." I smirked, and Grey rolled his eyes while Andre studied his water bottle.

"It wouldn't be a bad idea if we go to oversee our plans. But we'd have to be careful. Fly to the coast and take a boat into one of the private docks so Vicente doesn't know we're there."

Santa mierda. Andre was actually considering it.

I slapped my thigh. "Done. We'll also have to take a smaller contingent of guards. Be less conspicuous, and also make sure the compound is protected. We'll also have an escape route just in case."

"Agreed. We'll take ten," Andre said as he climbed over the ropes. Grey was shutting down the gym, not interested in logistics. The bastard only cared about fighting, fucking, and his freedom to do both as he pleased. I rolled my eyes.

"Five. Ten isn't that low-key, brother." I ripped the tape off and helped shut down the gym. "We'll meet at the chopper in," I glanced at the time on my phone, "two hours." That would give us plenty of time to see everything go down.

After a few disgruntled waves, we were getting ready in our apartments. I almost wished Little Love was going. I was fucking horny planning the demise of Vicente's reign, and this was absolutely the kind of outing where I'd pick a girl for a little public play.

Would Amorette let me force her to her knees in a crowded room?

I shivered.

Better yet, I'd love to bend her over in front of me as I stared my father in the eyes. He hated public displays of any kind. Like that said a man was weak.

Fuck that. I used sex as a weapon against him any chance I could, just because it made him angry. It was the little rebellions that made life worth living.

I turned on the shower as obscene images of Little Love repeatedly played inside my head.

Mm. Maybe I'd set her on the table before me and pull her panties to the side. Give her perfect little clit a slow lick. Then I'd tease her while men conducted business around us. No one would dare look at her.

She was ours.

I'd never eaten a woman out in public. It was all about my gratification and a big fuck you to Vicente. Not that I left them wanting. I definitely made sure they walked away satisfied. Why else would they come back in droves for a chance to play?

But for Little Love? I'd happily feast on her pussy.

I reached down and stroked my hard cock as I stepped under the hot spray. Her tiny hand would feel even better. Fucking Grey, the lucky *pendejo*.

Barely three strokes, and I came all over the white tile.

THE SMALL, chartered boat was barely more than a rusted-out heap.

"Really, Andre? This is the best you could do?" I asked, raising one brow at him.

His mirrored sunglasses showed my own reflection staring back at me.

"Anything flashier and Vicente would get word that we're here."

"Like he's not going to know we're here anyway?" Grey pushed his sunglasses up and started uncoiling the rope to tie us to the dock.

"I'm sure he will, but every minute counts."

Two very old men stood at the dock leaning on their walking sticks and watching us approach under the bill of their hats. We weren't moving that fast, with how shallow the water was. And this particular entrance to the island was more marsh than straight sand.

Still, it was a gorgeous day. The sun shone bright, and the crystalline water shimmered almost too brilliantly.

A perfect day for our revenge.

"*Hola! Hola!*" one of the men called and waved, while the other used his stick to pull the end of our boat to their dock. They both erupted into furious movements as Grey helped them tie us in place.

Water sloshed over the floor of the boat as we stepped out. Given its decrepit state, I wasn't convinced it wasn't from a hole in the boat.

Andre tipped the men and thanked them, and we piled into a waiting car. Our men were in a boat behind us, and they had their own vehicle waiting behind ours. This wasn't exactly the low-key traveling I'd had in mind, but I'd take my wins where I could get them.

Everything we had planned today shouldn't require us to do too much anyway. I just wanted a front-row seat to the bloodshed.

Andre, drumming his fingers on the steering wheel, watched the second boat dock. "You sure this is a good mission for Jorge?"

I shrugged. "He wanted to come."

"Blanca has become a friend to Amorette, though. It will go sour if her brother dies today." Grey pulled his glasses down to watch the men enter the car behind us in the side view mirror.

"Blanca understands life is short. She understands why. It's Little Love that doesn't," I murmured as I took out my phone to validate that everything was in place. "Think Doc will be happy to see you?" I flicked my gaze at Grey.

He was the one who "delivered" Vicente's message, after all.

Grey grinned and glanced over his shoulder at me in the backseat. "He loves me. Don't let him fool you."

Andre grunted under his breath, then pulled onto the

road. The men behind us followed but left enough space between us so it wasn't overtly obvious we were together. It also helped that we were in shitty seventies cars with a rusted-out paint job rather than the regular sleek bullet-proof SUVs we usually traveled in.

The fifteen-minute ride to Doc's was filled with tense silence. Andre because he thought too fucking much. He was probably reviewing all the different scenarios of how this could go wrong or how we could fuck it up if our plans went right.

I did the same thing, but without a giant stick up my ass. My silence was from the building anticipation. I could barely sit still; I was so fucking excited.

Then there was Grey. Who, if I had to bet, was thinking about being balls-deep inside Little Love right now.

When we pulled up to Doc's modest house, we pulled around back into his garage. His neighborhood was in the rougher part of the city. Not that this was rough. Not by any standards. He had a two-story house and the garage in the back alley fit four cars, and the building next to it was set up for his practice. He only saw his favorite patients in the house.

Vicente was always relegated to the building. I snickered.

The garage doors opened for us, and we pulled in without issues. The alley was clear. No one was around to see us enter. Not unusual since Doc owned this entire street.

"My boys," Doc greeted us with a wide gapped-tooth smile and open arms when we climbed out. He wasn't tall, and age seemed to diminish his height a little more each year. His skin was wrinkled like rough, old leather, and his cheeks and temples creased with a hundred lines as he smiled. But his eyes couldn't hide his intelligence with his thick glasses that magnified them.

He said his hellos to our men, looking them over and inquiring about some of their families. Our men mostly grew up close to our island, but Doc had been there a time or two to patch us up.

His pinky was gone, courtesy of Grey. He was also missing an extra tooth that he'd had the last time I'd seen him. Little Love would be mortified to know Grey dished out so much pain to someone who didn't deserve it.

Then again, maybe she'd understand a little pain was worth his life.

If Grey hadn't delivered a visible message, Vicente would have done much worse and delivered a brutal death that extended to his family too.

"Doc." Andre greeted, dipping his head. Doc was having none of the formality. He brought Andre into a hug and heartily slapped him on the back. Then he gave the same affectionate hello to Grey and me.

"I must say, I was surprised to hear from you this morning." He glanced at the men then back at us. "Why don't you boys hang out in the back while we go into my office?" He motioned for our men to go through the backdoor, where he had a sweet backyard set up. It was very domestic of him, though we'd never tease him about it.

They agreed and filed out in record time. No one mentioned they wouldn't be relaxing and shooting the shit back there. They'd travel around to the front and patrol the alley. Some would spread out a little farther.

Doc led the way into his clinic and his office at the back of the hallway. Where the clinic was anything you'd expect of a doctor's office—white, pristine walls and furniture soaked in strong disinfectant smells—his office was warm oak and plants on every available surface.

Amazing how he kept them all thriving on two small windows of natural light.

"So, now that we're in a trusted, sound-proof room, care to explain what you boys have been up to?"

Only Doc would have the guts to refer to us as boys. A hint of a smile slipped out as I looked to Andre. I should be the one to lay this out, but Andre was a bitch sometimes about his perceived role in our brotherhood.

He didn't say anything, so I jumped in.

"Vicente has to go." I started off strong.

Doc snorted. "This has nothing to do with him stealing Grey's lover? Don't get me wrong, I want to see Vicente go up in flames for the hell he's rained down on my family, but why now? Why are you boys suddenly fired up to take care of it?"

"It's no secret we're not on Vicente's good side anymore," I continued as Grey pulled out one of his knives and started cleaning under his nails. It wasn't an intimidation tactic. He used his glare and fists for that when he bothered to intimidate anyone at all. Although since we were kids, he preferred not to give warnings and just knock someone out. No, Grey was just bored. "We've been working on this for a long time. A long fucking time. This is just the opportunity we need to start putting plans in motion."

"Care to share these plans?" Doc skewered me with a sharp gaze as he leaned back on his desk. None of us had taken a seat as we crowded the small room.

"Nope," I said with a pop and a grin. "That would spoil the fun."

"Of course, we decided everything because of how much

fun it would be." Andre sent me a withering glare. It just ate him up that I found so much enjoyment in the process.

"And why reach out to me, then?"

Andre took this question. "Because you're no more in Vicente's pockets than we are. Of all the people we trusted to bring in, and there are less than a few, we knew you wouldn't flip us."

Doc glanced down and rubbed the place where his pinky used to be. For a second, I worried that I had played this wrong. Did he harbor ill will toward us for Grey following Vicente's bidding?

Then he glanced up over the rim of his wire glasses and glared. "I'd do everything I could and then some to make sure Vicente loses everything he holds dear. Which, as we all know, isn't people. It's his power over his ill-gotten empire."

Grey gave him a devil's grin, and we all shared in the delight of being able to trust someone outside of our circle.

"In answer to your earlier question, Doc. Vicente taking Little Love was just the catalyst. We've been waiting for this for years." I didn't mention this was my plan until recently. He was in the trust circle, but that didn't mean he needed the intimate details. As far as any outsider was concerned, we were always on the same page.

"Where am I supposed to take you?" Doc was back to his normal jolly self.

"We need a lift into the upper balcony overlooking the festival," I said lightly.

Today was the anniversary celebration of Vicente's decades-long reign. He'd be presiding over the parade and festivities from his own personal balcony, but several lined the streets for his top men. While Doc wasn't exactly welcome in that group of jackals, he was awarded a prime viewing spot as Vicente's head doctor.

"That's it?" Doc sounded like he questioned our intelligence.

"The plans are already in motion. We're just here to ensure everything goes smoothly," I inserted with confidence.

Doc lost his humor and even his support as he stared each of us down. "Don't play this for fools. Arrogant men die young."

"Then Vicente should have died long ago, no?" I asked.

He bah'd and shook his head. "*Most* arrogant men. Don't place yourself in danger because you're brats who have no understanding of Vicente's reach."

"We understand the dangers just fine," Andre argued. Like clockwork, his hackles rose anytime someone hinted he wasn't as good or worthy of Vicente. "He has no idea we're coming today. This will be a quick in and out, just to make sure everything runs the way we need it to."

Nodding slowly, Doc pushed away from the desk. "Okay, boys. I'll offer whatever help I can. It won't be an issue getting you in. Don't fuck this up."

THE FULL, rich notes of street music drifted up to the half-covered balcony. I leaned over the banister like any regular party goer getting a look at the half-dressed dancers down below. Doc's balcony was just out of sight of Vicente's, yet we had a view of almost all the other headmen in the Institution. Perfect.

Today was about pomp and ceremony, exhibiting big feather fans on the dancers, masks on the attendees, and loud, boisterous music to rival Bourbon street. With Andre, Grey, and I all sporting fitted, half-face black masks that covered our hair too, I wasn't too concerned about being recognized. Most of the balconies were well into the liquor anyway.

Oh, look. There was Gregor, the crusty-ass bastard from my childhood. He yelled at a dancer below to show him her tits as he fell into the banister and sloshed his drink onto the people below.

Everyone here loved Vicente and the Institution, so they cheered with the spray instead of responding with vitriol. Like it was some fucking gift from heaven to be treated like dirt by these assholes.

Andre checked his watch while Grey sprawled out in one of the chairs in the shade. "Shouldn't something have happened by now?"

I shook my head. You could never plan an exact timeline for this type of thing. The exposing of secrets among Vicente's most devoted henchmen? That took guts, and the rewards were hefty enough to be worth the risk.

Still.

"Be patient."

Jorge cleared his throat, and I glanced at him. Three of our men were on the balcony with us, and two were on the roof. Not optimal for security, but it worked in the chaos. If something went awry, we'd go to the roof to make our escape.

"Yes, Jorge?"

"Sir, I don't see any of our *men*." He emphasized men in a way that meant the players, not our guards.

I searched the balconies. Andre and Grey both joined me, pushing Jorge out of the way.

"Fuck," I hissed.

"These men, they were supposed to be here by now," Grey said under his breath, gripping the banister's hot metal.

"How likely is it that every one of the men with a part to play is missing?" Andre asked in a hushed whisper as he pulled out his phone. Some of these men were his. Getting contacts on the inside was tough enough as it was. To find men willing to play our game for us? Fucking impossible, yet we'd found two.

Added in with my two, we have four men ready to start fights in front of Vicente and lay all the shit bare of Vicente's five top men—the men who ran his security, travel, and finances.

A crippling blow to allow us time to strike again while he was scrambling.

Horns blared over the speakers like sirens as the music and dancing came to a halt.

"Oh shit, I don't have a good feeling about this," I muttered.

"Neither do I." Andre took a step back. "We should leave." Yet none of us moved.

Down below, a float rounded the corner straight from the mansion, and on the front were seven spikes. All with heads stabbed on top. Their mouths were gaping, as their sweaty hair stuck to their foreheads. Blood ran down the wood like they'd been recently killed and dismembered.

"Those are our four men," Andre whispered, shooting me a troubled glare.

I flared my nostrils. Those were our collective four and three of the five men who were to be exposed.

The float had a covered box conveniently uncovered to reveal Vicente sitting on a golden throne with an elaborate, cheesy crown on his head. He held his head high in a regal show for the crowd. His golden brown skin glowed as if he'd rubbed himself down in oil.

A woman kneeling at his feet stood up and handed him a microphone as the float stopped right in the midst of the balconies.

Fucking hell. If we could have seen his balcony, we would have known something was wrong when he wasn't there.

"My loyal friends, today is a glorious day. Not only is this the anniversary of the Institution, but this is also the day I've uncovered a scheme to try and tear me down." The crowd gasped. "I know, I know." He moved his hand downward to settle the crowd's growing unrest.

"Fuck," Grey muttered, glancing at the balconies.

"And by my most entrusted enforcers no less. The heads you see before you are the heads of traitors. They were the footmen who did my enforcers' dirty work. Thanks to my many trusted advisors who saw straight through their plot, I remain with you today as the leader of the Castillo Institution!" He threw a head up and the crowd went absolutely fucking insane.

"That's not what was supposed to happen," Jorge whispered beside me. "He's making it all sound like you four had an assassination attempt out on him."

I heard the words somehow over the racket of my pulse inside my ears. All of my hard work was gone in a matter of hours. This was a plan I was sure would gain us the upper hand. It was simple. Publicly spill their secrets and deprive Vicente of key players in his circle. It wouldn't have won the war, but it would have caused a resounding blow. I had felt it in my bones.

"We'd happily see him dead, and he knows it," I responded. I wasn't even sure how I was able to string words together as I stared at the heads of the men who laid it all on the line for a shot to get their own revenge on Vicente.

Christian, the first man on the spike, lost his mother to Vicente's gallery when he 'discovered' her.

The second, Regan, was whipped at the post four months ago for disagreeing with one of Vicente's favorites.

Then there were Andre's two men. The first, Jose, was bullied so severely by Vicente's in-house generals that he almost committed suicide twice before deciding to get revenge. Lastly, George, a man from the US who was abandoned on the island when he was a teenager. Vicente could have sent him home. But he put him to work, made him a slave to the Institution, until Vicente thought he was brainwashed enough to climb the ranks.

All that motivation wasted.

"Now," Vicente said as he stood, sticking one hand in his linen shorts. "The enforcers are here today. I know that because I caught another rat among us." He motioned a hand, and a beaten and bloody Doc was carried out between two men. He was still full of fight as he twisted and kicked at his handlers.

Grey groaned, covering his face.

"I'm going to ride in the parade through every street of the island so we can celebrate together the end of these pitiful, disgusting lives. For whoever brings me Andre Medina, Lafe Nilsen, Grey Morozov, or Parker Adair will be granted a small fortune and the esteem of my council. Alive...or dead." I could just make out the swell of his cheek from his sadistic fucking grin. The people pushed toward the float as they yelled, screamed, and reached for the chance to touch his feet. He ignored their growing blood lust. "Let the party continue!"

"We have to get out of here." Jorge gulped and started calling the other two men.

"He doesn't know everything, so that's at least one benefit in our favor," I said. "Let's head to the roof. We can call for a chopper and get out of here."

"He's got Doc. He knows where we are, even if he didn't tell the crowd." Andre glanced at me with such bleak defeat I wanted to shove him over the balcony.

I grabbed his shirt and gave him a shake. "Snap the fuck out of it. You can wallow in your own misery when we're back at the compound. Not yet." I shoved him inside, where the men were already waiting for us. "Not yet."

We took the steps up to the roof two at a time and busted through the door. There waiting was a shiny chopper with the blades already starting to spin.

The man running around checking the outside waved for us to hurry the fuck up.

"Do we trust this escape?" Jorge asked, glancing around. With every second, people were filing out onto the rooftops, pointing and jeering at us. They'd made us. It was a matter of minutes before they shot at us or found a way to hop over.

"We don't necessarily have a choice." I drew my gun from under my shirt and ran toward the chopper. They seemed to be here for us, but that was more suspicious than if we had hijacked a ride.

Grey was the first to dive in. Then Andre and I brought up the rear. Our men followed as we pushed up from the floor. In the pilot's seat was Matías, coldly staring back at us like we were wastes of space.

Fucking Matías, of all the people who could have rescued us.

What a joke.

26

AMORETTE

"**F**uck." Blanca paced the commons. Every few steps, she stopped and stared out the window as if willing Jorge to come running through the trees.

"He'd text you as soon as they got here, right? You don't need to stare at the trees." I sat on the stairs and watched her wear a circle in the stone.

"The last message was two hours ago, Amorette! All he said was I love you. You know how many times that man has told me he loved me in my life? Twice. When Papa died, and when I started working for the brothers." She turned to face me, and her dark eyes seemed scarily large in her pale face, set off even more by the white sundress. "I can't lose him, Am. I can't." She covered her face and took in a few shuddering breaths.

I almost went to her, but something kept me planted on the stairs.

When she lifted her head, she whipped around to face me, her dark hair flying behind her. "What am I supposed to tell *mamá*? He has to come back." Her chest quickly rose and fell as she turned back toward the glass.

"There's nothing to be worried about right now. Someone would have been alerted if something bad had happened." I stood and slowly stepped down the stairs. Edging closer, I waited for her to show any sign that she didn't want comfort.

When I worked with battered women, sometimes they welcomed physical comfort, and sometimes they just needed my presence. I'd learned that slow movements allowed them time to see what I was doing and to shut it down if they weren't okay with it.

Blanca wasn't a battered woman. Quite the opposite, actually.

But she was so distraught that I was falling back on old lessons.

"Would we? Lafe hasn't been seen in days. The men are always outside on patrol now, waiting for Vicente to attack us. How would we know!?" she yelled, still looking outside.

I hadn't seen Lafe since I'd walked out on him. I had knocked on his door a few times, and when I went to Grey, he brushed off my concern. He'd had enough brief conversations with him over text that he wasn't worried.

That last encounter with him had played over and over in my head. That wasn't him. I don't know what caused it, but he would never force me. Something had been off, and someone else had to have noticed it.

How did these brothers not care about each other the way I cared about Grace? It confounded me. Constantly.

"If something happened, and Lafe found out, he would tell us." I wasn't as confident as I sounded.

"Will you go with me to *mamá's* if I have to go?" Her voice trembled.

Blanca wasn't emotional. At least not in a sensitive way. And she'd never really spoken about Jorge. I only knew about him because of running into him in the commons kitchen, and she'd teased him about being her big, smelly brother. It had been a fight I'd expect from much younger siblings, but it made this whole world seem a little more real to me. Not one filled with vile people.

Her phone chimed, and she almost tossed it from whipping it out so fast. "*Dios mio.* Oh God, they're back. Let's go!"

She grabbed my hand and yanked until I ran across the courtyard with her. Even in sneakers and a pair of shorts, it was hard to keep up with her in fancy sandals and her dress.

The whirring of the blades got louder and louder as we cleared the trees. He must have texted her when they were a minute out because they had just touched down. The wind beat at us in waves until the blades slowed.

This wasn't their chopper. Theirs was black. This one was red and silver. Yet the position of the helicopter kept me from seeing who was inside, but this had to be them. Jorge texted Blanca.

The guards climbed out first. I recognized most of them. Jorge was the last, and he made a beeline straight for Blanca. They caught each other in a tight hold and muttered low words to each other in Spanish.

I kept my gaze trained on the helicopter, waiting for all three brothers to emerge. Andre jumped out, followed by Grey, then finally Parker. I didn't run as Blanca had, but I did pick up the pace. From the dire looks on their faces, something terrible had happened. Stress and concern tightened around my shoulders like a strangling jacket. Was this when they'd tell me it was over for all of us?

Andre and Grey reached for me simultaneously, but I stopped short when another man came out. *Matías.*

I sent a questioning look to Andre, then to the other two. Andre sighed as he dropped his arms, like he hadn't realized he had raised his arm, to begin with. "We're fucked. We might as well go inside and have this conversation."

The men were off to the sides, watching us with wide eyes and pinched expressions. None of them had even attempted to leave the pad.

Grey caught my hand, and we all collectively walked toward the compound. Their moods were somber, and it was terrifying what would make the guards this freaked out.

Parker stayed on his phone as we headed toward the offices. Finally, most of the men peeled away, except for Jorge. When Blanca tried to follow, Jorge stopped her, speaking quietly in her ear. Whatever he said, she wanted to fight it. She had that stubborn tilt to her jaw that said she was about to flay him with her words. But in the end, she nodded and left, shooting me one last worried glance before disappearing.

Should I even be here for this?

Maybe not, but I wasn't going anywhere. Knowledge was power, and these men seemed to parse it out to me as they saw fit. Which, fuck that. Steeling myself for a fight, I squared my shoulders as we moved through the compound. When we made it to Andre's office, no one batted an eye as I entered with them.

Andre caught my arm and tugged me over behind his desk. At first, I thought he was going to sit me in his lap, which would be weird in this setting and also out of character. Instead, he lifted me up to sit on the side of the desk closest to the window. Then he took his seat.

Grey took one of the chairs on the other side of the desk, but Parker, Matías, and Jorge all decided to remain standing.

No one spoke. They all traded glances; some bland, some hostile, ignoring me altogether. All except Matías, whose gaze touched on me every few seconds. It wasn't long, and it wasn't threatening or invasive. More curious. It warmed my skin.

Why was he so fascinated with my place here?

A minute later, the door opened and Lafe stepped in. I sucked in a soft breath. He looked like hell.

Dark circles ringed his eyes, and his hair was so greasy I doubted he'd showered within the last week. Then there were his eyes. Glossy. Not present.

Andre cursed as Grey sneered and Parker just glared.

"What the hell have you been doing, Lafe!" Andre pushed up out of his chair.

Lafe slowly lifted his gaze to Andre, but there was such a small level of care that I wasn't sure he even registered what was happening here. He spotted the empty chair next to Grey and settled down. This was different than when I was stuck in his apartment with him. He had been wired then. Paranoid. Now he was like goop that was going to slide onto the floor at any second. He had no idea what was going on. If he even knew what his name was.

"I'll take care of this after we're done here," Grey said as his gaze lingered on Lafe.

"It was useless to call him in." Parker shook his head, then turned to Matías. "We're here. You have the four of us. And then some. What the hell was that and why did you come to our rescue?"

Matías swept loose dark hair away from his face as he leveled Parker with a glare. "You're my brother. The four of you are my brothers. Why wouldn't I want to save you?"

"Did you know what was happening?" Andre asked as he used his fingers to rub at his temples.

"Not as early as you think." Matías looked down his nose at Andre. "Barely thirty minutes before his announcement– after he caught Doc."

Grey's hands gripped the ends of his chair with white knuckles.

I was dying to jump in, to ask what had happened to bring them to this point, but I couldn't. It wasn't the place. But they weren't watching their information either.

"Can you get him away from Vicente?" Grey asked through clenched teeth.

Tipping his head, Matías regarded Grey. "Does he mean that much to you?" There was a note in his voice that made me believe Matías was jealous.

Holy hell. Was that it? Was he jealous of the brothers and their relationships? From the few encounters I'd witnessed at Matías' house, he didn't have friends. He barely had acquaintances.

I couldn't imagine Vicente was the kind of man who fostered any kind of warmth in a childhood, even for his favorite.

"More than you," Grey said through a cruel smirk. My stomach plummeted. That was harsh. But still, I stayed quiet. Observing the back and forth between them.

Matías laughed, but there was something dry about it like he didn't do it very often. "Funny way to try and pry a favor out of me. Especially when you have nothing to trade, not with a ransom on your head. All of your heads." He skimmed his gaze through the room, altogether avoiding Jorge.

He had something he wanted to say. It was building, and Matías was either ramping up the courage or playing a sneaky hand in manipulation.

"How did you find out what was happening?" Andre asked a better question this time.

Jorge shifted from foot to foot, pulling Matías' attention to him. "Guard. Leave us."

Jorge ground his teeth as he glanced at Parker. When he nodded, Jorge bowed his head and excused himself.

I contemplated hopping down from the desk, but Matías shook his head. "You might as well stay, Amorette. Since you were the catalyst for all this."

"How is that?" Grey growled and pushed forward in his chair.

"One question at a time." Matías turned to Parker. "You've been playing a dangerous game with your spies and your schemes. You should have left that to Andre."

Parker took a step toward Matías, then caught himself. There was a visible war going on inside of him. He wanted to know what Matías knew, but he wanted to fight him too. That was obvious from the hatred burning in his eyes as his fists clenched at his sides.

"Vicente cracked one of your rats, who wasn't very good at whatever job you gave him. Regan, I believe his name was. He cracked so hard, he spilled every name he could and what they had planned."

"Fucking fuck," Parker cursed and pinched the bridge of his nose.

"It was a good plan. The public humiliation would have hurt Vicente's image. Except, he came out on top, like he always does," Matías sighed.

"You're supposed to be his heir. If he finds out what you're doing, if he doesn't already know, you're dead," Andre half said, half groaned.

"If you hadn't noticed, I've never wanted to be his heir," Matías spat. "And he doesn't truly want one. Otherwise, he would have tried to train me years ago."

A thought occurred to me. What if Matías hated Vicente as much as the brothers did? They at least had each other to lean on. Matías had only had Valentina, maybe.

What if this whole thing wasn't about me but him finding his way into their group?

None of the brothers said anything. I wasn't sure what there was to say, not until they had time to digest what had happened at least.

"You're safe enough here. For now. If I hear anything, I'll let you know. I'd prefer it if you don't die because you've been stupid and overestimated yourselves." Matías stepped toward the door, but Parker stopped him with a hand on his arm.

"You still didn't answer why you would take this risk for us. We've been nothing to each other. Not when we were kids, not as adults. It stinks of a trap."

The coldness in Matías' eyes would have seared me to the spot, but Parker acted as if he wasn't fazed at all. "That was never my choice." He looked at Andre. "If you need something, call me." Then to me. "It was a pleasure, as always." He dipped his head, then left.

Parker didn't stop him this time.

Once the office door was shut again, Parker swore.

"What happened?" I hopped off the desk, ready to pepper them with questions, but Andre groaned again.

"Long story. We're good for now. I have to get back to my apartment." Then he reached for the trashcan and lost his lunch.

"Shit, this is going to be a bad one." Parker grabbed his arm and helped him stand.

"I'll take care of Lafe," Grey said, helping him out of the chair. "You'll get Andre back to his apartment?"

"Yup," Parker grunted. I rushed forward to open the office door. When they left, I followed Parker. I knew nothing about helping someone come down from drugs, but I learned a thing or two about migraines.

Parker's gaze lingered on me as we stopped at Andre's door.

"What?" I asked, almost defensively, as Parker fished out Andre's keys and unlocked the door.

"What are you doing, Little Love?" he asked. Although, the playfulness was drained from both his tone and expression.

"Helping. What does it look like I'm doing?" The door swung open, and I raced ahead to Andre's bedroom. The bed was made almost to military standards, which wasn't surprising. I pulled down the covers and stood back for Parker to help get Andre into bed.

While he was situating him against the pillows, I took off his shoes.

"I'll stay here with him to make sure he's okay."

I expected a clever comment from Parker, or some kind of tease. It never came. When I glanced back, he watched me with an indecipherable expression. Stepping forward, he pressed a kiss to my forehead and walked toward the door.

"Take care of him," was all he said.

Distantly, I heard the door shut and the beeping of the lock.

I started prepping the room to ensure it was as comfortable as it could be while Andre was in this state. I closed the curtains and lowered the temperature. Then I grabbed a trashcan and stuck it by his bed.

"Medicine. Nightstand," he groaned.

Opening the top drawer, I found the bottle rolling around. It wasn't hard, since there was barely anything in here at all except a notebook and a couple of extra phones.

I got a glass of water and a cool washcloth. Then when I went back to the bedroom, he'd flopped onto his back and thrown the covers off.

"Here," I whispered and held out the medicine and water. He clumsily gulped it down, only getting a little water on his shirt, and then he fell back, moaning.

I glanced toward the door, then back to him. Taking a deep breath, I made a decision. The bed depressed as I climbed on and stepped over him. I settled with my back against the headboard and touched his shoulder. "Put your head on my lap."

He opened an eye, then shut it, but inched down the bed so he could place his head over my thighs. I folded the washcloth over his forehead and eyes and started running my fingers through his hair and over his scalp. Being careful, I massaged his temples and hit the pressure points the best I could without causing additional pain.

This was a fine line that I used to be good at walking. My roommate in college had terrible stress headaches and this used to help her.

I didn't mind doing this for Andre. In fact, I enjoyed being useful. It was a rare feeling here, especially when things seemed to be going up in flames around them.

"You're good at this," he said groggily.

I hummed, not wanting to bother him with conversation.

"You act tough, but the way you're taking care of me, you're a fucking regular little wifey." The words were almost intelligible.

There wasn't an opportunity to reply because shortly after, he fell asleep. I kept up the movements, helping alleviate the pain as long as I could, but eventually I got tired and dozed off and on against the headboard.

Andre wasn't as hard as he had made me first believe.

I just wasn't sure what to do with that information. Not

when I repeatedly found myself in the same position over and over again.

Vicente was escalating his attacks against the brothers. Who knew how long we'd be safe here.

Could I stay? Did I want to?

I wasn't sure what to do with that information either.

27

PARKER

I swung my keys around my finger as I prowled through the commons. Some of our men dipped their heads in greeting, but Anton jogged to catch me.

"Sir. Where are you going?"

"Out." I sent him a grin, but it dropped as soon as I faced forward again. Anton was more of Grey's man than he was mine. Still, he wouldn't jeopardize his life by trying to stop me. Which was precisely what he'd do if he tried.

Die. Painfully.

So much fury, the likes I'd never known before, simmered under my skin. Just behind my sternum was a swirling vat of molten rage thrashing against my ribs, threatening to spill over into the rest of my body. I could practically feel the ghost of it in my fingers and toes.

Fucking Vicente.

Fuck that motherfucker to his grave. Which is exactly where I wanted him.

Before the break in our bastard brother bond. Before Amorette. Hell, even before yesterday, I only wanted out. Yeah, I wanted to make it a painful break and give Vicente a dose of his own medicine. And take my part of the Institution with me.

But now?

Now, I wanted to take everything from the devil himself, and make him bleed while he watched. Then, once he knew he'd lost everything, I wanted to take one of Grey's serrated knives and have a go at his gut. Play around for a while.

I had a feeling nothing would be quite as satisfying as the warmth of his quickly cooling blood coating my skin. It would be one of those fleeting moments that I'd know only in that second and never again.

It would be worth every inch of required sacrifice to experience it.

"Andre said no one was to get in or out of the compound. It's too dangerous." Anton's voice shook, a sure sign that he knew what he was doing.

"Hmm." I slowed to a stop and turned to face him. "Is Andre the King of the compound, and I just didn't know it?"

I swiped my thumb over my bottom lip, highlighting the smile trying to break free. Some people frowned when they were angry. Some had faces twisted with terrible rage.

But since I'd been maybe twelve or thirteen, I smiled. It didn't matter if I was angry, frustrated, or sad. I smiled. All the ways I'd serve revenge cold were too good to not smile about. It was what kept me going.

Anton glanced at my mouth and gulped. He at least knew this little quirk about me, which wasn't saying much. I smiled all the fucking time. The smirk was my signature look.

Who knew... Maybe there was something in my eyes that gave away exactly how much patience I didn't have.

"No, sir. But we've talked to our friends outside the

island. It's not safe for you to leave. Andre gave the order until things died down a little."

"When are they going to die down?" I mused and took a step forward. "When Vicente has humiliated us until we can't show our faces? When our people who are *not* on the island are dead? Until one or all of my brothers are dead? How about when he razes the island to the ground for fucking giggles? Will it be safe for us then?"

His face paled as I took another step toward him. Then another until his back slammed against the wall. I reached up my hands, and he flinched.

I grinned even wider as I gently straightened the collar on his black button-down and smoothed my hands down his shoulders. "How about this? I'm leaving. I have shit to do, and unlike my weak-ass brother, I won't hide under a rock until the deck is so stacked against us we're dead, anyway."

Anton dropped his dark gaze, then glared back at me with false bravado. "Fine. But I'm going with you."

"Is that so? And what are you going to do when Andre asks why you disobeyed a direct order?"

He flexed his hands at his side, fear clinging to him like a bad perfume. "I'm going to tell him I kept his baby brother alive."

Well, well. What do you know? Maybe Anton should be my friend instead of Grey's.

I clapped his back and started pushing him toward the doors. "Why didn't you say you wanted to tag along from the beginning?"

He laughed, and it was almost as dark as Grey's. Not bad. He definitely had potential. I knew Grey had trained him, so he wasn't a complete waste of space if he was coming with me. Anton might even serve a purpose.

More of our underlings cast us curious glances, but no one else tried to get closer. The men at the gate just stepped back when I approached. Glad to see some of our men still had their wits about them.

"I'm going to do the checks and get the chopper ready. You can help, or you can sit in the front and look pretty." I let go of his scruff as I started walking around the chopper.

He helped, though that wasn't surprising.

By the time we were in the air, I still hadn't received a call from Andre. Either he was still down from his migraine yesterday, or none of the soldiers had ratted on me. I'd like to think the latter. Regardless, I'd find out soon enough.

"Where are we headed?" Anton's voice crackled over the headset.

The sun was setting and soon it would be dark. He should have had a clue. Maybe it *was* a mistake to bring him.

"A club in LA. It's Vicente's favorite money maker." I glanced at him. "And run by Maikel, my least favorite uncle."

"Your only uncle," Anton added.

I shrugged. Semantics didn't really matter. I wasn't fond of anyone in the Institution, but I did have a little extra hate in my heart for what Vicente loved the most. That was this club. And Maikel because he ran it.

"What is it? A nightclub?"

"The front is. The back is a strip club and a gambling hotbed for organized crime in the US."

"You're not worried about the Feds tracking you? Surely, you're a known member of the Castillo cartel." He glanced over at me with the lights on the dash highlighting his harsh features.

Of course, they knew. But there were bigger fish to fry

when we handed them pawns and enemies from time to time. Vicente got to keep his hands clean, and the Feds looked good. The public never knew they were taken as part of an agreement between the cartel and the Feds.

They even gave us special permission to fly this beauty over the border.

That wasn't a relationship I feared would turn on us anytime soon. Not while Andre was around. For all his faults, he handled his business with rigid precision.

"Not a concern," I answered as we dipped to the right.

Anton didn't say another word the rest of the flight. He kept his gaze locked on the horizon, probably wondering if this was to be his last trip to the US. He'd be fine, but the man was definitely gearing himself up for something.

When we landed and climbed into the car waiting for me, I called Jorge. He didn't waste my time with useless questions, instead jumping right into the thick of important information.

"Vicente is at his mansion like we suspected. Maikel is locked away in his gallery, but Sanders is there. In case you want to have a little fun. All our men are accounted for." He hung up.

Perfect. Sanders was a little bitch who thought he was a big shot because he ran guns for Vicente, among a few other dangerous items. Of all the factions, he was probably one of the savviest businessmen Vicente worked with, but he was also an American-born man who came over to the dark side after an unfortunate set of choices in college. He was also not much older than me.

He'd always had a chip on his shoulder because he thought my brothers and I were more important than we were.

"Please stop smiling. It's giving me the wrong impression of what we're about to do here."

"We're here to fuck shit up." I clapped him on the back as we moved through traffic. It wouldn't be long now, and I'd be able to upset Vicente just a little bit. It wasn't the satisfaction I was looking for, but it would do until that day came.

And it would. Eventually.

Hopefully, sooner rather than later.

At least for this trip, my brothers and our sweet little love were tucked safely away in the compound. I didn't like the guilt of Little Love's kidnapping on my shoulders. The looks my brothers gave me were enough to shrivel my balls up.

No, thank you. Let's not do that again.

Anton cursed periodically right up until we stopped at the front entrance. I hopped out and locked the vehicle.

"Sir," the valet said as he reached out his hands to take the keys. I pretended to toss them at his face, and when he flinched, I pocketed them instead.

"I'm a family friend. You won't want to tow it. Otherwise, it will be your head." I winked, letting the thicker part of my accent bleed through. I studied so many languages I didn't use one unless it suited me. And now, it suited.

The young kid of barely twenty-one paled and stepped back. Apparently, the cat got his tongue. Perfect. I wouldn't be here that long.

Neither would he.

This particular club sat outside the city proper, and Vicente owned the real estate two blocks in every direction. It made everyone's life much easier when there were fewer spying eyes.

The entrance line was primarily men and mostly wrapped around the side of the building well into the alley. There were a few women here and there, but the real beauties were either on the stage or had already been pulled from the line to enter.

"That's Mr. Adair." I heard whispered at the entrance as the bouncer stepped back. At least one of the people working the door recognized me. And it seemed from the reverence in their voice, they weren't aware of our little family squabble.

Fantastic.

The first floor was all stages and lights. Women in various levels of undress twined around the poles while one main dancer took the spotlight on the stage. But I wasn't here for this level. I was here for the back room. Or the gambling floor.

Anton walked two steps behind me. When I glanced back, he had his hand on his waist, where his conveniently tucked gun was, as he glared at anyone who looked like they would breathe in my direction.

At the back of the club, one woman with a shimmering evening gown stood with a clipboard. Something much too classy for the strip floor.

"They've been here for three hours. I don't care if you can't take them to the basement, they need to go." She dropped her hand from her headpiece and whirled around.

Her eyes widened when she saw me, and her bottom lip trembled.

"Uh, Mr. um, Mr. Adair. It's a pleasure to meet you," she stammered. Up close, she was close to fifty. Though from a distance, she didn't look a day over thirty. This must be the manager of Maikel's club. How progressive of that misogynistic asshole to have a woman running the LA club. Although, the US did things a little differently.

"Please, drop the ums, love. It's just Mr. Adair." I stopped close to her as I pulled a hand to my lips and pressed a kiss against her knuckles.

Could she see the chaos I was about to wreck in my eyes?

I hoped not. It was far more fun that way.

"Of-Of course. Mr. Adair." A flush crept up her neck, which must have been fierce to show with such brightness under the flashing neon lights. "What can we do for you this evening? Are you here to enjoy our hospitality? We can have a VIP room set up for you and your...." She most likely was going to say guest, but one look at Anton and anyone would know he was there to bring death at my behest. "Man."

"Unnecessary. I'm more intrigued by what you were just chatting about over your radio. What kind of problem is the club experiencing?"

"Oh. Oh!" She took on a disgruntled expression. "We have a few small celebrities here tonight. Isaac Kim and Atlas Jones are here with their manager, Joaquin Amaya. They're two of America's *It* faces for men right now. And at least one of them knows how to count cards. They're losing every few hands, then stealing everything from the house. We can't give them the standard treatment because their arrival was very public."

Models....The very ones Amorette believed had the Qing Dynasty vase. I couldn't have planned this better.

I bet they knew Grace.

"Show me their table. I'll take care of it."

"Sir," she said and cleared her throat, dropping her gaze to the floor like she was afraid to speak her next words. "You can't treat them the same here in the US. They're public figures. We—"

I waved a hand. "Absolutely understood. I won't make a

scene. Not a public one, anyway...And don't worry. I won't leave any physical marks on the men."

She relaxed when she saw my smile, not showing the same alarm Anton had. "Good, good. Right this way." She escorted us down the glossy black hallway until the room opened up into a gambling hall. The room was Old-World elegance with mahogany wood panels, rich tapestries, and burning candlesticks on podiums around the edges of the room. Tables and tables were stuffed into the middle to rival the best Las Vegas casinos. Only there was a more sinister vibe here.

Most of these players walked the darker side of the law. Not like the amateur gamblers in Vegas. I'd love to hear how the models heard about this club.

"There they are, sir." She nodded to a table right in the center of the room where a bouncer was arguing heatedly with a man.

There was the trio among two other groups of patrons. But they were all striking. The Asian man was slender and all angles with a shock of shimmering blue-black hair hanging in his face. He watched the table with a smirk and continued to play even as the tan man argued. The black man beside him had skin so smooth it practically glowed under the lights. Cut cheekbones and full lips. He looked bored as he skimmed between the cards and his other friend.

The tan man turned back around with a snarl on his lips. He was of some kind of Hispanic descent. No less beautiful than the other two.

"Which man did you say was their manager?" I played dumb.

The manager laughed. "It's hard to tell, right? They are all gorgeous. But the man who was arguing is their manager,

Joaquin. You just missed their fourth, who left about thirty minutes ago. He's their bodyguard and just as beautiful but in a more rugged way." Her appreciation oozed from her pores as she watched them.

"Perfect. I'm going to sit at this table here for a few minutes, and when I'm ready, I'll approach. No one else is to bother them until I've had time to make my own assessment."

The man standing over Joaquin touched his ear, mumbled something, and shot one final glare at Joaquin's head as he stomped away. Joaquin flipped him off over his shoulder without removing his eyes from the table.

Both Joaquin and the Asian man, Isaac Kim, watched the table with neutral intensity. Their faces showed no emotion, yet their eyes drank in everything from the minute movement of the dealer's hands to the cards being flipped and even what the other patrons at the table were doing.

Isaac grinned and struck up a light conversation with the man and woman next to him, who were dazzled by his looks. Or maybe his celebrity status. It could be either.

"They're skilled," Anton quietly noted.

I nodded. They certainly were. "They're young con-men in the making." With an eye for tricks and a head for numbers. Of course, they could be shit at it, but only time would tell. And luckily, I had plenty of it in this dark corner of the gambling hall.

We sat there for almost two hours, watching this young trio of men earn millions from the house. One man with a large cowboy hat and a mustache big enough to cover Texas realized what they were up to and he wasn't snowed by their good looks.

"What the fucking hell are you doing?" He stood up, all bluster and crude hand gestures. Yet, in the grand scheme of things, he was a small man with no muscle, no intimidation factor. "You fuckers are cheating."

He swung and hit Joaquin right in the face. His head snapped back. His buddies both jumped up to take his back, but I was already weaving around the table to stop an altercation. I raised a hand to let the approaching manager know I had this taken care of.

She stopped in her tracks but didn't look away. Mainly because she was drinking them in with a hungry gaze.

"Sanders," I said cheerily, slapping a heavy hand down on his nape. "Funny seeing you here." His eyes widened seconds before recognition dawned, and a sneer curled his top lip.

"You fucking traitor, you—"

"Shh." I placed a finger on his lips as I nodded Anton toward the trio. "Take these fine men back to our ride. I'd like to have a word with them."

"Hell no," Joaquin snarled. "We need to cash out. There's at least three mil in chips here." He tapped the chips harshly, knocking some over.

"You leave with the chips, or you leave with your lives. Your choice." I shrugged. The staff here wouldn't kill them, not if they were indeed celebrities, but they didn't know that. Anyone else scamming the system would get thrown in the basement with a bullet to the head and a few broken bones for good measure.

Atlas placed a hand on Joaquin's shoulder and shook his head. So, Joaquin was the hothead. He looked between his two friends and nodded. It was a chore, but he backed down from his anger.

"Fine," he grunted and shrugged out of Atlas' hold. Anton wasted no time moving them through the crowd, leaving me alone with good old Sanders.

"You a dead man, Adair," Sanders whispered gleefully.

"Is that right?" I turned back to him with a smirk.

"All the men in Vicente's inner circle are looking for you."

"They're not looking very hard," I remarked drily. "We've been at our home the entire time."

Some of the excitement dimmed in his eyes. Not because he was afraid of me but because he lacked a comeback. Vicente was an intelligent man—one of the smartest. Yet I couldn't understand why he kept this piece of shit around. Just because he had a head for business didn't mean he had the guts and wits to really survive in the Institution. Or outside of it.

"Listen, I just came here to cause some trouble." I smiled, confusing him even more.

"Why would you admit that?"

"Because you're going to help me." I peered past his shoulder to the candles burning next to the column. A column draped in a dark, mysterious tapestry like something from medieval England.

"Huh?"

I didn't give him any time to rub his two brain cells together. As if perfectly timed, a patron lightly brushed my back, and I stumbled into Sanders, giving him a helping push into the candles. His hat brushed them and immediately burst into flames, probably a by-product of whatever treatment he sprayed on the felt to keep it crisp.

His screams were music to my ears as he whipped it off his head and waved it in the air. Oh, look, he caught the tapestry on fire. In true old-fabric fashion, the fire raced up the column.

People yelled and raced toward the exits as the manager

grabbed my arm. The fire alarm started to blare and the water sprinklers kicked on.

"Mr. Adair! You have to get out of here!" She tried to pull me toward the door, but I waved her off.

"Help the patrons. I'll see myself out." Pivoting on my heel, I left her standing next to a now empty table. The patrons wasted no time exiting all on their own. They valued their lives more than the value of the chips.

I whistled as I took the long way out, knocking over candles and helping the other tapestries along. Might as well make sure the place truly burns. If you're taking the time to cause trouble, it better be worth it.

28

ANDRE

"He did what?" I slammed my fist down on the desk.

Juan, the youngest brother of our head of security, gulped and took a step back. He glanced at the door then back at me with more than a little fear in his eyes.

"Answer me!" I roared, pushing out of my chair and to my feet.

"H-h-he left. Parker left with Anton."

I took a deep breath through my nose to compose myself. Once I let it out, I asked, "When?"

"Yesterday. He took the chopper yesterday." Juan trembled as I took his measure. He was a good kid. His brother was the most competent man I'd met, and after he'd proven his incorruptible loyalty, we'd made him our head of security. It didn't hurt that his entire family lived on the island, making it hard for Vicente to get his hands on any leverage over Rodrigo.

"And it's..." I looked at my watch. "Ten-fucking-thirty in the morning, and he's still not back? What the fuck!" I spun and kicked my office chair into the desk. It clattered to the floor, and I kicked it again.

"Get the hell out," I yelled and slammed the door as soon as he left. Dialing Parker, I struggled to get my breathing under control. All the blood rushed to my face, and my head felt like it was about to burst.

No answer. Figures.

Next, I dialed. Garcia.

I didn't operate a faction like the brothers. More like a spy ring. I dealt in secrets and favors and occasionally threw people to the feds. Mostly it was under Vicente's orders, but I fostered relationships where I could in case he ever flipped against us.

Laughing, I shook my head. When, not if. We all knew it had only been a matter of time.

"Garcia." A raspy voice over the speaker.

"Has anything happened in the last eighteen hours I need to know about?"

He whistled, drawing it out. Garcia knew I hated that shit, but he did it anyway. He was loyal to the bone, so I put up with it.

"You mean the youngest bastard son of Vicente burning down Vicente's favorite club in LA? I thought you might not know about that."

He fucking did what?

I curled my fingers on the black mat under the keyboard.

And he was still unaccounted for. Because he was a fucking spoiled brat, who was retaliating against Vicente for cutting down his complex, thought-out plans before they ever left the ground.

"I can tell from the rage coming down the line that was exactly the information you were looking for. And to answer your question, no, Vicente doesn't have him. Vicente is currently balls-deep inside his two favorite concubines to fuck his anger away."

Flinching, I reeled back from the phone. Pilar was one of his favorites, and when he was in this shitty of a mood, he was never kind.

"Not Pilar," he said softly. "She lost her rank when you fell from his good graces."

I breathed a sigh of release. Except it only went so far. Being his favorite protected her. If she wasn't a favorite, any of his men could have her and snap her neck if they had the whim.

No consequences.

"Where is he?"

There was a pause. "That, I don't know. He's not at the mansion or in Vicente's hands. That's all I know."

"Thanks." I hit the end button and kicked my chair again.

Fuck Parker for tying my hands like this.

I could engage my contacts and try to find him, placing my network at risk of exposure. And fucking hoped we found him before he got himself tortured to death.

Burning down Vicente's favorite US hangout? He was a fucking idiot.

The laugh that spilled from my lips grated against my skin like jagged glass. If I did that, I could expose how much we didn't have our shit together. Going after him myself after he made a colossal move like that put me at risk too. Vicente probably had two or ten of his best men after Parker right now. And I would purely be a bonus if they caught me too.

Or I could sit on my ass and hope he returned in one piece.

When I saw him again, I was going to fucking strangle him.

I called Garcia back. "Keep your ears to the ground. If he's taken in, we need to extract him."

"Are you asking me to engage the network to find him?"

"No," I said with too much force. "No." I softened my tone. "You're not to engage anyone to find him. The only way you're to act is if he's actually taken. Outside of that, everything runs as normal."

We hung up a second time, and I reached into the cabinet and pulled out the tequila. I saved this particularly strong brand for the really shitty times in my life.

It was the one liquor that could knock me on my ass.

Uncapping it, I glanced at the glasses tucked away. Fuck it. Today's a straight-from-the-bottle type of day.

The first swig burned so good as it went down. I sputtered out a cough and pounded my chest. Whether it was an extra-large dose or wishful thinking, the warm tingling was already traveling through my limbs to my fingers and toes.

I took another drink for good measure.

Today was a wasted day. I'd get nothing done here, so I might as well head to my apartment to wallow in my self-hatred in peace.

Blanca hovered in the hallway, bouncing between the rooms on her cleaning routine. She took one look at me and the tequila in my hand, squeaked, then ducked into Parker's "office."

Fucking right. I was about to be on the bender from hell.

I'd avoid myself too.

Fifteen feet from my apartment and sweet Amorette stepped out of the movie room, muttering in elementary Spanish.

"Bate, bate, chocolate. Mixing choc—" She sealed her lips when she saw me.

"Watching Dora?" I snickered, then let out a bubbling laugh. Her eyes widened and dropped to the half-empty bottle of tequila still clutched in my hand. Oh yeah, I still had the liquor. I hadn't drunk half today, though. This was a cumulation of many terrible days.

I lifted it to my lips for a tiny sip. I wanted to feel good for the next few hours. And maybe forget the shit storm that was brewing right now. I didn't want to pass out before I got there.

She narrowed her eyes at me, and I loved it—the blue swirling into a darkening gray with her anger. Amorette was like a spitting kitten with her hackles up.

"Come on," I held out a hand.

She glanced at it with more than a little suspicion. I shook it.

"I won't bite, not unless you ask me to." She rolled her eyes and still didn't take it, so I stepped closer. My chest nearly brushed hers, and she held her breath as I breathed her in. Sweet pomegranate shampoo smelled good on her. "I've had a shit day, and it's only going to get worse from here. Come take care of me like the good wifey you are. Maybe I'll even share a secret or two for your time," I said, dropping my voice into a deep whisper.

She tipped her head back. "You don't play fair."

"I don't play at all. Maybe that's the problem. I should have more fun like Parker. Or fuck, even like Grey."

Throwing an arm out, she stepped back. "Lead the way, and I'll follow. I'll at least make sure you don't pass out in your own puke."

"I don't drink that much, Wifey. My stomach's too strong for that."

"Mm-hm."

"Believe it or not, my brothers and I know how to hold our liquor." She was deathly quiet behind me as I unlocked the door. I pushed it open and peeked over my shoulder. "Lafe can get carried away with the hardcore stuff, but liquor isn't a problem for him."

She nodded, not believing a word I said. No problem. Only time would show her I was telling the truth. If we had the time.

Fucking dark thoughts. It was time for another drink.

"Here," I said, holding out the bottle.

"I don't like that stuff." Amorette wrinkled up her nose.

"Live a little. I don't like to be the only one drinking. It's bad for the vibe." I pushed the bottle to her chest, and she took it.

"Vibe? That's not something I'd ever imagine you saying," she said as she lifted the bottle to her face and sniffed. She wrinkled her nose, and it was adorable as shit. "I'll take a drink, but I want you to talk to me."

"Done," I threw myself back on the couch, lining the back with my arm. "What do you want to know?" After she took a sip, I reached for the bottle and was soon left gasping.

"You don't have any lemon or salt or anything?"

"No, sorry. It's just you, me, and the bottle." I could have said something more salacious but left it at that.

"Why is this a drinking day?" she asked with her face still scrunched.

"Ah, that's a double-sip answer." I passed the bottle back to her, and she obediently took another swig. I could get behind an Amorette that followed orders. "My siblings are assholes and sometimes asshole idiots. Parker is currently out wreaking havoc that I'll have to clean up later. Although, with the current standing in the Institution, it might not be that clear cut anymore. So, I'm hiding my head in the sand for the time being."

She furrowed her brow and moved past me, but I snagged her thigh and pulled her down into the space next to my hip. "Shouldn't you go get him if he's in danger?"

"No, that's the last thing I should do. For all his idiocy, he's good at getting out of his own messes. Usually. Any attempt I make to retrieve him would just throw him off and put him *and me* in more danger. And everyone else by default, including you, Wifey." I bopped her cute nose.

Scowling, she turned to face me. "Why did he leave?"

"Arrogance? Hurt feelings? Who fucking knows." I used the remote to dim the lights and turn on the music.

Dropping her gaze, Amorette chewed her lip in thought as if she wanted to ask me something, but didn't know if she actually wanted to go through with it.

"Go ahead. Say whatever is on your mind." I scooted down to rest my head more firmly on the armrest.

"Do you think you'll win against Vicente?" She speared me with a gaze so intense it almost shocked me out of my buzz.

"It's either we win, or we die. There's no way to tell how the cards will fall right now."

Her fingers first brushed the buttons of my shirt on my chest, then she slid them down to my stomach. I grabbed her waist and rearranged her to straddle my hips. Not unlike the plane. Except this time, I wasn't caught off guard. And I wasn't flying a plane.

"What about you, hm? Why did you come back to us? Matías' would have been an easy place to escape from. His security is laughable, and you might, keyword *might* have found someone to take you to the airport."

She pushed against my chest, but when I didn't let her

up, she settled her weight firmly over my hardening cock. Fuck. This was a bad idea. I handed her the bottle. I needed her just a little more wasted, so she didn't suddenly jump up when she realized how she sat over me like last time.

Without hesitation, she took a healthy swig and gave the bottle back. She wiped her mouth with the back of her hand and wheezed through the burn.

"Damn, that's strong. Terrible aftertaste too."

"Don't worry, you'll get used to it." I set the bottle on the table and slid my hands up her thighs. She was in some kind of sundress that made her look too young and innocent for this world. Like a girl barely able to drink on holiday with her family, rather than a woman used to defending battered women and was now caught in the middle of the Institution.

"Oh, will I? You're acting like this will be a common occurrence." She raised one brow.

Was Amorette flirting with me? I gave her a half smile while smoothing my thumbs just under the edge of her dress.

"Why not? My brothers are endless headaches, and I could really use some company. Especially beautiful, feisty company."

She grinned ruefully. "And I'm not a headache? I thought I would have been the worst kind."

"You've never been *that* kind of headache. I always understood you and your actions, even when you struggled with what was right and wrong. You wanted to get back to your life, and you wanted away from us criminals. But you came back to us all on your own." That was a stretch, but I was going off of her own admission.

She stiffened, and instead of letting her have her moment of hesitation, I reached around, flattening my palm against her lower back. With the barest amount of pressure, she leaned forward, until we were almost chest-to-chest.

And she let me.

I used my thumb to tip her face up. Her sparkling gray eyes were just glazed enough that I knew she was good and tipsy.

"Why did you come back, Wifey?"

"Why are you calling me wifey?" she whispered, her gaze dropping to my lips.

"Why are you avoiding the question?" I couldn't help the closed-lipped smile. Even with a few drinks under her belt, she still answered a question with a question. That must have been drilled into her during law school.

She blew out a breath and dropped her forehead on my shoulder. Rubbing both hands up and down her back, I enjoyed the feel of her small, curvy body.

"I wanted to, and I think that makes me an idiot," she mumbled against my chest.

Laughing, I sat up, holding a hand to the back of her head and using her other to adjust her legs around my waist. "Then that's idiocy I can get behind. I'm the fucking idiot who's trying to keep us all together."

"I'd love to see Grace again," she sighed against my neck.

"You will, I promise. As soon as Vicente is a non-issue, we'll bring her to a safe location to meet you. It just can't be here...or in the US." I grabbed the bottle for another sip.

"But you won't let me go?" She leaned back to grab the bottle and take her own sip.

"Never." I wasn't even sure where that came from. The tequila? The feel of her pressed up against my hard cock? Fuck it. Even if I would let her go, Grey wouldn't. And I had a feeling neither would Lafe or Parker.

I slammed my lips against hers and her hands instantly buried in my hair.

The erotic beat of the music pulsed through my body as I turned to sit Amorette on the couch. Untwining her legs, I pushed my fingers under the sides of her panties and pulled them down.

I tossed them in the corner as soon as they were off and she spread her legs, baring that sweet pussy. Just a small thatch of short black hair covering the top.

Groaning, I dropped my head and buried my face. I ate her out like she was my last meal. I licked, bit, teased. Every feminine noise I drew from her, every grasp of her fingers in my hair. I lived for this. The control, the struggle that she had in letting go.

I loved every single fucking minute of it.

The light from the stereo flashed across her face, lighting up the ecstasy that was fast approaching. I memorized the way her brows pulled together, and her lids dropped to cover her eyes. The deep indent of her teeth in her bottom lip was especially captivating. Like I made her feel so good she couldn't help but cause herself a little pain to balance out the pleasure.

"MORE," she pleaded.

Amorette wanted something inside her, but I wanted her to come like this. The first time I felt her grip, I wanted it on my cock. Not my fingers. Not my tongue.

On my cock as I thrust deep inside her.

Her hips flexed, and her fingers twitched. She was almost there.

Her lips pulsed lightly against my tongue when I dipped down to lick around her entrance, then back up to suck on her clit. So responsive, exactly what I enjoyed in my lovers.

She groaned, tossing her head back, pulling tight on my hair. So close.

I whisked the sundress off her body, leaving her clad in a tiny bralette. Who had bought that sinful garment? Fuck, she was so sweet in it.

That went too.

Reaching down, I used one hand to free my aching cock, all while drinking in the beauty of her naked body. Smooth, flawless skin. Perky round tits. So fucking tiny.

And a gorgeous pussy so red and wet. I used my thumb to trace around her slit as I sucked that sensitive bundle of nerves. Over and over, I ran my tongue across it until suddenly, she gasped and cried my name.

Now.

I slammed home, giving her all of my cock until I was fully seated.

Fuck... so wet. She was so damn wet.

I braced her hips with my hands and they nearly spanned her entire waist. Then I started furiously pumping. I couldn't help it. Her head thrashed back and forth against the cushion as her fingernails bit into my biceps.

"You take my cock so fucking good," I growled and started to pull her back as I thrust forward, getting as deep as I could.

She fluttered and squeezed me, nearly making my eyes cross. Then her gaze snapped to mine as her pussy clamped down so hard, I exploded on the spot. Jet after jet, I pumped everything I had into her.

"Holy. Fucking. Shit." I gasped. I couldn't stop. I continued to thrust into her with short, hard movements. "So. Hot. Fuck."

Even in her second orgasm, her eyes stayed glued to mine, until we were both panting. She'd have bruises on her hips and in the back of my mind, the idea of her going to my brothers with my mark on her thrilled me.

Let them see how much we enjoyed each other.

Lethargy swept over me, and somehow, in my hazy mind, we arranged ourselves on the couch, with me still tucked inside.

This was exactly the medicine I needed.

Or at least, that was my last thought before I passed out. I couldn't even remember why I'd needed to drink in the first place.

29

GREY

Where the fuck was Amorette?

It was just after ten, and she wasn't in the apartment or the movie room. Unlikely, but I checked the gym and the offices too. Parker had given her a laptop, but she was only allowed to use it at his place.

Where was she?

I banged my fist on Lafe's door. He'd been helping her with Spanish, so it wasn't crazy to think that he was helping her study, and she lost track of time.

Footsteps creaked closer, and when he opened the door, he barely looked present. Dark purple circles covered the bags under his eyes, and his hair was a sopping wet mess.

"What happened to you?" I barked. When I'd left him, he was sober and going to bed. He still looked like shit.

Lafe shrugged. "I just got out of the shower."

His voice was strong, and his eyes were focused. Good, but he hadn't slept. He started to close the door, but I kicked it open. "We're going to revisit this, but first, is Amorette in there with you?"

Some of the life popped back into his eyes for a brief

second. "No, why would she be?" And then he sunk back into his pathetic existence.

I shook my head and backed away. Parker wasn't here. Enrique had told me all about that shit show Parker had conducted yesterday. He still wasn't back, but who the fuck cared. He did what he wanted and didn't give a damn about anyone else.

"What's wrong?" Lafe called after me, but I was already marching down the hallway.

My phone rang. "What?"

Enrique coughed. "*Hielo*! It's burning down! Someone set fire to the building!"

"Argh!" I dropped my head back and screamed at the ceiling. "My fucking *hotel*?" My entire life had been put into that business. I lived for the fights, but I'd build that hotel up from the ground.

"What happened?" Lafe caught up to me and yanked on my arm. "What happened?"

"Vicente is burning down my fucking hotel."

"How do you know it's Vicente?" Clarity hit Lafe's eyes as the seriousness of the situation sobered him up.

"Because Parker torched his favorite spot yesterday." I brought the phone back up to my ear. "Enrique, how bad is it?"

More coughing and sirens in the background. "We've called for help, but the sprinkler system isn't working. We're trying...We're trying."

Unimaginable rage set in as I stomped to Andre's door. Flames should have sprouted in my steps because I was so fucking incensed.

Lafe's phone rang, and he ran back to his apartment to get it.

"I'll be there. Two hours. I'll be there if I have to fucking take the boat." I hung up and sent out a series of texts to my contacts in the city.

First, I'd save what I could of the hotel. That was my first priority. Then set up safeguards to keep Vicente's men out of it.

When that was done, Vicente would die—a horribly painful death.

I'd strap him to the whipping post and dare his people to save his old ass.

I rained down my anger on Andre's door. It took almost three minutes for him to shout from inside, then finally unlock and open it.

His eyes were bloodshot with his shirt half open and the top of his pants were undone. I narrowed my eyes. He was never disheveled, not like this. His cock was tucked away with the base showing.

Before I brought my gaze back to his face, I knew with a sinking in my stomach where Amorette was. It seemed to take eons for my eyes to meet his. When we finally locked eyes, my green to his brown.

"I fucking hate you," I whispered. He'd really fucked with Lafe's head at one time, but I stayed out of it. I understood it. We all did. And at the end of the day, it wasn't any of my concern. We tried to live our lives the best we could.

I'd never had an issue with Andre, personally.

Except right now, seeing him standing there after fucking Amorette minutes or even hours ago, I hated his fucking guts.

Because my already bubbling rage needed somewhere to go, I attacked Andre, using my shoulder to slam into his stomach and tackling him to the ground. I wailed on his face, and he was still so wasted he didn't stand a chance.

Amorette yelled, but it was a minute before she popped

into the hallway. When she did, her sundress was askew, and she dove to knock me off of Andre.

Glad to see where her loyalties lie.

"Get your fucking hands off me." I pried her arms from around my shoulders, careful not to hurt her.

"Stop! What are you doing?" she yelled right in my ear as she wrapped her arms and legs around me. Automatically, I dropped my hands to her ass, only to find her bare underneath.

I glared at Andre as he blinked and sat up. A little blood trickled from his lip and he wiped it away. "What is your problem?"

"My problem is my hotel is burning down, and you're in here fucking *my girl*."

"Your girl? You mean the girl we've all been taking care of? The one you watched ride my lap on the plane? *That girl*?" Andre struggled to push to his feet, and when he stood, he fell into the wall. Then slapped it. "Fuck. Did you say your hotel is on fire?" He turned and stumbled down the hall, disappearing from sight and moaning about his aching head.

Amorette still clung to me, her body trembling. I tried to pull her back, but she wouldn't budge.

Sighing, I stood and followed Andre into the living room. Amorette's panties were discarded in the corner, and a half-empty bottle of tequila was turned over on the floor. Music still played on the speakers like Andre had tried to set the mood.

How long had she been here? Now that I had a minute to think, he'd been passed out. They fucked hours ago, then took a nap. *How fucking precious.*

I sneered.

"*Mamí,* I need you to get down." I pulled at her arms, but

she still wouldn't let go. Her trembling turned to full-on shakes as she sniffed against my neck. "Are you...are you *crying*?"

I wanted to punch Andre's face in again. What the hell had he done to her to make her cry?

"I—" Then she stopped.

Moving to the couch, I sat down in the middle and tried to urge her to sit up. She refused. Everything inside of me screamed for me to run to the chopper and fly to the hotel, salvage what I could. Help the people, if possible.

But I had a crying girl on my lap, which did more to dampen the rage than anything I'd ever experienced. I drew in a deep breath, closing my eyes. When I was under control, I tipped her face to meet her gaze.

"Did he hurt you?" I asked slowly.

That got her to sit back. "No, absolutely not." She shook her head vigorously.

Her eyes were impossibly blue next to the pink and shiny whites of her eyes. Tears clung to her lashes and wetted the skin underneath. She cried so pretty.

I wiped her face of tears and leaned forward to taste them. Salty but sweet. Just like our wicked little love. Breathing out a soft sigh, I dropped my forehead to hers.

"Tell me why you're crying." A command.

"I'm sorry. I shouldn't have done this." *This*. Fucked Andre.

I wanted to tell her no she shouldn't have. But had I told her he was off limits? Had I told her to stay the hell away from my brothers and their cocks?

They all wanted her. I knew it. They each knew it.

The only one who might be struggling with it was Lafe, but on some level, he couldn't deny his attraction either.

She'd begged me to tell her what I planned and if I wanted to share her.

I hadn't wanted to. But I never found the words to tell her that. And when Parker watched us? Or when she rode Andre? I'd burned for an entirely different reason.

My cock twitched under her ass. Goddamn it.

Grimacing, I wanted to tell her it wasn't her fault, that Andre could fuck a nun seven ways from Sunday when he wanted to, but I also couldn't give her an out either.

Because I was still fucking furious with her.

"I'm sorry. We're not really together, but we are. Even if I did nothing wrong, this still makes me feel like a bad person." She sniffed and turned her face away.

"I'll take you back to my apartment." I needed to take care of shit, and she needed time to gather herself.

"No!" She pressed a hand to my chest. "Take me to the birdcages."

"Hell no. Those are people we don't trust. Whether you fucked Andre or all of my brothers, you're not our enemy."

Her bottom lip trembled as she met my stare. She seemed to be trying to decipher how truthful I was.

"Stop making Amorette cry. We have bigger shit to worry about." Andre breezed back into the room, dressed, hair brushed, and his phone in his hand.

"This is because of you, not me. She thinks she's a bad person because she fucked you." She stiffened in my arms but said nothing. Andre just tossed me a look that said, 'are you serious?'

"Here," I tapped her thigh, and she finally climbed off me. She stopped in the corner to grab her panties, purposely facing the wall as she put them back on. We both watched, and when she turned around, Andre resumed with the shit we should actually be focusing on.

"While I was...occupied," Andre flicked a guilty gaze to Amorette, "Vicente has operated a series of attacks. One on your hotel, burning it like Parker burned his LA club. Another was hanging one of my men from his gates." His mouth pressed together in a grim line. When he glanced up, his eyes showed more emotion than I'd seen in a decade. "He's also taken over one of Lafe's warehouses. It seems the only person he hasn't retaliated against is Parker."

"Because he knows Parker is the one who torched the club..." It made sense. He would have pulled the footage. Talked to the employees.

"What was he thinking?" Andre rubbed his temples. "Vicente wouldn't just take that sitting down. Parker wouldn't be able to hide that shit."

Amorette sat on the end of the couch, not too close to Andre or me, and kept her gaze on the table between us.

"I need to get to the hotel. There's probably a fuck ton of work to be done." I started to stand.

"No," Andre shouted. "That's exactly what Vicente is hoping for. He's trying to draw us out. He'll take us, then use us against Parker."

I laughed. "Like Parker gives a fuck if Vicente has us. He only cares about his revenge and getting out of there. But you know who does give a fuck? I do. For the people that run the hotel. About the fights that I run there." I started for the door.

"You know who else cares? I fucking do!" He pounded his chest. "Good luck getting off the island. All the toys are grounded and shored."

Slowing to a stop, I turned around. "You forget that you're not the only leader around here. I have men just as loyal to me as they are to you."

I skimmed my gaze over Amorette, taking in her sad eyes

and the downturn to her mouth. Then I turned and walked out.

Twenty minutes later, I'd packed a bag and arranged as much backup for the hotel as I could. The boat was my best bet to get there quickly since Parker still had the chopper.

A loud, harsh pounding came at my door like it would splinter the damn thing open. Andre's panicked face met mine when I unlocked it and swung it open with a snarl.

"Lafe's missing. Is he with you?"

No, he fucking wasn't with me. I dropped the bag and ran toward his door.

"I've already checked there!"

"Where the hell is he?"

Andre stopped and typed on his phone. Within seconds it chimed, and his face paled. "He's gone. Lafe left."

"To where?"

"I don't know." Andre gulped and looked up at me.

30

LAFE

Everything Grey said into the phone was like garbled music. I couldn't understand a word after he dropped that bomb.

Vicente burned down Grey's hotel. Because of Parker.

Everything I'd ever been afraid of was happening. All these years, I'd hated everything about the Institution. I'd even hated myself. And for what?

We weren't even in our thirties, and Vicente turned on us. Andre had us hiding out here at the compound because his men were looking for us. There was practically a bounty on our heads.

Parker was right. We should have gotten out of this life years ago. Fled to the US or something. I could have gone to Sweden to see my mom's family. Assuming they'd want to see me.

Hell, they could look at me as the reason that they lost their daughter and sister.

My phone went off. Not the one I used for my brothers, but the one Vicente always used for enforcer jobs.

I ran back, leaving Grey in the hallway. My door had

been left ajar, and I slammed it shut, so Grey didn't follow me. I doubted he would. He had enough to worry about if the hotel was burning.

The burner was in the corner of the kitchen and went off again as I approached it. My heart tumbled over and over inside my chest like it was stuck in the dryer. It beat wildly but seemed to flip with each breath.

My hands were sweaty, and I swiped them on my pants.

This wasn't a coincidence. If Parker had really retaliated by burning down one of his clubs, he wouldn't stop at Grey's hotel. He would target each of us for fun.

Andre and Grey had both been certain that Vicente was after us because of Parker's efforts to break away. I wasn't convinced. He was a psychopath. Turning on us, turning the institution against us, was a hell of a good time for him. If Maikel wasn't such a lap dog, he would have killed him years ago.

Hell, Vicente could be threatened by the small army we'd amassed for ourselves. It was no secret that we lived in a fortress with our own men not associated with the Institution.

I wasn't sure we'd ever find out the real reason he wanted us dead.

That irritating metal chime went off again. That was three, maybe four messages.

He could be taunting me with my men. Or one of my suppliers. It could be any number of threats.

Making the split-second decision to rip the band aid off, I picked up the phone and opened the screen.

It was worse than anything I could have ever imagined.

It was a picture of Amorette.

No.

It was her twin. At a photoshoot.

She was dressed in a classy suit with bold sunglasses in the golden hour. She was so different from Killer. Softer. Sassier maybe.

Hanging industrial lights were scattered overhead, and a large camera was discarded on the table behind her. This had to be taken during the shoot but from a different angle.

And it was on my burner phone from Vicente.

Looks like you were the one to bring the weakness to my house.

And there are two. Are you going to save her too?

The location drop was my warehouse in Brazil. Fuck. That's where most of the product was made and stored. Was the warehouse even mine? Did I even still need to do this business anymore if Vicente was pushing us out?

For a moment, I let that thought sink in. Running drugs for Vicente had become my entire identity. If I stopped, what would I be?

Alive?

I couldn't stay here and fuck it all while Vicente had Amorette's twin. She already hated me, but if I let her sister be taken...I couldn't stomach the look that would be on her face when we had to tell her where Grace was.

I wouldn't be able to do it. Fucking Andre could do it. He was good at making hard decisions for people and destroying their lives.

"*Helvete*," I muttered and pressed the meat of my palms into my eyes. I needed sleep. And food. My current state would get me killed.

Fuck.

Parker was gone.

If I went to Andre, he'd ban me from leaving.

Grey...Grey might help. But if it came down to saving Grace or keeping Amorette, he'd choose to keep her.

Not giving myself time to second guess my decision, I snagged the shoes under the couch and roughly stuffed my feet in them. I grabbed my other phone and ran out the door.

Yelling was coming from Andre's apartment. About...

Shit—I tripped over my feet.

Andre... Andre fucked Amorette.

I wasn't prepared for the way that would punch me in the stomach. He wasn't even *nice* to her.

But I hadn't been either.

No, I needed to focus. Otherwise, Andre would put the island on lockdown. I could do this one thing.

I couldn't save her years ago. And that had stolen a piece of my humanity.

What I could do was save Grace for Amorette. If Vicente took me out after...that would be a mercy.

A few guards shouted to me when I burst through the glass doors. I waved them away and headed for the pad.

That was empty.

Fuck!

There was the plane. That would work. It was a couple of hours' flight, anyway. I pivoted and headed toward the plane. We had a few, and the one I needed was a small two-person Mach business jet. It was much smaller than our other plane, but one person could easily fly this one.

I'd have room to get Grace out too.

But I wouldn't bring her back here. I think Amorette would almost hate that as much as her being in Vicente's hands.

A few soldiers watched from a distance. Some called to each other on their radios, but no one moved to stop me.

Good. Either Andre hadn't given the lockdown order yet, or they were too afraid to stop the junkie brother.

Starting cold, I'd be lucky to get the plane off the ground in an hour. Usually, it took two. Yet as I raced around doing my checks, no one approached. None of my brothers called my phone. They didn't know what Vicente had done.

Or at least not this one act.

I wanted to be thankful. So much could go wrong if he messaged any of them the same picture he'd sent me. But all I had in me right then was an unhealthy level of fear and adrenaline.

Finally, after fifty-one minutes, I was off the ground. Once I was coasting, I opened the burner and looked at the photo of Grace again.

She was Amorette's entire world.

I couldn't—wouldn't let her lose this last piece of herself.

I wouldn't do to her what Andre did to me.

THE LANDING STRIP was on the property, allowing me a good look at the place as I circled around for landing. This warehouse had been part of the drug business long before I took it over, and about five local families worked in the lab. They were compensated handsomely by my company, or by Vicente, if you chose to look at it that way.

No fires were sprouting out of the windows. None of Vicente's men were patrolling the roof. The only oddity was how empty it seemed to be.

After I landed the plane, I armed myself from the stash we always kept onboard. Scanning my surroundings, I pulled my gun out and pointed it at the ground. I had another in the back holster, a knife inside my jeans, and one strapped to my ankle.

This was a suicide mission, but I couldn't walk in empty-handed.

Still, no one came out to greet me.

At any other time, a guard would have been working the tower next to the strip. Guards would have come out to meet me and check my business here. Even if they recognized the plane, they would have come to check on why I'd make a surprise appearance.

Blowing out a breath, I pressed my ear to the door while looking right at the security camera. The light burned bright red, signaling it was turned on. I didn't smile. I didn't try to mouth any words. I glared and flipped my middle finger.

I hoped Vicente was at the monitor station to see exactly how much I hated him. He wouldn't care. But I'd get a tiny bit of satisfaction from it. Andre had never let us show so much to him in the past.

It didn't matter anymore.

I wanted him to know how much I loathed him. If he could know a taste of the hate I had for him, I'd die happy.

No sounds traveled through the door. It was eerily quiet on the other side. The usual sounds of people coming and going and the typical sounds of manufacturing were all missing.

It was a ghost town.

I twisted the handle, and it opened easily. Also wrong.

The Garcias always had the locks engaged and required a badge.

Inside the lobby, papers were scattered over the floor, and some of the equipment was turned over. Not a single sign of life.

Moving deeper into the warehouse, I cased all the hallways before stepping in, checking rooms as I went by. The feeling that I'd been incredibly stupid coming here pressed harder and harder against my temples.

This was a trap.

I knew it with certainty as I reached the end of the last hallway, and no one came into sight. There was no blood, no signs of a struggle. Just one giant mess like a hurricane had blown through years ago. In the last office, a coffee mug was turned over and the coffee was dried to the floor like it happened at least a day ago. Maybe more.

A loud bang traveled through the warehouse as if someone had entered and they weren't being discreet.

Fuck.

I pulled the small canister out, twisted the lid, and snorted the powder right off the prong. Then took another hit just for good measure.

My nose tingled, and I sniffed again for good measure as I put the canister away. How did I forget to do that before I left the compound?

"Lafe!" Maikel called. What was he doing here? Vicente never trusted him, not for enforcer jobs.

But maybe he was feeling the pressure if we weren't there to pick up the slack. Slim pickings.

He had to be the one to tell Vicente that I had taken Amorette. Was it worth it to leak how he skimmed off the top of Vicente's profits? Or offered favors that weren't his to give?

Only if Vicente was here.

I slowly walked back to the entrance where Maikel was whistling and banging stuff around. It sounded like he was swinging a bat into the shelves and counters.

"I know you're here! We saw you on the cameras." He was too cheery. But he'd said *we.* Someone else was here too. If it were Vicente, I'd blow his shit wide open.

"You're such a soft prick. How'd you hide that all these years?" Maikel called, sounding amused more than curious. "Vicente was quite disappointed, you know. He always favored Parker the most. Even with his idiocy, the boy has plans. He admires that. But he thought you had more grit than this."

I peered around the doorframe to the lobby. Maikel had his back turned to me with a sledgehammer over his shoulder. Two men stood at the doors and watched the outside.

Suddenly, a palm landed between my shoulder blades and rammed me forward. I grunted as I fell into the lobby, my gun coasting across the tile floor.

Maikel stopped it by stepping on it with his designer loafer.

When I brought my gaze up his suit-clad body to his face, he grinned down at me.

"Gotcha."

31

AMORETTE

"**B**lanca!" I screamed down the hallway where the offices were. No answer. I ran to the next wing of the compound and screamed for her again. Nothing.

When I was in the commons, I tried one final time.

"What?" A smattering of incensed Spanish followed, and Blanca popped her head out of the hall for the birdcages.

"I need you!" I whisper-shouted, but it was pointless. The hall was empty, and all the guards were outside. Andre and Grey had run off toward the helicopter pad ten minutes ago.

"What's wrong?" Blanca raced down the stairs, a frown on her lips.

"Lafe's missing." I waved her after me and started toward the apartments. She had a master key. They made a big deal out of no one having access to their homes, but I knew for a fact that Blanca cleaned their apartments occasionally. "I need you to open his place up. I want to see if there are any clues as to where he went."

"Amorette! If I open his apartment for you, they'll strip me of my job." She tried to tug on my arm, but I shook her off.

"We have to find him!"

"Let his brothers find him! Where is Andre? Parker? Grey?" She ran in front of me and stopped, putting her arms out. I ducked to the right and slid right past her.

"I think Parker's gone. That's what they said. He hasn't come back yet. And they just ran out."

"Then let them find him. Lafe is their brother." She stepped forward and caught both of my arms, looking deep in my eyes. "You don't have any skills to find him. Or an obligation. Let the brothers do their thing."

"That's not good enough for me!" I swiped my hands through my hair, my fingers catching on the tangles. They hadn't told me everything, but I knew enough.

They had a plan against Vicente, and it didn't work.

Parker retaliated, and instead of going after Parker, Andre decided to get wasted and...Damn. We got wasted and had sex.

Then Vicente served his own revenge against Grey. And now Lafe was missing? That wasn't a coincidence. It couldn't be. I didn't think he could come in and steal Lafe, but how the hell should I know what Vicente was capable of.

Over the last few weeks, I'd tried to learn more, but there were no opportunities to understand the Institution. The brothers didn't even seem like they understood it anymore.

"That's not good enough," I whispered, dropping my hands on Blanca's shoulders. "They forced me to be here. Now I'm here. They don't get to decide how I live beside them. Life doesn't work that way. If they wanted a prisoner, they should have locked me up in one of those apartments they keep for visitors."

She struggled with what I was asking her. I got it. If she helped me, she could be in trouble. But I'd fight for her, and if there was one thing I was damn good at, it was arguing in someone's defense.

"I want to help you, but I don't even know of a way to search for Lafe. If he's gone, and Parker's gone, that leaves at most one plane and a boat. If Andre and Grey went together, that would leave us one way off the island. If they went separately, we're stuck. Say they did leave something behind, do you know how to drive a boat? Fly a plane?"

Shit. She had a point.

"There has to be something we can do, Blanca. I can't sit here and wait for them to get back. I won't put myself out there. I won't do anything stupid, but there has to be something we can do to make sure Lafe is okay. Open his apartment, and let's look around. There might be a clue as to where he went."

"Andre could have done that already," she argued.

"He didn't," I assured her, stepping closer. "Both he and Grey left the compound. They ran out without checking his place." I nodded, trying to get her to agree with me.

She bit her lip and furrowed her brow, clearly distraught at the position I was placing her in. Blanca was a good woman. She'd been sheltered by her brother and the men at the compound. She should want to keep them safe.

"Fine. I'll open his door."

I waited for her to warn me against telling them, but she just muttered under her breath as she turned and stomped toward his door. Following behind her, I rushed to keep up.

She punched in a key code that I should have paid attention to, then used a key for the lock. The door swung open, and I pushed past her, ready for something to stick out at me.

There was nothing. No open laptops. No broken phones or dated pictures scattered on the floor. Nothing that could shed some light on anything that was going through his head. We searched the entire apartment, and with each passing second, I grew hotter and hotter.

"Fuck!" I yelled to the ceiling after finding nothing in the guest room.

"Amorette, it's not a bad thing that we didn't find anything," Blanca said softly as she walked toward me.

"Yes, it is." My voice shook, and I was on the verge of fucking tears. Couldn't she see? This was bad. Not being able to do anything while something terrible was happening was almost worse than having a choice and not acting on it.

It was the fear of the unknown. Could Vicente have Lafe? Could he be torturing him to death, plucking the brothers off one by one while I sat on my ass in this jail of a compound?

I couldn't even defend myself here. Not really. I could lock myself in a room. That was the extent. None of them ever left weapons out. I'd have to knock one of the guards unconscious to steal theirs. Like that would happen. Their guards were beasts of men.

And I...wasn't.

Thirty minutes later, my tears had dried up with the numbness that settled over me. If something bad was happening, it was probably over. There was nothing I could do to stop it.

I had no way to contact any of the brothers. The best I could do was sit here and wait.

"It's okay." Blanca rubbed circles on my back as we made our way back toward the commons.

I sniffed but didn't answer her. What was there to say?

We'd just reached the commons when the glass door banged against the wall. Anton was laughing with Parker while they strolled in like they were having the time of their lives.

"Blanca," Anton smiled and held his arms open.

She erupted into a stream of Spanish, waving her arms and getting up in his face. His broad smile quickly faded as he listened to everything she had to say. Parker lost his amusement, too, as he stepped close to the pair, his gaze intent on Blanca.

When she stopped for air, Parker spun around and got to work making calls.

"Stop!" I ran around them and stuck myself right in his path. He couldn't leave again. I was going with him whether he wanted me to or not. I'd be damned if I sat here.

His gaze burned me up as he said something into the phone. I thought he said 'talk to me', but I wasn't sure. It was too fast, and I hadn't learned that much yet.

Whatever he heard on the other end of the line wasn't good. His black gaze only grew frosty.

He said a few more rolling phrases and hung up. "Anton," he said over his shoulder without looking away from me. "We need the chopper refueled. We're leaving."

"I'm going with you."

"No, no, Little Love. You'll stay here where my brothers left you." He tried to move me to the side, but I refused.

"Like hell!" I moved with him, clutching his waist. "After everything you assholes put me through to keep me, the least you can do is take me with you," I growled.

He laughed, but it was dark and menacing, rolling over

me and leaving ice in its wake. "Lafe is currently being held hostage by our uncle, at the very least. Grey and Andre haven't found him yet. And you want me to take you there?" He bent forward until his nose almost touched mine. "You could die, Little Love. Is that what you want? To lose any hope of seeing your twin ever again?"

I sucked in a sharp breath. Of course, that wasn't what I wanted, but I couldn't not help. That wasn't who I was. A piece of me would die if he left me behind, and I could have done something.

"I'm going with you."

One side of his mouth kicked up into a cruel smile. "And what? Offer yourself up in his place?"

I dropped my gaze. No, I didn't want to do that. Did I?

If I was willing to, I doubted it would work. I meant nothing to Vicente or the Institution. I was a pawn. A means to hurt the brothers. Nothing more. But we didn't know I couldn't help unless I had a chance. And how could I have a chance if I didn't go?

"All right, Amorette." I widened my eyes at the use of my actual name. I'd never heard him use it. "You can come, but if you *die*, it's on you and I'll be pissed. If Lafe survives, he'll be livid too. Are *you* prepared to be the wedge between us?"

He was trying to deter me with his words, but I gritted my teeth. If he thought I was easily manipulated, he was wrong. And I couldn't wait to show him.

WITHIN FIFTEEN MINUTES of reaching the pad, we were up in the air. Parker had arranged for ten of their best sharpshooters to come with us. While they got it ready, Blanca found black jeans and a black T-shirt for me to wear, and when I came out, she had a pair of old black boots in her hand. I was more than a little thankful to have something practical to wear instead of the stale sundress from earlier.

Anton monitored the controls while Parker briefed the men on where we were going, the layout, and what he expected of them. The short of it was, if anyone not in our group twitched suspiciously, they died.

Bullet to the head. No exceptions.

He didn't try to keep me out of the conversation, but he certainly didn't invite me in. I might as well have been useless eye candy for all the attention he paid me.

The men too. It turned out that they were single-minded machines when there was actual danger.

As they brought us to a smooth landing, I worked to control my breathing.

Breathe in, breathe out, I chanted to myself.

Lafe was so close. It hurt to think how close he was but yet so unreachable. All because he'd been born into a self-centered, deranged family with no empathy for anyone. And now he was being held hostage by at least his uncle. My stomach rolled. He was being held by the very man he'd stolen me from. That alone gave Maikel reason to want to put him in his place.

Shit, this might have been a bad idea. How was I going to make sure I was an asset and not a liability?

The doors opened, and Parker appeared in front of me. Immediately, he and Anton started pulling open some of the compartments and strapping on enough weapons to fuel a small army.

Once he was decked out, he turned and held out a hand.

"Come on, Little Love. It's time for you to get introduced to the Institution."

"What does that mean?" I asked as I placed my hand in

his. We turned toward the main door, and he rested his other hand on an automatic weapon hanging over his shoulder.

"Being at the fights with us as a piece of ass is one thing. For you to show up here, assuming we all make it out, this says something quite different. We're making a statement that you're more than a pretty face with a tight ass. You're important to us, and you have a use. They won't know what it is, but you'll be on their radar because of it."

We held each other's stare. He was warning me there was no going back.

No warning needed. I'd already made that choice by choosing to come back with Andre and Lafe.

The sun was just rising and we were out in the middle of nowhere. A familiar plane and hanger were maybe a hundred yards away, and a string of black SUVs were parked on the other side.

"Do you hear that?" Anton stopped and tipped his head to the side.

The helicopter was still loud as it cooled down, but I tilted my head, anyway.

Then I figured out what it was. A soft, rhythmic whomping was fast approaching. Parker and I turned to face the trees when two helicopters appeared over the top of the branches.

Shots immediately erupted, and I ducked while Parker raised his gun to fire back at the helicopter. "Run!" He yelled to his men. Then he lifted me over his shoulder and tossed me in the open door.

Screaming, I covered my ears as men called orders to each other. Metal pings bounced around the stairs and Parker cursed, ducking.

"Stay here," he yelled.

I couldn't drag my gaze away from the two men face down on the pavement with dark red blood pooling beneath them. They were practically sitting ducks out here. Why weren't they getting back into the helicopter?

"Amorette!"

I jerked my gaze to Parker. His mouth pressed into a thin line as he looked between my eyes. "Stay here," he repeated. I nodded, and he ran around the nose to the other side.

Minutes passed like hours, and I crouched down, trying to stay out of sight. A couple of our men made it to the hangar, one to the SUVs and were driving back to us, but several were severely injured.

Or dead.

Then the ropes dropped.

Men climbed down, jumping off when they were just a few feet from the ground. I turned to look for Parker, but I didn't see him anywhere. I didn't think he'd leave me, but I didn't see him anywhere.

Fuck! Why hadn't I watched him instead of what was happening around me?

One of the men caught sight of me and yelled to his buddies. I glanced around, then jumped out. In there, I was trapped. The SUV was almost here. It was flying. If I could make it to them, I could—

"Oomph!" I grunted as a man tackled me to the ground.

"Amorette!" Parker yelled, but I had no fucking idea where he was.

In seconds, the man had me bundled up in his arms and he was back on the rope. The swinging was so violent as they pulled us up, I was going to be sick. The ground swirled under us as we spun around in a circle, but I finally found Parker.

He fought one of the men on the ground, shouting and

pointing up at me. Terror seemed to light his face right before I lost track of him, but I couldn't really tell in the soft glow of morning.

Just like Parker warned, I just proved I was the liability. And worse, I had a feeling I was about to be the bait.

EPILOGUE
LAFE

"I didn't actually think the picture of Grace Black would work," Vicente said with a smug smile as he sat on the office chair across from me.

Maikel leaned against the desk in the lobby and crossed his arms, having a good laugh with Vicente.

"I'm glad I can amuse you," I snarled but jerked to the right when a shadow passed.

"You have to lay off the drugs." Maikel shook his head in mock sympathy. "The way you've jerked all over the place? That kind of paranoia is deadly. You'll get yourself killed, or someone else."

"Isn't that what you want?" I directed my stare at Vicente, pushing against the ropes they used to tie me to the chair.

"Lafe, there are many things I want. I wouldn't say your death is one of them." Vicente tsked like I was a naughty child who didn't grasp the whole picture.

I didn't. My brain felt like stretched-out cotton as I tried to understand what he was saying. If he didn't want us dead, why put a bounty on our heads? My runners practically had to go to the ground to avoid his people hunting for me.

"But if it happens..." Vicente shrugged.

Skitstövel.

Familiar screaming caught my attention right before the door opened. One of Vicente's men—Manuel—grunted as he carried a raging Amorette over his shoulder. She kicked and punched, landing any kind of hurt on him that she could, even grabbing a fist of his hair and pulling.

He cursed and threw her to the hard tile. "Fucking bitch! Ouch." He rubbed his head.

"What a treat." Vicente leaned forward to get a good look at Amorette. "You're that cunt my sons can't keep their hands off of. Why are you here?" He asked her like he actually expected an answer.

She twisted until she sat on her butt and pushed away from him as fast as she could. Her wide-eyed gaze swung around the room, but relief hit as she saw me.

My heart twisted inside my chest. After everything I'd said to her, did to her, I never thought she'd want to speak to me again, much less be relieved that I was alive.

"Parker Adair brought her and a chopper full of men. They're mostly dead, but we brought her before the rest of our men finished the job. We thought she might be valuable."

"Is Parker dead?" Vicente glared at the man.

He paled, making the scratches on his face stand out in stark contrast. "N-no, sir. He was still alive when I left."

"Your men were shooting at him?"

The man dropped his gaze and didn't answer. Of course, they were fucking shooting at him. Vicente had given the order that he wanted us placed at his feet, dead or alive.

Vicente let his gaze linger on the man as he addressed

Amorette. "I hear from my daughter that you're an attorney. For battered women. Is that right?"

Amorette didn't answer, her gaze shooting between Vicente and me like she wasn't sure how to handle his sudden switch of topics.

"I also hear you have a nasty moral compass. You tried to fight for the girls because you thought they were being mistreated, right?" Vicente glanced at Maikel, who rolled his eyes.

"You mean raped and beaten," she blurted out with so much venom.

"I told you, she's too stupid to live. She thinks she's a white knight, even though it just got her extra time with Randall. He sends his regards, by the way." Maikel kissed his palm then blew it to her.

Her top lip curled and her brows dropped low.

Vicente smirked as he dragged his gaze from Maikel to Amorette. "How about a game?" He slapped his knees.

"A...game?"

"A game. I'll let you go if you dirty up that moral compass. Show me how easily you'll fall to save yourself."

"Fuck you," she spat.

That only pulled a chuckle from Vicente.

"No? How about Lafe?" He pulled a gun from inside his jacket and pointed it at me. "Carve up the man who brought you here, or I'll shoot him."

Maikel pulled a knife off of his belt and tossed it to Amorette. Manuel started to turn for the door, but Vicente stopped him. "I wouldn't do that if I were you. Your sister is at the mansion, and I'd hate to think what will happen to her if you disobey me."

He stopped and turned around slowly, closing his eyes.

Horror took over Amorette's entire face as she turned

her wide blue eyes to mine before dropping her gaze to the knife and then to the man behind her.

No. I started thrashing my head back and forth and pushing against the rope. This was everything Amorette would hate. He might as well shoot me. He couldn't fucking ask her to make that kind of choice. She was a hero, not a fucking villain.

I wasn't worth this stain on her soul, and she knew it.

When she met my gaze again, her eyes were brimming with unshed tears.

"What do you say? His life, or Lafe's?"

To be continued in <u>Killer</u>...

AFTERWORD

Wow. That was intense! Right?

But in a good way? I'd love to hear your thoughts on what you think Amorette will do. Will she save Lafe? Will she stick to her rigid morals because she just can't let go? There are so many possibilities!

Come see me in my Facebook group Blake's Book Babes and let me know! There will be a spoiler post pinned!

We also met some new faces in Convict, but did you recognize any you already knew?

Something my very own Master Po has taught me—how much fun cameos are. If you don't know who that is, it's. Heather Long. She's Po. LOL

One last nugget to help you lose sleep at night, and then I'll get onto other housekeeping things...

Actually, nah. I can't give too much away. ;)

If you want to see the Killer cover (no pun intended LOL!) early, make sure to join my newsletter! Disclosure, the cover will be sent out via newsletter a few days to maybe a week before it's released to the public.

Join the newsletter here.

If you want to read something else in my backlist with a similar—but not quite as dark—vibe, try Pin-up Girl. That's a secret society stand-alone so no cliffys!

And... If you're stalking game is strong, follow me here too.

Facebook Author Page Bookbub TikTok Instagram Amazon

Thanks for reading and I'll see you in the next book!

XOXO
Blake

OTHER TITLES

Bastard Brothers of Carnage Series
    Addict
    Convict
    Killer

Mazza Series
    Marks of the Mazza
    Bonds of the Mazza
    Secrets of the Mazza
    War of the Mazza

Astrid Scott Series
    Pretty Lies
    Ugly Truths
    Busted Dreams
    Vivid Fears
    Brittle Hope

Fragile Minds Duet
    Fractured

Altered

Standalone RH Romance
Pin-up Girl

Co-Writes with my Co-wrifey
  Standalone Series
  Kiss of Fate
  Taste of Karma
  Cardinal Sins Series
  Kill Song
  First Chorus
  High Note
  Last Word

Standalone MF Romance
Full Glasses and Burju Shoes

WHO IS BLAKE?

Blake Blessing is no longer new on the Indie scene, but she's still ecstatic about this chapter in life. She is a mom, wife, art enthusiast, and author.

She attended ten different schools growing up, so books became her constant friend. Escaping into books of all different genres made life fun and exciting. Blake was also raised on music and still blasts it through the house and car at every opportunity.

She has a weird sense of humor and a penchant for chocolate milk. It only makes sense she would one day go on to write her own stories.